Become the Night

Book One Of the Undying Series

Can she still be a mother after becoming a monster?

Trinity Showalter

AuthorHouse™
1663 Liberty Drive
Bloomington, IN 47403
www.authorhouse.com
Phone: 1 (800) 839-8640

Published by AuthorHouse 02/03/2019

ISBN: 978-1-7283-3495-0 (sc)
ISBN: 978-1-7283-3494-3 (e)

Print information available on the last page.

Any people depicted in stock imagery provided by Getty Images are models,
and such images are being used for illustrative purposes only.
Certain stock imagery © Getty Images.

This book is printed on acid-free paper.

Bitten

It was late when Kendra Hughes came home from working a double shift at the hospital. She opened the door to her two-story, four-bedroom house in Cumming, Georgia. Thankful that the kids were at their aunt's house, she dumped her bags on the couch and headed for the kitchen. The left-over spaghetti in the fridge was a welcome sight to Kendra's empty stomach. After eating, she sat down in the living room to watch a few shows recorded on her DVR. She, the tired mom of three, flopped down on her sofa, cuddled up with a blanket, and within minutes, was fast asleep.

Kendra bolted up from her reclined position, knocking down her floor lamp. She cursed under her breath, then got up to go to the kitchen for the broom and dustpan. She swept up the mess absentmindedly and thought to the reason why she jumped like that. She was having a weird dream, but all she could remember from it was fire and a melting face. The face was familiar, but she couldn't place who she dreamed of, it was like the answer was right on the tip of her tongue. Kendra shivered at the memory and tried to just push it out of her mind. It was only a dream after all.

Kendra dumped the broken light bulb into her trash bin then headed upstairs to her bedroom. She passed her kids' bedrooms in the hallway and wondered how they were doing. She had promised Zeke she wouldn't take any more night shifts, though, that was a promise she had to break

— money was tight right now. Kendra knew she would have to make it up to him somehow, but her hands were tied until the settlement went through.

Travis. His death left a huge hole in everyone's hearts and lives. Kendra and him had promised each other they would live forever, so long as they had each other. As she stared into Zeke's room, she muttered: "Guess broken promises are contagious, huh kiddo?" A tear escaped and she quickly wiped it away before heading down the hall to the bathroom. Kendra washed her make-up off in the sink; it wasn't much, mostly eye make-up, but it still proved to be stubborn nonetheless.

Once all the make-up was gone, she stared at herself in the mirror. Her pale skin seemed to have lost some of its luster since the accident. Depression can really kick you hard. Kendra tries keep up the act, tries to not let what happened affect her so that she can be strong for her children. But on the inside, she feels like she is dying, like some part of her wants to give up and be with Travis. She doesn't want to be away from her kids, but not having him there with her was the worst feeling in the world.

Suddenly, she remembered whose face she had seen melting in the fire, and tears flowed down her face. She slumped to the bathroom floor, unable to hold back the torrent of bottled up emotions anymore. The love of her life was gone; her heart felt like it was breaking all over again, the fresh scars breaking open like burst seams. They were supposed to last forever. Why did he have to die? Memories of his funeral came rushing back. She had felt so cold and distant then, she couldn't even remember what anyone had said.

Kendra lay on the bathroom floor, sobbing for what seemed like an eternity before she got the strength to get back up and go to her bedroom. Her kids were coming home tomorrow, a thought that brought a rare, though small smile to her face. Kendra sat at the edge of her bed, staring at the bottle of sleep aid on her nightstand. The raging maelstrom of emotions that twisted her gut into knots surely wasn't going to let her sleep that night. With some reluctance, she popped a recommended dose of pills into her mouth and washed it down with a glass of water from the bathroom sink. Kendra settled down under her down comforter and waited for the numbing bliss of dreamless sleep.

***

Janet knocked on Kendra's front door. Aveline squirmed in her arms; her cherry-red hair danced as she turned her head this way and that way. Zeke kicked a small rock off the top stair of the porch and seemed to take great satisfaction in hearing it land in the dirt underneath. "Come in!" Kendra hollered from the kitchen. Janet opened the door and entered her sister-in-law's house, one niece in her arms, the other holding her brother's hand; the house smelled wonderfully of eggs and bacon.

"Kendra?" Janet inquired. "In the kitchen," came the response. Zeke and Sasha ran ahead to greet their mom, a chorus of "Mommy" left in their wake. The two kids were hugging Kendra when Janet walked in with little Aveline. A big bright smile graced her face as she embraced her children. Kendra looked up at Janet and Aveline in the kitchen doorway; the one-year-old babbled happily at the sight of her mommy.

"Hi there, Sweetie!" Kendra gushed back, taking the toddler into her arms. "Were they any trouble?" she asked Janet. Zeke started tugging at his mother's shirt, and Kendra ruffled his light auburn hair. "No, not at all. At least, not for me. It would seem Zeke had some trouble at school yesterday. The teacher left a note in his bookbag. Something about not cooperating with the class. I figured I'd leave him to your capable hands." Janet folded her arms and glared lovingly at Zeke, who looked down at the floor and toed the grout between the tiles. "May I see you for a moment, please?" Janet asked.

"Sure," Kendra bent down to Zeke. "Would you take your sister upstairs to play for a little while?" Zeke beamed innocently up at his mother. "Yes, Mommy," came the reply before he took Sasha's hand and pulled her out of the kitchen. The adults watched them leave the room and remained in silence for a moment after. "How have you been? You know, since ..." Janet trailed off, not seeming able to put a coherent sentence together.

Kendra hugged her sister-in-law. It was more impulsive than usual, but was rewarded when Janet hugged her back. "I miss him so much." She sobbed into Kendra's clothes. "Can you believe it's only been a month since the funeral? It seems like it was only yesterday." Kendra nodded, her tears leaving a wet spot on Janet's shirt.

"I know. I still look at the clock and expect him to be headed home." Janet whispered softly.

"Zeke is just like him, you know." Kendra nodded again. The two women stood there in the kitchen, lost in their embrace and taking comfort in one another's presence. Slowly, they both broke off their embrace and faced each other once again.

"Anyway, I need to get going, if you need anything, just call. Ok?" Janet said, wiping away tears. "And thanks. I think we both needed that." Kendra walked with Janet to the front door, each wiping their faces dry. They said their goodbyes and, for the time being, parted ways.

***

Rick watched the two women on the porch as they talked briefly. The blonde turned and walked off the porch, heading toward what Rick assumed was the woman's car. However, the blonde was not his target. He focused on the redhead as she waved from the front window. Rick leaned back in the driver seat of his rental and looked over at the man sitting next to him in the passenger seat.

"She's the one?" Rick seemed incredulous about the Council's choice.

"Are you questioning your superiors, Rick? You know that is a death sentence." the man replied.

"No, James, I'm not questioning them. Just wondering why." James sighed

"Look, Rick. You know the law. There is a reason for everything the Council decides. You have been evading this for too long. If you don't do this …" James shrugged. Rick looked straight ahead for a time without speaking, James could see his eyes were slightly glazed and knew that Rick was miles away, possibly even centuries.

When he snapped back into reality, Rick asked, "Why her? I just don't understand. Don't they know what she'll go through once this is done." James sighed.

"I don't know, Rick. You've been around them longer than I have. I don't have all the answers here." Rick chuckled.

"Well, if someone as long in the tooth as me doesn't have all the answers by now, what hope does anyone else have." Rick started up the car and eased back out onto the road, he had sat there long enough. He knew what had to be done; the rest he'll figure out later.

***

The weekend came and went, but such is life these days for Kendra. Zeke had spent most of it indoors as a punishment for a poor report from his kindergarten teacher, Ms. Bings. He had to watch from his bedroom window as his sister played outside with her friend from daycare. On Monday morning, Kendra got her three kids up, dressed, fed, and out the door. Her daughters had to be dropped off at daycare by 6:30 am, Zeke had to be at school by 7:15 am, and her shift at the hospital began at 10 am. She got the kids to their respective locations and was back home in record time.

It was a little after 8 am when the hot water flowed from the bathtub faucet, turning her bathroom into a sauna. Kendra walked into her bedroom in her favorite bathrobe to fetch the work clothes that she had laid out on the bed earlier, when suddenly her bedroom door shut behind her. She whipped around to find a man standing between her and the door. He was tall — very tall. At a minimum of six feet, he had broad shoulders and thick arms barely hidden under a long, tan trench coat. His ashy brown hair hung loosely just above his ears, barely framing his roman facial features. But what stood out the most was his eyes — hazel eyes that shimmered with a light that was almost supernatural and very intoxicating.

Kendra managed to shake herself loose of the hypnotic hold those haunting hazel eyes had on her. She lunged to the left where her cordless phone sat virtually unused on her bedside table. He caught her arm in mid-reach with a strong grip, almost too strong, and jerked her away from the phone. She screamed but was muffled by his big meaty hand.

"Don't scream. I promise this won't hurt," his voice rasped in her ear. Kendra bit hard into his hand and he yelped, giving him pause enough for her to make her escape.

He grabbed for her again but only managed to knock her to the floor as she tried to slip away from him. Kendra banged her head on the bed frame in the struggle. Through the stairs she was able to see that her cell phone, still attached to its charger, had landed on the floor. She scrambled to get her legs underneath her and had the phone in hand when she was yanked once again into the arms of her attacker. He snatched the phone out of her hand and pushed her onto her bed. Kendra watched horror-struck as he crushed her cell with one hand — protective case and all.

What kind of man could do that! How much strength does it take to do something like that! He approached her prone form on the bed. She opened her mouth to scream, but before a sound made it out, he was on top of her. His weight was enough that breathing was difficult, forget screaming or even talking. He dug his fingers in her hair and pulled her head to one side. The thought crossed her mind that she was probably going get rapped and then killed, but the more she fought, the harder it was to continue fighting. His body was as immovable as a stone statue.

He bit into her neck, but all she could feel were two needle-like teeth. It didn't hurt really, though it was strange. She had no idea what was going on, but Kendra could feel her blood being drained from her body, like when she gave a donation to the Red Cross. He was drinking her blood! Kendra had seen some horror films and her addle mind thought about the monsters that fed on human blood. But this was real life, wasn't it? Vampires weren't real. Or were they?

At the rate he was going, though, she knew without a doubt she was going to die from blood loss. Her suspicions seemed to be correct as her eyelids grew heavy and her body slumped. She fought just to stay awake, but that was a losing battle. Before death could claim her, her last thoughts were of her kids and it gained her a small burst of adrenaline. She struggled more, pushing against him, her limbs growing heavy and numb. Her strength left her, leaving behind nothing but a deep blackness that threatened to consume her completely.

Breakfast

Kendra opened her eyes. At first she couldn't remember anything. She looked around at a room that seemed quite familiar, but she couldn't put her finger on why. Her head felt like it weighed a thousand tons and took all of five minutes for her to sit up in the bed she was laying in. After a moment, her memory started to come back. She was in her room, in her house. She had been getting ready for work, but couldn't remember anything after that. Kendra gasped and looked over at her alarm clock. It was 10 o'clock — she was late for work. She got up and began to put her uniform on when a reddish-brown spot on her bed caught her eye. *Is that blood?*

Kendra swooned with the flood of a memory. No, not a memory — a nightmare. She glanced at the clock again. It wasn't 10 am, it was 10 pm — she had been out for over 12 hours. Panic began to set in; everything she missed today came crashing down on her. Where were her kids, did she still have a job, and how come no one has called or tried to check in on her? Kendra figured she must have been knocked out too hard to hear her phone go off.

She looked for it and found it in pieces at the foot of her bed. The memory of a man's big hand crushing it like it was nothing more than a peanut shell danced through her mind, but was gone before she could get a grasp on it. She looked at her mainline laying on the floor and she picked it up gently as if it would break, there had been no calls. She placed it back in its base on her nightstand.

Then it hit her — the smell of breakfast wafted into her room and her stomach growled loudly. She followed the smell out into the hallway and the sound of cooking food hit her at the top of the stairs. *I was sick,* Kendra rationalized, *Yeah I must have been, and that's Janet in the kitchen now. She's making dinner for me and the kids. She didn't have to go through all the trouble.* Kendra rushed down the stairs to greet her sister-in-law and thank her for all the help.

She walked into the kitchen — mouth ready to begin apologizing for being a space cadet — when she stopped cold in her tracts. It was him, the man from her nightmare. His eyes trained on her and they still had that shiny, hypnotic gaze. Kendra felt cold. It seemed her blood drained out of her body once again. She stood frozen in place, staring into the face of evil, the memory of his teeth in her neck. She rubbed the spot instinctively, still feeling the slight twinge of pain as he had drank from her.

"Afternoon, sleepyhead. So good of you to join the living. Well, in a manner of speaking, anyway." He grinned wide, showing all his teeth, even the pointed ones. "Come, sit down, I hope you don't mind, I've helped myself to your kitchen. I've made plenty, though. Figured you'd be hungry after your big nap." Kendra's knees wanted to buckle under her weight, but she quickly got a hold of herself.

"I'm calling the police." She announced, grabbing for the kitchen phone. He was suddenly standing next to her, gently taking the receiver from her hand and placing it in the base.

"Hey, now, let's not be hasty, it's only breakfast," he said with another toothy grin.

"Why?" Kendra asked, finally able to use her voice again. She stood firmly rooted to the floor even as all her instincts told her to run. He blinked at her

"Because I was hungry, and thought you would be, too," he said slowly, then grinned sheepishly. Her eyebrows furrowed as she stared at him. His was like that from a child who was trying to be cute.

"I don't mean why are you cooking in my kitchen. I mean why are you here? Why did you stay? Why did you attack me? What did you do to me?" She was yelling in the end, the insanity of it all causing her to break for a moment. His features grew dark and he turned back to the stove to pile the sausage links onto a plate in his hand. It was already partially filled with scrambled eggs and a stack of about six pancakes.

"Please sit, we shall discuss it over breakfast." His voice became oddly monotoned as he used the tongs in his hand to point her to the table. For a moment, the idea of rebellion skittered through her mind as she contemplated her own dinette set. Kendra then realized she had been holding her breath, the smell of food filled her nostrils when she allowed herself to breathe again, making her stomach growl. Kendra took a deep breath, filling her lungs with the wonderful aromas, she could smell each individual spice in the sausage, the buttermilk in the pancakes, and even the butter used to coat the pan so the eggs wouldn't stick.

As she took a seat at the dinette set, giving in to the temptation of food, she wondered if she was always able to smell with such precision. The table had been set very nicely with orange juice and coffee gracing the middle. The man who still had not revealed his name set a bottle of pancake syrup in the middle of the table next to the coffee. He then put a plate of food in front of Kendra pilled so high that it bordered on daunting. Kendra eyed the huge plate of food to figure out a good place to start eating.

"So am I going to get some answers, or what?" she asked, cutting into the mountain of pancakes. He sipped on his coffee.

"Yes, yes, the question is where to begin." He pondered on it for a moment then said "Well, how about we start with an introduction. My name is Richard Blake. Most people just call me Rick, though." He stabbed a link with his fork, then bit half of it off. "I work for a highly secret organization, my sign is Pisces, favorite color is green, and I was recently given the task to ... ah ... 'recruit' you, I guess would be an appropriate term," Rick said before eating the other half of his sausage. He gulped down some OJ and dug into the eggs.

"Recruit me for what?" Kendra asked, cramming a fork full of pancake into her mouth. "I'm not exactly secret agent material." Rick sputtered, almost choking on his eggs.

"Oh, no, you have it wrong," he said, barely containing his laughter. "No, this isn't a recruitment for the position of 'secret agent.' It's much more than that. You see, I'm not human and thanks to me, neither are you." Kendra's fork clanged against her plate. A memory flashed through her mind; the feeling of teeth piercing her neck, being held down by the man sitting across from her, his body like stone.

"What did you do to me?" Kendra's voice dripped with venom, her hand clasped protectively on her neck. "What are you?" the man smirked.

"The question here isn't what am I; the question is, what have you become?" Rick said, a twinkle danced in his inhuman eyes as he chuckled softly. Kendra shot up from the table so quick her chair fell backward. She rushed to the half bath down the hall where she stood before the mirror. Shock overcame her, then a flood of relief as she stared into her own eyes reflected back at her. It was only a moment that she felt this relief, however, because in her reflection she could see she was changed somehow. Her eyes had the same unnatural light dancing in them as Rick did; her skin seemed lighter, if that was even possible for Kendra's naturally milky skin.

"Were you expecting to not have a reflection?" Rick chuckled from the hallway. Kendra turned around to face him.

"I don't understand, please explain it to me, what is going on?" Rick smiled at her, and this time it touched his eyes. It almost seemed genuine, welcoming even, his smile was one that you'd give to a friendly stranger.

"Come, let's finish eating and I'll explain everything." He turned back to the kitchen, Kendra in tow.

"Where are my kids? Why hasn't my job called? I never showed up. They should have called me by now." Rick held up his hand to stop the barrage of questions and motioned for Kendra to sit down.

"Your children are safe," he began once they were both seated. "They have been picked up and are being cared for by a reputable sitter within my organization. As far as your work is concerned, you called in sick today. Your sister-in-law came by to check up on you when she found out the kids were already picked up. I made sure she left here knowing you are pretty ill and needed lots of rest. She had even brought you some chicken noodle soup. It's in the fridge." Rick dug into his stack of pancakes again while he let all that sink in.

After a moment's thought, Kendra asked: "How were you able to accomplish all that with me being out cold for the last twelve hours?" Rick swallowed his food. "Easy, one of my associates went to your job and 'convinced' your boss that you had called in. Also I had to do some 'convincing' myself when Janet showed up at your doorstep." He sipped his coffee and made a face. "It's gone cold. Would you like me to heat up your cup as well?" Kendra nodded and handed him her coffee.

"So when you say you 'convinced' these people, you're saying ..." Kendra began.

"I hypnotized them, yes." Rick finished for her. "Well, hypnotized doesn't really cover it. It's more like I replaced their memory, but we'll go with hypnotism for the hell of it, and for the record, *I* only hypnotized Janet. It was my associates that took care of your boss, the daycare attendant, and the secretary at little Ezekiel's school." The microwave beeped and he returned with two cups of reheated coffee.

"So you're a vampire, a real vampire, a blood-sucking, only comes out at night — vampire?" Kendra started to freak, as the realization that she too was a vampire sank in.

"Yes, but slow down on the occult fiction there. We don't come out only at night. Well, most of us don't, anyway. Yes, we drink blood, no we don't kill people. Yes, we have numerous powers and abilities, no we are not allergic to garlic, crosses, holy water, silver, or any other mundane 'Holly Relic' nonsense. Actually, many vampires still attend various churches and practice many faiths, though I personally can't fathom why. These things were thought up and planted into human society to protect our kind from prosecution and the like."

Kendra cocked her head. "You don't believe in a god, Mr. Blake?" she asked. Rick shook his head.

"Just call me Rick — Mr. Blake just sounds weird. The god thing, though, that's all fairy tales and gibberish made by humans to control other weaker-minded humans." He waved his hand dismissively. "Anywho, let me lay it all out for you. In this day and age, we have been able to study ourselves just as humans do. The truth is vampirism is a disease of unknown origins that humans are actually immune to, and always have been. "The way vampirism works is the victim has to be drained of blood until near death — roughly 3-4 pints of blood— then the host vampire has to introduce the disease into the victim's bloodstream. You see, a humans' white blood cell count is key here. The draining of blood leaves the human immune system vulnerable and the introduction of the vampire virus begins the change from human to immortal. You see, we aren't dead things wandering the earth. In fact, some would say we're the next evolution."

Rick talked between bites. Kendra ate as she listened, not wanting to end the stream of information; it was all quite fascinating to her. She could understand the science of it well enough. Rick chugged his orange juice and wiped his mouth with a napkin. She was a lot hungrier than she had thought before and by the time Rick was near finishing his tale, her plate was almost clean. Her orange juice was gone and she sipped on her coffee as Rick came to a conclusion.

"There was once a group of vampires about 400 years ago that believed we are the superior species on the planet. While they aren't wrong when you think about it, what they did was. They tried to overthrow the world and either turn or kill all humans. So in 1616, a board of lawmakers was formed to quell the surging population of New World Order cultists. There wasn't any war or anything, but a treaty was signed as the vast majority of the vampire population wanted to live among humans peacefully. The Vampire Council was established right in the heart of Rome afterward and they serve as lawmakers, judges, and jury, among other things."

"The Council likes to keep to the old ways of vampires, such as keeping a low profile in human cities and most will follow these laws. However, there are those who don't and that's where the organization I work for comes in. The simple truth is, any vampire that goes against the Council and is found guilty of their crimes can face confinement or even death. Going against the Council's will is considered an act of treason. Breaking any one of our laws can merit a death penalty depending on the Councilman acting as judge, but thankfully there aren't that many laws.

"As a new fledgling, you too must follow these laws, which are: 1) Do not break the laws in other lands. 2) Do not reveal yourself to anyone human — remain hidden. 3) Do not kill, unless your true nature is in danger, then turn or kill — no exceptions. 4) Every vampire must turn between one and five people every 50 years unless otherwise authorized by the Council. 5) The Council is law above all else, the decisions made in the Council are to be respected and directions followed.

"It works kind of like a democracy in that Council members are elected every 12 years and it's the job of the Council members to select senators."

Kendra sat back in her chair — her plate cleaned of the mountain of food — and thought on the vampire laws.

"That's it? Just those five laws?" Rick nodded.

"Yeah, basically. There are several amendments and a few unwritten laws, but they all fall under these five categories. What I've just listed are the vampire laws as they were written roughly 400 years ago, similar to the US Constitution, with some improvising made in the more modern world. The organization I work for is called AIVA, or Agents of Internal Vampire Affairs. We are the Council's right arm, basically a glorified police force."

"Is that what I'm being recruited for? This vampire police force?" Kendra asked.

"No, you were chosen for me to turn; you were selected for commissioning into our world. You see, one of the unwritten laws is that vampires cannot turn others without permission. It helps cull the herd, so to speak, by keeping tabs on who is turned, when, why, and by who. The Council is able to control the outcome and keep out any unsavory individuals who would threaten our way of life. Vampires are required by law to turn someone every 50 years for population control. It's kind of like renewing a license and mine, by the way, was expired by about 10 years." Rick chuckled at his little joke.

"So what happens when it comes time to turn someone? They just tell you who to go to and that if you don't, it's a death sentence?" Kendra asked mortified.

"You'd think with as much power that a vampire possesses, we wouldn't be on such a tight leash." Rick shook his head, "No that's not how it is. You're free to choose anyone you want to turn, and I've never known the Council to turn down a well-submitted request for a Bloodening. I wasn't given a choice because I refused to choose, so the Council chose for me. It's the law. It's what perpetuates the species without harming the delicate ecosystem of humanity."

"A Bloodening?" Kendra found the term kind of ritualistic, saying it even brought out some goosebumps on her arm. "Yes, that's the actual term for turning someone. It's the act of trading bloods to change a human into a vampire. Most find the term a bit unnerving at first," Rick explained.

"Is there any other way of … perpetuating the species?" Kendra asked, forming the words carefully.

"Well, vampires have been known to be born. Purebloods are rather uncommon, though, and I don't think there are any living today. Contrary to human lore, vampires are not infertile. We're not undead things — we're still very much alive. Immortality doesn't seem to have a factor in this either, unlike what some might think."

"Purebloods are rare due to simple biology. A woman is born with all the eggs she will ever carry. Her body is incapable of making more and for whatever reason, the virus replenishes everything but that. So the problem is, with a vampire's life being measured in centuries rather than in decades, a woman's body tries to conserve the eggs and only releases one somewhere between every 10 – 20 years on average." Rick finished his cup of coffee and sat back in his chair.

"So, are you telling me that even though I'm a vampire, I'll still have a period every decade or so?" Kendra asked. "Well, at least it isn't every month. After a few hundred years that would be unbearable. Do vampires go through menopause at some point? Why are you laughing?" Rick had begun to laugh so hard he could barely stand it; he almost fell out of his chair with the force of it. Once he got his composure back, he looked across the table at very mad Kendra, and the look on her face almost sent him back over the edge.

"No, you won't ever have a period again, I promise." Rick wiped the tears from his eyes. "I'm sorry for the outburst, I just never pictured myself having this conversation with you. I found it to be rather amusing, but to continue, your vampire blood will keep you from shedding your uterine lining. As a matter of fact, your body doesn't even need the estrogen that comes from absorbing the egg. Vampires have very different hormones which are currently being subjected to lab studies. This is why trying to tell whether or not a female vampire is ovulating is harder than when dealing with a human. Have I answered all your questions?"

Kendra thought for a moment, going over in her mind all they had discussed. "I have only one more question." She said after about a 10 minutes' reflection.

"Ok, shoot." Rick nodded.

"How old are you?" Kendra looked intensely at him as she waited for his response. After some calculating, Rick answered her.

"It would seem that I am 665 years old." He chuckled "Ah, how time flies, I was born in Rome, Italy in 1351, during the height of the Renaissance." Rick stood from the table. "And as long as you don't have any more questions, it's time to go."

"Go? Go where?" Kendra blinked, Rick grabbed her arm and pulled her up out of her chair. "To complete your transformation," Rick said simply. "Did you think all you had to do was lay there?" he said with a wink. "And you might want to go get dressed before we head out. Pick something sensible; it's your first time. This could get messy." He grinned mischievously and eyed her fuzzy bathrobe with meaning. Kendra blushed deep red as she rushed upstairs.

Feeding

Kendra came downstairs in a pair of blue jeans and an old band t-shirt. Rick read at the name on her shirt, *The Vipers*, and recognized it as a local rock band. They had been broken up for some time, though, before Kendra was even born. He guessed her parents were fans and that she probably got the tee online.

"What are you staring at?" Kendra snapped "You said to put on something I wouldn't mind getting dirty. What are we going to do anyway? Dig around in the dirt?" Rick laughed

"I'm sorry, I was just admiring your shirt. I hadn't heard them play in a long time. No, we are not going to be doing any such thing, I promise." Rick extended his hand to give her the option of taking it in hers. Kendra eyed his hand suspiciously before she placed hers into his waiting grasp. Rick opened the front door and off they flew.

The wind rushed past her and the quick movements left her disoriented — when they landed on a rooftop, she lost her footing. She felt like a newborn foal as she flailed for purchase on the sloping roof. Rick's strong arm wrapped around her waist and held her until she was steady. Looking out at the rooftops and the street below, Kendra knew where she was and that was about eight blocks away from her house.

"We didn't fly very far, did we?" she said, a bit disappointed.

"Fly? Oh, that was just a jump. Vampires can't fly, we can jump higher and farther than anything on this earth. Actually, some believe Superman's abilities are based on vampire powers, though, nobody knows if there is any truth to that or not. Our jump is a lot like his. It's more about controlling the gravity around you than your muscle mass. You bend the force of gravity to propel yourself up and then you come down in a sort of controlled free fall. The better control you have over it, the farther you can go and the closer to flying you can get. Just remember what Newton had said: what goes up must come down."

"Oh, ok. Well, let me try." She closed her eyes and tried to force herself to go up. It didn't seem to be working when Rick said:

"Reach into your belly. Make gravity move you from your core. You'll have more control that way." Then she felt it; it was like a tightening, not uncomfortable, but noticeable. She could also smell something like gunpowder or maybe a match being lit as she built up energy. She opened her eyes to see Rick beaming at her. He must have smelled it too because he knew she had found what she needed. Then he looked at her with this mischievous grin and said: "Now, let's have some fun."

In a flash, he was gone. Kendra's new vampire eyes spotted him quickly, though. He was another eight blocks away. She let the power that had been building in her body go. It shot her high into the air. She came to a slow stop about twenty stories above the roof she was just standing on. The air around her was colder and strangely invigorating, and she would have giggled with glee if it weren't for the fact that she felt the pressure change. She felt herself begin to fall and remembered what Rick had said about a controlled free fall. Kendra aimed herself at Rick and gave herself a small push with the reserves of her newfound power. The wind rushed past her and made her feel like she really was flying through the air, her ears popped some, and the grin on her face was ever-present.

In minutes, she and Rick were playing a game of tag across rooftops and chasing each other over impossible miles. For a moment, Kendra forgot about everything. She lost herself in the freedom of near flight with the wind whipping through her hair. The whirl images of the night swirled past her as moved faster than most things on Earth. She would have been happy just to continue living as a blur, moving so fast that life's troubles couldn't catch her.

Then, it happened. She stopped in the middle of a cornfield. She had traveled miles in a time period that would have been impossible by car. The smell was what stopped her, it was so good that it caused a rumble from deep within her so fierce it couldn't be ignored. She suddenly felt hallow and the need to fill the space was painfully present in her mind. She followed the smell through the endless corn until it broke open. There she could see a farm house and the smell was drawing her in; it must be coming from inside.

Rick landed lightly next to her. "You feel the hunger, don't you?" Kendra nodded. "Well, this is as good a place as any. Let's go get you a bite." He grinned at his own joke knowing it would be lost on Kendra. Her mind was more involved with the intoxicating aroma of fresh blood nearby. They made their way up to the house, Kendra moved toward the front door, but Rick had other plans. He pulled her to a window close to the ground and easy to open. Kendra watched as Rick used some sort of vampire trick to pull the lock on the window open, then he pushed his fingers under the window and pulled it open as well.

They slipped inside and closed the window gently. The smell was stronger inside. Kendra could hardly bear it. Rick gave a quick sniff before saying, "Ah, now I know what drew you to this place. There is a menstruating teenager here. Yes, that is a rather alluring scent indeed. Shall we continue then?" Rick let Kendra lead the way, Kendra followed her nose to an upstairs bedroom. She stood at the door with the aroma wafting out from underneath, tantalizing her senses. Hesitant, she stood there wondering if she should choose another but unable to pull herself away from the smell.

"Will it kill her if I feed on this young girl?" Rick put his hands on her shoulders.

"If you don't want her to die, then pay attention to what I'm about to say. When you walk in there, focus on her heartbeat, listen to the way it rhythmically pushes the blood through her veins. Keep that in mind and monitor it like you would as a nurse. Vampires are not the gluttonous beasts Hollywood makes us out to be. Take it slow and only take what you need. When you are finished, lick the wound on her neck to make it heal so she doesn't bleed out. You got all that?" Kendra nodded.

"I'm ready" she breathed.

The door creaked slightly as she walked in. Rick closed it behind them in case someone else in the house got up in the night. Kendra stopped next to the young girl's bed. She looked to be no older than 14, and for a moment she lost her resolve. The beating of the girl's heart kept her in place; the sound was almost as enticing as the smell of blood that permeated the room. The teen's jugular pulsed with the beat of the heart, only a fraction off. It was more like an echo that was coming from her heart.

Kendra wanted what pulsed in her veins, wanted nothing more than to drink the precious life force that flowed through her. *She is just a child. I should pick another. This is wrong.* But the smell of blood confused her with an instinctive need; she knew she couldn't leave. Saliva pooled in her mouth and her gums ached — to pull away now would be torture. She battled with the part of herself that said she was a nurse and a mom, sworn to protect life, and the new part that craved this child's blood. The rhythmic thumps, the intoxicating aroma — her head swam with the sensory overload.

Before Kendra knew it, she was kneeling at the girl's bedside, fangs broke through her gums, pushing her original canines out of their place. The two teeth dropped to the floor with barely a sound, Kendra leaned forward and sank her new teeth into her first victim. She gave in to her primal desires and the reward was worth it. The blood gushed into her mouth, sweet and warm. The girl stirred but didn't wake up. Kendra drank deeply like she had never eaten before in her life. The blood flowed across her tongue tasting both sweet and bitter, salty with a hint of coppery iron. Yet, it was by far the best thing she had ever tasted.

The girl's heart began to flutter some, just before Kendra had had her fill. The flutter startled her and she stopped. She licked the girl's wound, pleased that it started healing so quickly. Once the blood stopped flowing, Kendra looked up at Rick, who stood in a dark corner with his arms folded across his chest. He smiled back at her.

"Well done," came the approval Kendra didn't think she wanted, but found that it made her feel better about successfully feeding without the loss of a life.

Rick bent down and picked up Kendra's lost teeth. "I'll be taking those." Kendra stared at the teeth in his hand, "What? You want me to give you a dollar for them or something? I'm not the tooth fairy, you know." Rick smirked. Kendra shook her head.

"I was just wondering if that will happen every time now," she said, pointing at them. Rick chuckled.

"Nah, you just got your adult fangs in. You're a big, bad vampire now, and you won't be losing any more teeth." He patted her head and jokingly acted like he was talking to a child while Kendra fumed. "Now, how about we get out of here before we're found out, hmm?" In two long strides, he was standing near the girl's window, Rick opened it wide and climbed out, hanging from the frame he waved Kendra to join him. Kendra went to the window and climbed out with him. She dug her fingers into the wood of the outer wall and hung with her feet bracing her. He closed the window and was about to lock it from the outside when Kendra stopped him.

"How do you do that? Show me, please."

Rick sighed, "Ok, remember when you were focused on the teen's heartbeat?" Kendra nodded. "Use that focus now. Put your hand on the glass and focus on the lock. Find the pull of gravity you used to get here. Use that to move the lock. Focus, then give it a small push." Kendra obeyed and, in an instant, was rewarded with an audible click indicated the window was locked. They pushed off from the wall and landed on the grass below, Kendra was alight with new energy and new powers at her fingertips.

"Race you home?" she wagged her eyebrows at Rick.

"You're on!" he said and they were off, racing through the night.

***

He lurked in the shadows, waiting for their return. His position was prime, hidden by houses around him, downwind so they couldn't smell him, and with a perfect view of the front porch of Kendra's house. Well, a perfect view for a vampire, that is. He stood there for a long time, almost too long.

How long does it take to finish the Bloodening process? He pondered, *is she a picky eater or something? That would not bode well for her.* He chuckled to himself at the idea of such a thing. It was five in the morning when the two returned to the house; the girl's red hair stood out in the moonlight, which said something due it being a crescent moon. They landed on the steps to the front porch and spoke for a while before the man in the shadows decided to let his presence be known.

***

Kendra landed on the top two steps of her front porch. She turned in time to see Rick land right on the bottom step. "What else should I know about being a vampire?" she asked, "Are there more perks like this?" Rick grinned wide.

"Oh, many more, and we will explore them together. I guess the next thing you should know is that among our peers I would be known as your sire. We will have a sort of bond for about five years, during which I will always know roughly where you are and if you are in any danger. For the first year, however, it's customary for me to stay close and teach you, so we have plenty of time for you to learn all that a vampire needs to know."

Rick began his ascent up the stairs as Kendra turned to unlock her door. She heard a soft scuffle behind her and looked back. Rick was gone. Panic struck her and she looked frantically around the area trying to get a glimpse of where he had gone. *This has to be a test.* She thought, *Nothing more than a test, right?* Just as she finished rationalizing his disappearance she saw him in the distance, some ways down the road, and he wasn't alone.

Her new vampire instincts kicked in and in moments, she was on top of the mysterious man. She held him down and was about to claw his eyes out when Rick stopped her, "Kendra, stop! He's a friend, it's just James, he's a friend!" It took a minute for her rage to clear from her eyes.

"A friend?" she blinked "He's a friend?"

Rick smiled "Yes, yes, his name is James. He works with me. He's an AIVA agent. James is just here to make sure I fulfilled the requirements of the Bloodening." Kendra looked at the man sitting on the ground, who was rubbing his throat where Kendra had him pinned.

"Oh, God! I'm so sorry. Here let me help you up." She extended her hand, the man known as James took it and with Kendra's help pulled himself up off the ground.

"I have to say, Rick, she is a strong one, the Council will be pleased. You did a good job, man," James said, patting Rick on the back. Kendra couldn't help but notice the man spoke with a slight British accent, though it seemed like he was trying to hide it. Rick grinned.

"Kendra, this is James Wilson, he's an old friend of mine."

"Now, when you say old …?" Kendra asked.

"Oh, we've known each other for roughly 100 years." James pipped up with a smile that split his face in half. "Quite literally, actually"

Kendra gaped at the two men before her, wide-eyed as a child who had just met the boogieman and found out he wasn't a bad guy. James clapped.

"Alright, we're not getting much done standing around here. How about we head inside for a cup of t … coffee and begin Phase Two, hmm?"

The three of them walked back to Kendra's house, moving like normal humans because now the sun was raising and cars began to pass them on the road. Kendra caught up to Rick and asked: "What's Phase Two?" Rick's eyes took on a mischievous twinkle as he answered her.

"Your Initiation"

Plans

The three of them stood in Kendra's living room, a heavy silence settled around them, and Kendra found herself staring at the man named James. He was dressed in a dark tan suit and a black duster. James was quite shorter than Rick, maybe by as much as a head but slightly stockier. His hair was a dark blond that was neatly trimmed and professionally layered. His eyes were an ice burg blue that stood out in contrast to his bushy eyebrows, which were a shade or two darker than his hair. The only thing the two shared in common was their preference in being clean-shaven.

"Well," Kendra pipped up, feeling awkward. "How about that coffee?"

"Oh, yes, um, that sounds delightful," James said with a slight grimace. Rick raised his eyebrows, a smirk danced briefly across his face and Kendra got the impression that she was missing out on some inside joke.

"Ok, I give up. What's with you?" Kendra asked James; him hiding his Britishness was getting on her nerves.

"Hmm? What? Nothing's wrong." Came his startled reply.

"You know exactly what I'm talking about. You're British, but you're trying to hide it for some reason," she said, though she was not really trying to pry. "I mean, unless it's a big secret," Kendra added feeling guilty.

"Oh, um, it's not a secret, really. I'm just trying to fit in with others in this country. I've been told my accent isn't very becoming here," James said, a blotch of red showing on his cheeks. "I guess I don't have a very good American accent."

"Well, the cat's out of the bag and that's that. Moving on, I do believe our hostess was just about to make some coffee or tea or something. We have lots to discuss, so we had better get moving." Rick started nudging Kendra to the kitchen rather impatiently and Kendra got the feeling he wanted to talk to James alone. Hoping she would get filled in later, she obligingly went into the other room to get some drinks for her unexpected house guests.

Kendra came to a halt in the doorway of her kitchen. Before her was a scene that came from one of her darkest nightmares. Her kitchen was a victim of the biggest mess she had ever encountered. Her dishes were piled in the sink looking like a replica of the leaning tower of Pisa. The stovetop was so covered in grease, it shinned under her 40-watt light bulbs, not to mention the counters were covered in flour, egg, and more grease. Staring into the abyss of what was left of her kitchen, a rolling heat started in her belly and began to make its way up to her head. A strong urge to kill filled her body, as rage like nothing she had ever felt before filled her being.

***

James and Rick huddled together talking low, so low that if Kendra had been eavesdropping from the kitchen, she wouldn't hear anything, even with her new vamp ears. The conversation was cut short, however, when Kendra came back into the room. She carried a wooden tray with three mugs of coffee and a plate of sugar cookies. It was a welcoming sight to the two men, but the smile that spread across her face had an unnerving edge to it.

She sat the tray on the mahogany coffee table in the living room and sat on the edge of the armchair across from them.

"Please, dig in." she said, "we have much to discuss." Her mood seemed to change the temperature in the room as a shiver ran down Rick's back. He wasn't sure what she was so pissed about, but it was palpable. Rick looked over at James, who shrugged, confirming to Rick that James could feel it too.

"Uh, ok, I get the feeling you want to talk about something, so why don't you start." With a wave of his hand, Rick gave Kendra the floor to which she sat straight up and her smile disappeared.

"Yes, as a matter of fact, I would like to talk about the state in which you left my kitchen. It is a disaster area. It looks like a bakery exploded all over my countertop and stove. Did you have to use all of my dishes to prepare your breakfast extravaganza?"

Rick began laughing. He couldn't help it. *That's* what she's angry about? He tried to stop himself, knowing his amusement was only going to piss her off more, but her angry face was so cute and funny that the laughter just kept coming. She glared daggers at him with a deep purple-red that filled her face and made her look like an angry cherry. He lost it, rolling with laughter with no end in sight. Kendra tried to talk over him but he couldn't hear a word of it. What finally made him stop was the nervous look he was getting from James.

When the seemingly endless laughter ended, Rick wiped tears from his eyes for the second time in 24 hours. "Right, right, well, now that that is over with, down to business. We have to get you in front of the Council before too long. So I suggest you get your affairs in order before then." Kendra looked at him with a baffled expression.

"So that's it then? Screw the dirty dishes, let's take a trip to where ever and meet with this Council of yours, hmm? What about my kitchen? Aren't you going to at least help me clean it up?" Kendra was near shouting by this point and Rick really didn't care one bit about the kitchen. What was funny was she forgot she's a vampire now. Household chores are pretty much a thing of the past. She could have that kitchen done in minutes if she wanted to. The problem here wasn't a dirty kitchen; it was getting Kendra to realize her new potential. Why not have a little fun getting her there, though. Right?

He smiled,

"I knew you would understand. Sorry for the trouble, but I'm sure you can take care of that." Rick said as he stood up, "Thanks for the tea and cookies but James and I have some work to do before the three of us take off for Rome in about four days. Like I said before you'll want to get your plans in order, tie up loose ends and so forth. All the information you need is in this folder."

Rick pulled a plain blue folder out from inside his trench coat and dropped it on her coffee table. "Ok, James, my friend. I think it's time we skedaddle out of here."

"Wait a minute, you're not going to just leave without cleaning my kitchen, are you?" Kendra yelled but they were gone before she completed that sentence. Rick heard every word of it, though, and couldn't help chuckling to himself. James gave him a disapproving side look, but Rick didn't have to explain himself to him. He was pushed into this so why shouldn't he have some fun.

***

Kendra sat in her living room, staring at the empty couch were James and Rick had been sitting moments earlier. She couldn't believe him; he had some nerve destroying her kitchen and leaving it a mess for her to clean up. She stood briskly and carried the tray back into the kitchen, deciding to put her ager to good use. As she walked back through her kitchen doorway, she was again struck by the piggish mess left in Rick's wake.

She sighed as she figured out the best starting point; her breathing deeply helped clear her head. She stood there slowly breathing and then almost like magic she began to move, really move. She had the dishes done in under two minutes, the counters cleaned in half that. Next was the stove. Before she knew it, five minutes had passed and her kitchen was spotless again. It wasn't just clean, it was better than that. In about 10 minutes, she had cleaned the mess Rick left behind, reorganized her cabinets like she had been wanting to, swept and mopped the floor, then made a cup of hot tea. She stood at the island, sipping her hot chamomile tea, thinking.

I wonder if Rick did that so I would learn more about my powers. Kendra pondered that for a moment. She came to the conclusion that Rick was just an asshole before finishing her tea. She placed the cup in the sink and headed out of the kitchen. The hall bathroom light was still on from earlier and Kendra was about to turn it off, dreading her next electric bill, when her reflection caught her eye. She walked in to get a better look at herself, trying to see the differences that vampirism brought on.

While her skin was lighter and more opaque, it still had a warmth behind it, perhaps from her recent feeding. Kendra opened her mouth and looked at her two new canine teeth. They didn't look much different from her previous teeth, save for being much sharper, though, you couldn't tell just by looking at them. Other than the unnatural shine of her eyes, she looked pretty much the same.

"Of course I look the same, how else would vampires get away with blending in for so long." She spoke angrily at her reflection. Feeling foolish, she went back into the living room where the ominous blue folder that held her destiny awaited, still in its place on her coffee table. She sat on the couch and picked it up. It was much lighter than she thought it would be.

Inside was a flight schedule and a roundtrip ticket for to Rome, Italy. Kendra's eyes grew large as she stared at the ticket in her hand. It was First Class. She had never flown First Class. She had never flown — period. Feeling apprehensive about the trip to come in four days, she put the ticket in the empty left pocket of the folder. The next piece of paper was the directions to the overnight babysitting facility where her children were.

She didn't recognize the name of the facility, but the location was familiar; it was near Fort Benning. Kendra groaned. That's a two-and-a-half-hour drive. *Why?* She could almost hear Rick's laughter at what must be his version of hazing the new guy. Thankfully it was only 9 am and her work was under the impression that she was sick. There was a strange blank, white card attached to the directions and apparently, she was to show it to them when she went to retrieve her children.

The last paper had a bank card bearing her name in a clear plastic sleeve attached to it. The paper was a handwritten letter from the jerk himself. It stated that the card was for her use, so she didn't have to spend her own money. He had apparently given her some money from his personal funds to spend on herself. He even sounded very condescending in his letter as he instructed her to "buy herself something nice to wear." The letter didn't mention the available balance on the card but that was easy enough to figure out.

Aside from the huge creep factor that played into his unique brand of "charm," it was quite thoughtful of him to help her out financially. She wasn't sure if she had the gas money to drive to Columbus, Georgia. Kendra got up and grabbed the house phone off the stand in the kitchen. She dialed the 800-number on the back to get the balance. It took five minutes to set up the pin and phone passcode, then she got to the point where the automated system told her the amount available. Kendra almost dropped the phone when she heard how much money was there.

She pressed the pound key to hear it repeated just to make sure she heard it right. Rick had strangely enough been very generous in the money he was throwing her way. *Seriously, who has $80,000 readily available to just toss at someone?* She was beside herself; she knew she needed gas money and maybe some extra for the outfit he wanted her to buy, as well as other travel expenses, but what the hell made him think she needed 80 grand?

Shaking her head, she gathered her things and walked out the door. Kendra had been away from her kids long enough.

***

The drive was long and tedious; she had filled her tank before leaving and was at half tank by the time she reached the mysterious building that was in spitting distance of the military base. From what she could tell, it wasn't a part of the actual base, but it was definitely a government-run facility. There was an automatic gate with an intercom and keypad sporting a big red button. Kendra pressed it and after about a minute was answered with a nasally, monotoned voice.

"State your business." At first, Kendra wasn't sure what to say. She looked at the speaker as though it just asked her to do *The Macarena*. "State your business" the voice, now sounding annoyed, asked again.

"I'm here to pick up my kids, I was told …" Kendra began, after finding her voice.

"One moment" came the response that cut her off. Within minutes, the gate started to swing open. She drove through and was met by a guard about halfway up the drive. He waved her toward the second gate, which was opening as she drove forward.

Kendra pulled into a parking lot to a large brick building with a sign posted in front that read *AVIA CCD*. She got out of her car and looked around. There was only one door to the building. It was a darkly tinted glass door with no indication as to what lay behind it. Kendra sighed, "Only one path to take, I guess." She closed her car door and started up the walkway. She pressed a button on her key fob. Her car beeped twice, indicating it was locked and the alarm set.

Kendra opened the door and was greeted by a small room with a desk.

Two chairs sat on the wall with the door, serving as the waiting area of the room. The sound of a fan was all that the room offered and Kendra was the only person in the room. The desk sported a silver bell and a little sign that read *Ring for Service.* Kendra walked up to the bell and rang it. After ten minutes, she grew impatient and started tapping the ringer again and again.

Kendra must have rung the bell twenty times before the white door behind the desk opened. A pudgy man, about a head shorter then Kendra, stepped out; a tablet of some sort in his hands. He wore a pair of black prescription glasses that had a piece of tape wrapped around the nose piece. He had an agitated look on his face that told Kendra it wouldn't have mattered if she rang that damn bell twenty more times — he was still going to take his time getting to her.

He stood there sneering at her, a pungent aroma of body odor and stinky men's cologne assaulted her nostrils. The collar of his white button-up shirt was a dingy gray where sweat beaded up at his neck. He had pit stains and a pocket protector — classic nerd. The only thing that wasn't classic about this guy was his upturned nose as he looked down on her from an imaginary high pedestal. He stood in cold silence as if waiting for her to speak first.

"I'm here to pick up my ..." Kendra began before Mr. Pudgy's hand came up to stop her before she said any more.

"I.D. card" he said with the same nasally voice from the intercom. Kendra blinked; she wasn't sure what he was talking about, but she had a theory. She moved almost robotically, putting her hand in her purse. She pulled out the blank, white, plastic card and handed it to the man. He snatched it from her hand and shoved it into a card reader on his tablet.

The card almost disappeared into the device as the man tapped on the tablet's surface. "Wait here," he said before disappearing behind the white door. About ten to twenty minutes passed before the white door opened again. This time the pudgy man was not alone. Two women, almost a head taller than Kendra, came out wearing strange white and red uniforms. They had identical facial features that made them look like they were relatives, maybe even twins. One was carrying Aveline in her arms, the other had Kendra's two oldest at hand. They slipped the woman's grip and ran up to Kendra. Wrapping their arms around their mommy's legs, the two began talking together excitedly, wanting to tell of their experience in this place.

Kendra shushed them and looked up at Mr. Pudgy. He ignored the children and handed Kendra the tablet.

"These are a few finalizing forms. I need you to sign on the dotted line." He said as he handed her a stylis, "This form ensures us that you have successfully retrieved your offspring." The man said as Kendra signed her name. He swiped up on the tablet to show another form under the first one. "By signing this form, you confirm they were received with no damages." Kendra signed as he explained, but she was getting tired of him talking about her kids as if they were property. "And this one is to waive all storage fees." Kendra signed the stupid form with a strong urge to bury her fist in his pimply face. Then he and the twins retreated back behind the white door. No goodbye, no "Have a nice day" — nothing. *How rude!*

Kendra strapped her kids in their car seats and pulled out of the facility's gates with every intention of getting as far away from this mysterious place and its weird inhabitants.

Preperation

"Yes, I understand," Rick spoke into the speaker of the throw-away flip phone. "Believe me, I know. It will be done, Councilman." Then, with a curt goodbye, Rick hung up the phone. James leaned against the exposed brick wall of the back ally motel where they were instructed to go to find the phone. His head hung low like he had fallen asleep in that position. "Go on, say what's on your mind." Rick said, the tension in the room making the air feel heavy.

James straightened up; the light glinted in his eyes. A piercing fire seemed to dance behind them as he stared Rick down.

"I can't believe you're ok with this," James said with a dagger-sharp tongue.

"It must be done, James." Rick looked away; he couldn't stand to look into those eyes.

"The hell it does! Rick, they're just children!" James was shaking with fury. He couldn't believe Rick would be a part of this. Rick continued to avoid looking at James.

After a few minutes passed, James turned to leave with a huff. "James," Rick's voice cracked, making James stop in place. "What do you want me to do? I'm just as bound to the Council as you are." Rick looked over at James with what seemed like hopelessness, but James knew batter.

James turned around, squared his shoulders, and said: "Out of all the vampires in this world, I would have never figured you to be one of those content with being the Council's lap dog. In the short time I've known you, Rick, I would have never figured you to be one to give up or give in. I will not be a part of this." And with that, James turned on his heel and walked out.

***

Kendra parked outside of Janet's house. Yesterday was spent getting her kids back from that strange facility near Ft. Benning, after which she spent some much-needed quality time with her kids. They told her all about the indoor slide with the giant ball pit and the nice nurse lady that watched after Aveline. Kendra was pleased that, despite her initial impression, the facility seemed to be very good with children. She drove home with them talking excitedly about a little girl they had befriended while they stayed there. She was glad they didn't ask why they didn't go to their aunt's house and once home, she tucked them snuggly into bed.

Shortly after that, she found it very difficult to sleep and ended up lying in bed awake all night. Despite not getting a wink of sleep, she felt really good, like she could take on the world. Today, however, she had to get a new cell phone to replace the one Rick had broken the other night and figure a way to convince Janet that she has to go to Rome without telling her why. Her new cell phone was active and in her hand as she stared at Janet's ranch style house. Kendra rolled down the two windows in the back to about halfway and opened her door.

"Stay here. I'll be back. I have to talk to aunt Janet and uncle Marcus." She told her kids as she got out of the car. Kendra walked up to the door and stood there for a moment, trying to get herself together. She breathed deep and focused on being "convincing." Kendra knocked three times on the door in rapid succession. She could hear Marcus inside say he was getting it and then the door opened.

"Hey Kendra, what brings you to this neck of the woods?" Marcus greeted her when he opened the door. "Weren't you really sick or something?" Kendra smiled, remembering that that was what Rick had made Janet believe. "Yep, but I'm all better now." She stared into his round, light brown eyes and tapped into the power she could feel deep inside, hoping this would work. "I have to go to Rome in three days. I need you and Janet to watch the kids for a while. If anyone asks, I'm still not feeling well." As Kendra spoke, a strange look came over Marcus's face, like he lost all strength in his facial muscles. When Kendra released her power, he snapped back to himself.

"Sure, Kendra, anything you say," came the creepy automatic response, "Did you want to talk to Janet?" he asked. Kendra nodded and Marcus stepped aside for Kendra to come in. She shook her head and said: "My kids are still in the car. I'd like it if they could still see me." With that, Marcus smiled and left her on the porch to fetch Janet. Kendra fidgeted while she waited, but it wasn't long before Janet stood in front of her.

"Hey, Kendra, is everything alright? Usually you call before stopping by." Kendra smiled warmly at her sister-in-law.

"Yeah, I'm fine. My cell broke and I had to get a new one. Here, this is my new number." Kendra handed Janet a small piece of paper torn from a notebook with her cell number on it. She repeated the process that she did with Marcus once Janet made eye contact. After Kendra was certain that Janet was thoroughly "convinced," she walked with Janet over to her car to fetch the kids.

"Mommy! Tell Zeke to stop pinching me, pleeaassee!" came the wailing of Sasha as they got close.

"I am not!" Zeke protested. Janet stifled a laugh as Kendra poked her head into the open window.

"That's enough you two. Now behave and keep your hands to yourselves." Kendra reprimanded them before opening the car door. Janet helped unload the kids and take them with their overnight bags into the house. Once the kids were settled and Janet had all she needed to care for them, Kendra gave her kids goodbye hugs before leaving.

***

The day after Kendra left her kids with Janet, she stopped by her job to put in a request for vacation time. Still unable to sleep but also not feeling tired in the slightest, she walked into the hospital through the front entrance thinking not sleeping must be a vampire thing. She made a mental note to ask Rick about it when she got the chance. After filling out the paperwork, she submitted it to her supervisor. She was just about to leave when someone called her name.

Kendra turned to see Linsey, the lead nurse for that day's shift, running up to her.

"Kendra, thank goodness I caught you before you left." She panted, "John wants to see you before you leave." Kendra blinked, "What does he want? I'm kind of in a hurry."

"He said something about a request you put in. That's all I know, sorry." Linsey said before running back down the hallway to the nurse's station. Kendra grumbled and began walking back down the hallway until she came across a door that read *Supervisor* on the paned glass. A pair of door blinds clinked against the door as Kendra opened it.

"You wanted to see me?" she asked.

The man at the desk looked up. He had grey-blue eyes and a receding dark blond hairline.

"Ah, yes, Kendra, come in." He wore a pin-striped blue and white button-up shirt with a dark blue tie. A dark black stain was forming on his chest where a pocket and three pens resided.

"Um, sir, your shirt." Kendra pointed at his pocket. He looked down quickly and cursed before pulling the three pens out. The middle one appeared to be the culprit as it was sticky with ink, but John threw all three of them in the trash, nonetheless.

"Come, sit down, I'll take care of this in a minute." He said. "We need to talk about this," he continued once Kendra was in the room. He held up the vacation time request form Kendra had just filled out. "You know our policy, Kendra. This request is too last minute; I need you here. You being out sick is one thing, but then you waltz in here and expect me to approve a three-week vacation time starting ..." He paused to look at the paper, "Today! What I would like to know is, why? Why do you need this, Kendra, what is going on? Why should I approve this?" Kendra shrunk down a little in her seat as he began a tirade about being shorthanded.

Once he calmed down some, Kendra sat up a little straighter. She focused on her newfound power and the moment he looked her straight in the eye, she had him.

"You will sign the vacation request and you will mark it as a family emergency. I've been called to attend a family member's funeral." She then released him from her hold, he shook himself and looked at her with a more apologetic look.

"I'm so sorry for your loss, Kendra. Please excuse the outburst from earlier," he said. Kendra decided that she didn't really like using this ability but it was very useful. They said their goodbyes and Kendra left the hospital feeling like she never wanted to do that again.

Kendra needed to unwind a little and found great pleasure in just driving around a bit; she especially liked driving on back roads. She could lose herself just driving, getting a little lost at times, and getting to know the area a little more each time. Kendra drove around for a while before it sunk in how late it was getting, she swung by a fast food place and went through the drive threw. After ordering, she headed home, munching down the burger and fries.

She had to make a stop to get gas before getting home and didn't arrive until almost 8 pm. When she walked in the door, she was feeling hungry again, fast food never stayed with her too long, but this is ridiculous. She walked into the kitchen and dug around in the fridge but couldn't find anything that piqued her interest. Then she felt a strange twinge in her gums around her canine teeth. She swirled her tongue around her teeth, pondering it before she remembered that she's a vampire now and the hunger she is feeling is probably for something other than food.

Panic struck her — she had never fed alone before, and Kendra wasn't sure she could do it by herself without killing. She started to think of everything Rick had taught her and remembered that he had said vampires aren't murderous killing machines. *There must be a reason for that, maybe a vampire doesn't need to take in a lot of blood to survive. I've certainly gone a couple of days without feeling the need, so why not? I'll have to learn how to do this on my own anyway, right?* She thought about it a little longer and after a quick pep-talk, left the house in search for her second meal for the night.

Hunter

It seemed like only minutes had passed by the time Kendra was on the other side of Atlanta hanging on to a third-story window and looking in at a young man. She had found herself at a college dorm building and rather attracted to the smell of this particular college student. He was fast asleep on a twin-sized bed in your classic styled male dorm room. He looked to be in his early 20's with dark brown hair and had some stubble on his chin and upper lip. There was another twin bed on the opposite side of the room, but it was empty. In addition, there were some personal effects decorating the other side, suggesting an absent roommate.

It was a risk, but she was going to take it. At the very least, she could make it seem like she was screwing him, giving him a better reputation than he probably had, considering he was alone while a party blared nearby. The window was unlocked, of course. What normal person would be able to climb up here without a tree in sight. She slid the window up and slipped in, leaving the window open for an easy escape. When she got to his bedside, she found out why he smelled so strongly. He had apparently taken a beating pretty recently, which also explains why he wasn't out partying like the other students.

His face was bruised on one side and a cut above his left eye still bled even with the bandage. The smell of his blood was very strong the closer she got. The fangs that she had grown with her last feeding extended down and ached to sink into his neck. Kendra moved closer, the throbbing of the vein in his neck calling to her. She went to her knees at his bedside and turned his head toward the wall so as to get to his neck better.

Kendra felt her fangs pierce his skin and the hot rush of fresh blood spilled into her mouth. She stifled a moan as it filled her with a pleasure that begged her to drink deeply of the hot blood as it pumped out of the two wounds in his neck. It only took moments before she had had her fill and she didn't have to keep drinking until his heart fluttered with impending death. She licked the wounds until they healed and not a mark was left to be seen.

Suddenly, there were voices just outside the dorm room door. When the door handle started to jiggle, Kendra was on the move. Before the door swung open, she was closing the window and out of sight. She could hear them inside yelling and shouting about the events of the party. Kendra's victim just moaned, yelled something back, and went back to sleep. With that, she slipped away into the night.

The trek back home took a little longer, mainly because Kendra got the strange sense that someone was following her. She kept stopping every so often to look around but couldn't find anything. She focused on all her senses to try to detect whoever it was that could be following her and still got nothing back. She chalked it up to her being a little paranoid and decided not to stop again.

Pain suddenly blinded her, and she was flung through the air like she had been broadsided by a semi. When her vision cleared, she saw a hulking man standing roughly six feet away from her. Her nose told her he was human, but his eyes said something else entirely. In an instant she was on her feet and ready to faceoff with this monstrous man when she heard laughing. At first, she thought it was the mountainous man in front of her but the laughter wasn't coming from his direction at all.

She looked around, trying to keep the lumbering hulk in front of her but she wasn't able to pinpoint the laughter before it had stopped. The rustling of a nearby pine tree caught her attention and she focused in on its branches. A skinny man stood near the top on one of thickest branches. He leaned on the trunk of the tree, staring down at her.

"See me now little Vampira, hmm?" he said and continued to cackle some more. The skinny man jumped down landing next to his hulking compadre, an impressive 30-foot drop that would have killed a normal human, and he landed softly on the grass.

Something about his landing bothered Kendra, but she couldn't put her finger on it. She pushed it out of her mind for a time and returned her focus on the strange pair.

"What do you want? Who are you?" She yelled at them. The skinny man pipped up first with more manic laughter, "One question at a time, little Vampira. First, let me introduce myself. I'm Phaze and this large oaf next to me is Zackery. Say hello, Zackery." And with that the giant lug let out a loud, snarling, roar. Thee monster looked like he had been taking some really bad steroids because he was nothing but muscle and stood about seven-foot tall.

"Ok, that barely answers one question. What about the other. What do you want from me?" Kendra said folding her arms across her chest. On the outside, she tried to seem calm and unaffected by the monster's outburst. On the inside, however, she was scared to death and trying to hide her shaking.

"Oh, that can be easily answered" Phaze said with a spreading grin. "Zackery, sic her!" Mount Zackery lunged into a blur before Kendra's eyes; he was fast. Kendra was faster, though, and she easily dodged the hulking figure that charged at her. She landed about a foot away from where Zackery came crashing down. He left a small crater where she had stood. Dirt plumed above him before falling back to earth. Kendra stood straighter and looking over at Phaze she asked: "So are you here to kill me or did Rick send you to test me?"

"Rick?" Phaze took on an unconvincingly innocent look, "Rick, who?" he asked, "Is he your dark father, Vampira?" Kendra didn't know what to make of these two. Phaze seemed to be the brains and Zackery was his wrecking ball. However, Phaze was also a bit off his rocker.

"Dark father? If you mean my sire, then yes. Your confusion answers my question, though." Kendra replied. She charged at Phaze. *Cut off the head and the snake dies,* she thought. Kendra could hear Zackery barreling behind her. She zigged and zagged to keep him from catching up easily. She was almost on top of Phaze when she realized he wasn't moving and the thought crossed her mind that maybe Phaze was playing bait for Zackery.

At the last minute, she jumped up and over Phaze, out of the way of Zackery's charge. Phaze's smiling face quickly turned into a blanched white look of fear just before Zackery bowled him over. Kendra stood at the ready, watching the two tumble end over end and became a mass of tangled limbs. A strong, highly intoxicating aroma wafted over to her. At first she wasn't sure, but Kendra believed it to be the smell of their blood as it was the only possible thing that could have this effect over her.

They didn't move for a few minutes and Kendra became impatient. She started to walk over to them, wanting to inspect the damage and figure out more about what she had just faced. Then the pile moved and the mass of limbs began to disentangle themselves. Zackery stood, looking down at was must be a puddle of Phaze, and then roared so loud Kendra was sure someone was going to report it. For a moment, the thought of the poor bastard who would have to give Zackery a ticket for disturbing the peace made her chuckle.

Bad idea, Kendra thought. Zackery snapped around, his trained red eyes on her; the shine of revenge had Kendra nervous. She readied herself. Kendra wasn't sure what was about to happen, but she knew it was fight or die. And seeing as she didn't plan on dying tonight, she geared up for the fight. Zackery snarled, a thick line of saliva dripped down as he breathed deeply. The vapors of his breath enveloped his frame and caught the moonlight. He was aimed right at her, digging his heels in he began to charge. His feet caused the dirt to fly, like every step was propelled by an explosion.

Here he comes! Kendra let instinct take over, and just as Zackery was about to bowl her over, time seemed to stand still. She moved faster than him; to her eyes it was like he was moving in slow motion. She ran at him and using her newfound talent, pushed off of the ground. Like something she had seen in karate movies, Kendra pulled off a roundhouse kick in mid-air, her heal slammed into Zachery's temple.

The hulking behemoth went tumbling end over end into a couple of trees, snapping them at the base. The odd angle of his head told Kendra he wasn't getting up from that position any time soon. Kendra waited some time before moving forward, the reality of what she had just done sinking in. The sound of blood dripping from his mangled body called to her and she walked closer to him. The sound of movement where Phaze had been pummeled caught her attention and she looked away for a moment.

Zackery's big meaty hand swooped up and grabbed Kendra by the throat, lifting her into the air. His head was crooked, and she could not hear his heart. Zackery seemed to breathe for the sole purpose of huffing air through his nostrils. Kendra dug her boots into his huge chest and pushed off as hard as she could, the force staggered Zackery and Kendra landed on her feet some distance away.

She charged him, running at top speed. Kendra aimed for his chest and rammed her hand straight through, grabbing his heart on the way out. *Let's see you live through this big guy!* She pulled her hand out with a sick wet sound, the heart getting lost somewhere inside. Blood coated her arm up to her shoulder, and Zachery's big body fell with a thud.

The smell was intense as Kendra dropped down to her knees by the hulking body of Zackery. Almost like she was hypnotized, she started licking the blood that dripped off her hand and down her elbow. She couldn't stop herself and part of her didn't want to as she moved to get more from his chest. His blood tingled her tongue and she could feel power in it. The small wounds she had sustained healed rapidly and a new strength washed through her.

Something rustled nearby, Kendra popped her head up, the blood forgotten. The sight of movement from Phaze's spot of demise surprised her. She stood, trying to get a better look. *There is no way that Phaze survived that,* but he did. Crawling up from the ground like a scene from a bad zombie movie, Phaze pulled his mangled body up with one arm.

"Zackery! Where are you? I need help!" Kendra walked over to Phaze with the intent of putting her foot through his skull.

"He's dead, and you're next."

When Kendra got close enough, she could see he was quite literally a broken man. The only thing that wasn't broken on him was his left arm and apparently his will to live. Kendra figured he wouldn't live very long and the fact he was still alive was very surprising. He was in pain, lots of pain; his death would probably be agonizing. "On second thought, I think I'll just leave you here to die. Killing you now would just be an act of mercy." Kendra turned to leave but he grabbed her ankle.

"Please, kill me. I can't stand it. The pain." He gurgled through his own blood. Kendra ripped her ankle free of his hold and walked way. "You'll regret this, I promise you! I'll have my revenge! There are others, they know who we hunted tonight, and they will find you!" Phaze yelled after her. The fact that there were others was a troubling thought, but she kept walking, pondering over how they knew of her when she had only been a vampire for three days.

When Kendra walked through her front door, she froze. A tall figure was standing in her living room. For a moment, she panicked, thinking it was one of the hunters that Phaze had mentioned. Instinctively, she smelled the air and a familiar scent calmed her down.

"Rick, you startled me." She breathed "Why are you standing in my living room with the lights off?" Kendra flicked the switch by the door.

"I was just waiting for your return. What kept you?" Rick blinked as light blinded him.

"I was ambushed on my way back from feeding." Kendra closed the front door. Rick snorted.

"Ambushed? By who?" Kendra sat on the couch.

"I don't know who they were, but there were two of them and they seemed to know me."

Rick's eyebrows furrowed "Two of them? Did either of them say anything?" Rick sat on the chair in front of Kendra. "Yes, actually one of them was very talkative. Although he really didn't say much about anything." Kendra watched as Rick's expressions displayed his nervousness.

"Did either of them give a name?" he fidgeted. "Yes, the skinny one said his name was Phaze and introduced the big guy as Zachery. Rick, is something wrong?" Rick stood from the chair and started to pace.

"Phaze, huh? That's bad, really bad. He's a hunter and a really good one." Kendra smiled and with a small giggle said: "You mean 'was.'" Kendra sat straighter with pride.

Rick stared at her a bit wide-eyed.

"He's dead? You're sure? Where's his body?" Rick was quickly standing in front of Kendra with his hands on her shoulders.

"About forty blocks from here, in the middle of Central Park, near the tennis court." After Kendra finished speaking, Rick pulled out his cell phone and dialed a number.

"This is agent Richard Blake. I need a clean-up crew at Central Park, tennis court grounds. Code 018-259. I also want a full report of the scene: number of DBs, forensic evidence, and the identity of the DBs, ASAP." After a moment's pause, Rick continued. "You leave the Chief to me. I'll handle all the loose ends. You just need to get me that report." Then Rick hung up the phone.

When he looked back a Kendra, her eyebrows were furrowed with worry. "I have to go. I'm sorry there's just no time to explain. We'll talk on the plane." That was all he said, and he was gone again, leaving Kendra in the dark. Pissed off, Kendra went upstairs to change her torn dirty, blood cover cloths. She walked past her kid's rooms and headed for the master bedroom at the end of the hall. Kendra couldn't help but notice that the rooms were in disarray as per usual with children. She wanted to go in but couldn't bear the thought of touching anything in the state she was in.

She mustered up whatever kind of power it was that allowed her to move a lightning speed and changed her clothes very literally in a flash. Despite even taking time to figure out what she wanted to wear, it took her less than half the time it normally took to get dressed. Coming back to the rooms, she was tempted to move through it quickly, but she stopped herself. She was going to be gone from her children for some time; Kendra wanted to savor the feeling of being a mom.

With tender loving care, she replaced everything in their rooms, making them neat and tidy for the day her kids would return to them. Satisfied with what she had accomplished, Kendra went down the stairs. She still found it strange that she didn't feel the least bit tired. She looked around at her living room, not sure what she wanted to do. Not really in the mood for TV, she walked out her back door and stared up at the starry night sky. She witnessed a shooting star and, though she knew it was just a meteor, Kendra made a wish anyway.

***

Rick dashed across rooftops until they became too scarce and then just ran. He made it to the sight before any of his people. Just like the AVIA responder had said earlier, local authorities had already fallen upon the scene; now he had to do damage control. *They get quicker every decade.* Pulling out his FBI badge to flash to the police, he walked at a normal brisk pace to the closest officer. He tapped the man and asked to speak to the lead investigator, to which Rick was pointed in the direction of a portly man in a sheriff's uniform.

"Sheriff Rhodes, I'm FBI agent Richard Blake," Rick said, flashing his FBI badge at the man. "I'm taking over this investigation. It's a matter of national security, so I'm going to have to take everything you have here. My people will be here shortly to take over." The sheriff looked like he was rather relieved to hear it until he gave Rick a quizzical look.

"Um, Agent Blake, is it? Sorry, you don't look like an FBI agent. Could I see your credentials again, just to be sure." Rick smiled.

"Of course, Sheriff." He held the badge open so the sheriff could inspect it, thankfully AVIA was able to communicate with the FBI. Though his badge was quite genuine, he wasn't an agent of the FBI. AVIA didn't exist as far as the general public was concerned. It was only one of the various and very real badges and I.D.'s in Rick's arsenal. The further you got in AVIA, the broader your reach.

"Ok, sorry about that, Agent Blake," the sheriff tipped his hat. "Can't be too careful these days, what with youngsters runnin' 'round with their fake I.D.'s an all." Rick tucked his badge back into his coat pocket.

"Understood, Sheriff. Now, if you wouldn't mind, I need you to clear the scene. You're CSI's can continue to collect until my people get here, I know how important it is to get the evidence quickly. They will need to hand over everything, however, as well as all the reports made by your officers."

"Right, right. So, uh, you think this was some sort of terrorist attack? It's mighty bloody, but it doesn't seem very significant." The sheriff drawled, prying for a bit of juicy info. Rick bit back a smirk. Their guys in the FBI told them to make sure that anyone carrying badges remained professional. "Sorry, Sheriff. I'm afraid that information is classified." The sheriff grimaced.

"I was afraid you'd say somethin' like that. Alright, lemme go tell the fellas," Sheriff Rhodes ambled off to start shutting down his people's investigation.

Before long, all that was left were the CSI techs photographing, bagging, and tagging evidence. Sheriff Rhodes had his key officers stand off to the side. They waited to pass off the case specifics to the "FBI" people that were en route. There weren't any witnesses to question. As a matter of fact, it was an officer on patrol who called in the scene. After talking with the other officers, Rick was pointed in the direction of a thin, pasty looking rookie.

Officer Johnson seemed to be roughly 25 years old. Of course, in these modern times, Rick had a hard time telling age by looks alone. Even the men looked younger than they appeared thanks to advancements made in technology and medicine. When the officer began to talk, however, it really showed his age and Rick was delighted in the fact that he could still tell a rookie from a mile away. Officer Johnson was a gas cloud of perspiration and nervousness.

While Rick questioned the young officer about what he had seen, the "FBI" crew showed up to begin their investigation. The majority of the group were blooded vampires with a few "in the know" humans thrown in, the ones the Council keeps on a tight leash. One person, in particular, stood out in the crown. Her scent wafted over Rick before he caught a glimpse of her. Even working in this line of work, he doesn't run into her very often.

Her brown hair bounced in its usual short curls, reminding Rick every bit of her mother. When she turned to see him, the smile that spread across her round face lit up her light brown eyes. She walked over to him, looking very comfy in her beige cargo pants and light blue blouse.

"Well, well, look what the cat dragged in," she laughed good-naturedly "Haven't seen you around much lately. The agency keeping you busy?"

"Hello, Sarah. Nice to see you, too. Oh, I'm fine, thanks for asking." Rick smirked "You never were one for small talk, so how about we just jump into it. I didn't get much of a look at the crime scene. Do you have anything to tell me yet or no?" Sarah frowned but didn't argue.

"So far not much, one DB, and a lot of wreckage. The agents on ground control are taking care of the officers, working their hypnotic magic on their memories. There are two downed trees over there, and a whole that looks like a small meteor landed over there." Sarah pointed to two locations.

"Wait, only one DB? There aren't any more?" Rick asked. Sarah gave him an odd look, "No, only one, a John Doe. A big John Doe; we'll have to bring in the super-size me gurney. There are also some tire tracks leading further into the park over here. One of the local CSI's had already made a mold of it for analysis." Sarah spoke as she led Rick to the crime scene tape boundaries. Just beyond were the tire treads she had mentioned; Central Park was pretty huge — they could be anywhere by now.

"Rick, what's going on here? You have a strange look in your eyes." Sarah squatted next to Rick, trying to get a better look at him. Rick rubbed the bridge of his nose.

"It's complicated, Sarah. I'm going to give James a call and see if he'll help, but I'm not sure he'll answer me right now." Rick stood. Sarah mirrored his moves, worry knotting her forehead.

"What did you do to piss him off this time?"

Rick chuckled slightly. "Everything I do seems to piss him off these days. Keep me updated. You got it from here, right?" Sarah nodded and watched Rick turn to leave.

"Hey, Rick. If he picks up, will you tell Dad I said hi?" Rick smiled and nodded.

"Will do."

First Class

Hartsfield Atlanta Airport was gigantic. Kendra had to go to the information desk to ask where she had to go, thankful she had arrived four hours early. It took her almost two hours to find someone who could point her in the right direction. Walking up to the twentieth person behind a flight podium, she handed the lady her ticket and asked if she was in the right place. The lady, who's name tag read *Jessica*, tapped on her computer before looking back at Kendra.

"I'm sorry, ma'am. I don't see your ticket in our system." Kendra gapped at Jessica like a fish who needed air.

"What do you mean you don't see my ticket?" Kendra wanted to pull her hair by its roots, mentally swearing that this would be the only time she'd fly ever. Even if flying cars were invented, she'd rather walk.

"Hold on. I think I found the problem," Jessica said before Kendra could have a mental break down.

"I found the ticket in the system. It seems like it had been canceled. Now, before you panic," Jessica said, noticing the startled look on Kendra's face, "there is a note on the cancelation that the bearer of this ticket is to board a private jet. The private aircrafts are located off the international terminals. If you head that way," Jessica pointed to her left, "you'll find them no problem. Take this card and show it to the attendant at the F-10 terminal and they will take it from there."

Jessica waved Kendra off with a smile and a "have a nice flight." Kendra thanked the woman and ran at a fast, yet still human, speed. *Private jet? Why a private jet? It wasn't enough that he had me sitting in first class. No, let's make it more expensive and flashy. I'll have her board a private jet. But not before having her run around the fucking place like a lunatic with a canceled ticket.* Kendra fumed to the point that the chance if steam coming out of her ears was becoming more of a possibility.

It would seem like that was exactly what had happened by the look on the attendant's face. Kendra's anger must have shown through because the man looked at her like she was a bomb about to go off. Kendra handed the poor man the card that had the flight number on it and tried to calm down before they labeled her a potential terrorist. The last thing she needed was some swat team wannabe security guards tackling her in the middle of the world's busiest airport. That would really put a damper on things and will not help improve her mood.

He ushered her to a door that led downstairs and to the flight pad, then he escorted her to a black, unmarked jet. She wasn't sure if it was large in comparison to other jets, but it was definitely the largest vehicle she had ever been close to. The engine hummed and the steps were pulled down for her to board. Kendra wasn't sure if it was possible, but the inside seemed bigger than the outside.

There was a bar, four tables with chairs surrounding them, a couple of couches with end tables, and a small two or three-person hot tub in the middle. The attendant took her bags and put them into a compartment near the front, next to the door leading to the cockpit. A stewardess stood with her hands clasped in the middle of the plane, just off to the left of the hot tub. Her name tag announced her as Cindy and her smile was well-practiced, though not very genuine.

"Welcome, Ms. Blake. If you need anything please don't hesitate to ask." Cindy chimed while Kendra took in the sights.

"Yeah, no problem. Wait, what did you call me?" Kendra snapped her head around to look at the woman. Cindy's smile drooped a little,

"Ms. Blake, Don't worry. Mr. Blake explained that you're his sister and that you're not accustomed to this kind of treatment. Although, I'm afraid

I've never known Mr. Blake to have a sister, or any family for that matter. He simply said to make sure you are comfortable during the journey."

"Oh, he did, did he?" Kendra questioned, the wheels in her head already turning on how she was going to get back at him. "Well, maybe you could answer a few questions, Cindy. When is takeoff and do you know if my *brother* will be joining us?" Kendra's voice darkened when she was forced to refer to Rick as her brother.

"We depart in 30 minutes and Mr. Blake is already on board." Cindy left then with Kendra looking about the cabin for the elusive Mr. Blake. The male attendant had left long ago, rolling the stairs away and closing the door behind him. It had seemed she was alone until the familiar snickering drew her attention to a chair facing away from her.

Like a villain from some cheesy movie, Rick sat in the turning chair, barely able to contain his girlish giggles. The heat rose in Kendra's cheeks, anger boiled her innards, and an outburst of profanity danced on her tongue. Before she could open her mouth, Rick stood and had somehow gained control of himself. "It would seem I've left you speechless. The look on your face, however, seems to be doing the talking for you. Look, I did what I did for a good reason. A private jet is the best place to conduct business. Something has come up that you have to be made aware of." Rick paused, "As of this moment, you have been temporarily deputized as an AVIA agent, Council's orders. Here is your paperwork." Rick handed Kendra a manila envelope that was so full it felt as though it would burst in her hands.

"There is a matter of utmost urgency that we have to deal with once we land in Rome. A small horde of ghouls were spotted and dealt with near the outskirts of the city. We have to figure out what happened and fast. I'm sure you have a few questions, so, by all means, ask away." Rick finished and sat back down in his seat motioning for Kendra to be seated herself.

Kendra sat opposite him, dumbfounded, anger forgotten, and gapping again, like a fish. Her head reeled with so many questions that she felt it might explode. She asked the first question she could get a grasp on.

"Ghouls? What are ghouls?" She sat the envelope down on the table next to her before it could break open in her hand.

"Where to begin?" Rick sighed. He sat back rubbing his temples. "Ok, you and I are a class of vampire known as 'blooded.' There are four total classes. These are the pure vampires, blooded vampires, pure dhampirs, and dhampirs — in order of strength. Dhampirs are the result of vampires breeding with humans. Pure dhampirs are the result of dhampirs breeding with vampires or other dhampirs. They are the most common among us, and the deadliest if left unchecked. If a pure dhampir stops feeding on blood for an extended amount of time, they run the risk of becoming what we call a 'ghoul.'

"AVIA was founded to police our own kind and dhampirs are a part of us, so a major part of AVIA is to wipe out threats, including rogue vampires. Ghouls are a class of rogue vampire, but what makes this bad is that there was a horde of ghouls. It was large for a group of ghouls, about six or seven, but even with that in mind, this is a very strange situation. This isn't something that happens often. It takes roughly six years of starvation before a pure dhampir will go rogue, so there is some presumption that someone else is behind this, we need to find out who and why." Rick sat back eyes trained on Kendra. He was soon lost in thought, the wheels turning behind his hazel eyes, as Kendra pondered the information.

The plane began to move and the pilot came over the intercom.

"We have been cleared for takeoff, please take your seats and fasten your seat belts. We will be arriving in Rome, Italy in approximately nine and a half hours." Kendra watched Rick buckle up before strapping herself into her own seat.

"Why do I have to be a part of this? Why deputize me?" she asked as she tested the belt that lay across her lap. Rick shrugged, "I don't know. Honestly, the Council is the one who made the call."

"Ok, so why all the run around back there?" Kendra jerked her thumb in the direction of the airport. Rick shrugged again.

"Couldn't have been helped, sorry." Kendra squinted at him.

"You could have called, you know." Rick grinned.

"I know, but where's the fun in that?" Kendra stared at him as the vision of cheesy villain came back to mind. She could almost picture him laughing maniacally and twirling a long, curled, pencil-thin mustache between his thumb and forefinger. She put it aside for now and picked up the manila envelope, intent on opening it. "Wait on that a moment, at least until we're in the air. We wouldn't want all those papers to go flying when the plane takes off," Rick warned and Kendra resigned to simply hold the large package in her lap. The plane started to pick up speed as it started down the runway. Kendra could feel the pull as the wheels left the ground and the jet started to point up. She felt like she was about to lose her lunch and bit back the urge to let everything in her stomach coat the jet's interior. Once the small jet had stabilized in the air, it was much more tolerable even with her ears popping here and there.

Kendra pushed her finger into the sealed envelope a little impatiently and pulled it open. Inside were five different badges from high-up Italian government groups with her information printed on them. There were stacks of documents outlining what looked like the incident Rick had described, as well as a few that may have been tied in, thankfully typed up in English. She scanned the papers, looking at the details and trying to piece together the scene.

Words like *massacre, carnage*, and *zombies* stood out in bold contrast as Kendra scanned the pages. I was horrible, but what made Kendra wonder the most is how connected the members of the Vampire Council had to be to keep this kind of thing out of the public eye. Another thing that kept popping up was the word *Sanctuary* and the fact that it was capitalized seemed to make it mean something.

"What is Sanctuary?" Rick was staring out the plane window and didn't seem to hear her. His eyes were distant, like he was lost in his thoughts, and Kendra could only guess at what memories a 600-year old vampire would dwell on. She cleared her throat, but he was still lost to her, his eyes dancing like fire. Kendra was at first resigned to simply let him reminisce and looked back down at the report. As she read, *Sanctuary* kept popping up with no explanation or further details. Then something sparkled in her peripheral vision.

She looked to her left to find a silver cup sitting in a cup holder built into the table. Kendra picked up the cup and found that it wasn't silver but aluminum, and it was full of ice water. A devilish thought crossed her mind and before she could talk herself out of it, she sent the water flying, cup and all at Rick, and for an instant, revenge had never felt sweeter. The cold water splashed down on him like a tidal wave and Rick jumped, straining against the seat belt he still wore. Swearing loudly, he ripped the seat belt off the chair and stood in front of Kendra, the tattered remains of the belt dangling in his hand.

His breathing was quick, his eyes were unfocused, and the temperature in the room dropped a few degrees. For the second time since they first met, Kendra felt pure fear. Before her stood a predator, a killing machine, savage and unforgiving, and for the second time since they met, Kendra feared this man. He slowly came back to himself, blinking deliberately, he looked down at the belt in his hand, somewhat bewildered.

"Rick, are you ok? I'm sorry, it was just water, I just figured I'd get back at you …" Kendra trailed off as Rick continued to stare at the belt in his hand. When he finally looked at her all she could see in his eyes was fear. "It's been a long time since I … I can't believe I just …" he stammered, she unbuckled herself and stood to face him.

"It's ok, you don't have to explain. I didn't think — I just did it."

Rick grabbed her shoulders hard and looked intensely at her, multiple emotions flickered across his eyes. "I could have hurt you." was all he said.

Kendra couldn't help but smirk, in an effort to pull him out of this state, she said: "Hurt me, please. You forget I'm also a vamp; it would take a lot to hurt me." Rick knew Kendra was blowing out hot air and to some degree so did she. It worked, though, and got him to chuckle a little. He released the vice grip he had on her and sat back down in the now buckle-less chair.

"I wonder how the cabin cleaners are going to react when they see what I've done to this." He chuckled, twirling the belt in his left hand. "Oh, to be a fly on the wall at that moment." Glade to have the old Rick back, Kendra tried to remember the reason she wanted his attention in the first place. She glanced at the envelope next to her, its contents spread out on the table, and her memory came back.

"Rick, what is *Sanctuary*?" She picked a piece of paper up that had the words *The Attack on Sanctuary* in bold print. Without lifting his gaze, he responded:

"A dhampir village, basically. Though some vamps live there, too. Most of the attacks happened there, which was something of a lucky break. The town's existence and location are confidential, even I haven't been there. It was founded roughly 300 years ago, and I only know about it because of my time on the Council. It was a pet project of a vamp known as Ilium during my last year serving. Its purpose is to house dhampirs and vampires in a safe place, where they can be themselves and live without the fear of being found out by humans and other species."

"Other species?" Kendra's head popped up, "What other species?" Rick sighed.

"Really, Kendra, just a few days ago you found out that vampires exist, do you really think that other beings would be that much of a stretch?" He chuckled "That's beside the point, though. Sanctuary is highly top secret, so the fact that the Council is even letting you this close is huge. All I'm saying is just be on your guard; something else is going on here." Rick stopped there, without any further details, and was content to leave it at that. Kendra, on the other hand, was not content. She had questions that demanded answers.

"Ok, first of all, when were you going to tell me that you had served on the Council? What exactly are these "other species"? Also how does the Council keep a whole town secret? And why would it be kept secret from me? I'm a vampire, too. Don't they trust me?" Kendra was on the edge of her seat hoping she would get some answers out of Rick. He stared at her for a moment before answering.

"One, I have lived for over 600 years. I figured it would have been evident that at some point I would have served on the Council. Second, other species — as in not human, not vampire, not dhampir. Third, the Council is everywhere. They have their fingers in all the pies. It's not hard for them to keep something secret. And finally, no, they don't trust you. They don't trust anyone outside of their little circle. The town of Sanctuary is Top Secret — on a need-to-know basis, basically, for the protection of its inhabitants. Did I answer all of your questions?" Rick had surprisingly remained pretty nonchalant during his explanation.

"No, actually, you haven't. But it'll have to do for now." Kendra sighed and she slumped back in her chair. Picking the papers up again, she scanned over them with a new light, trying to piece the puzzle together. "I do have another question, after all. It's about what happened the other day, with Phaze. Who was he?

"Phaze, as I had told you, is a hunter. If I had known that night you were taking him on, I would have been there in a heartbeat. He's devious, conniving, and somehow always survives." Kendra gasped.

"You mean …" Rick nodded, "But how? How did he survive? I almost literally crushed him like a bug." Rick shrugged.

"I don't know, but his body wasn't at the scene; he was nowhere to be found. The evidence of your battle was very strong. Everyone was quite impressed. As a matter of fact, that might be the reason the Council wanted you to tag along on this new mission." Kendra felt a strong surge of pride; she still had questions but was content to leave well enough alone.

***

Rome, Italy
Pontifical Academy of Sciences

A knock came at the office door of Niccola Francesco. His secretary had just left for the evening and he had stayed to finish up some paperwork. Cursing under his breath, he stood, his bones creaking, and went to open the door. In the doorway stood an old friend, who, despite the years has stood the test of time. The man that now stood before him was a vampire and Niccola knew it through his connections, it also helps that his mother is a dhampir.

"Luca, my dearest friend. What brings you here to see me this evening? Come, sit down." Niccola led the tall, raven-haired vamp into his cluttered office. He picked up a stack of papers that had sat in one of the chairs so long it had begun to collect dust. After finding a new home for the stack, Niccola pointed to the seat and said, "Sit, sit, I'm sure you haven't come all this way just to stand in around. Please, make yourself comfortable, don't mind the mess. I'm old, I know that doesn't mean much to you but my old human body just isn't what it used to be." Niccola chuckled.

The younger-looking man sat quietly in the chair Niccola had so swiftly cleaned off for him. The vamp cleared his throat before speaking, "It really has been a long time, my friend, and I wish my visit here was for more social reasons. I'm here on business from the Council. I'm afraid I bring bad news." He paused for a moment, a sad expression on his face, "Niccola, your mother — she's missing."

Niccola straightened in his seat, "What? What do you mean she is missing? She was in Sanctuary — it's supposed to be one the safest places on earth! How could this have happened?" Luca was going to explain, but first, he needed to know what Niccola knew, so he asked, "Did you hear about the recent ghoul attacks?"

Niccola's brows furrowed. "Yes, I've heard, I have other friends on the inside. From what I've gathered, it was quite dreadful. Please, don't try to change the subject, Luca. this is serious." Luca looked hurt for a moment.

"I'm not changing the subject, my friend. Your mother, along with at least twenty others, were taken sometime during the attacks. I was just checking to see if you had heard about them. We believe the attacks were a cover for whatever is actually going on."

"Why take her? I don't understand. My mother never hurt anybody. For a Dhampir, she is soft natured. I promised my pop I would take care of her when he died, and I have. I worked hard to get to a position to be able to have my mom go live in Sanctuary where she would be safe. Please, my friend, find the person responsible for this and bring them down."

"Don't worry, Niccola. We have the whole Italian branch of AVIA on the case. We're even bringing in some American agents to help out, we will find her." Luca comforted his friend as he stood to leave.

"Pfft, Americans. Why do we need to bring in Americans?" A rare smile slowly spread across Luca's face.

"Oh, I'm sure you would speak differently if you knew who the Council had called in, my friend"

Niccola stared at Luca for a moment before the implication set in. "You don't mean they called *him* in, do you?" Luca nodded.

"The very one." The men stood in silence, reflecting on the events soon to take place, after which Luca said his goodbyes and left. Almost two hours passed before Niccola left his office, locking it up tight. He began the walk to his car when he felt as though he was being watched. He quickened his pace, pulling his keys out of his pocket. Just as he was about to unlock his car, a hand landed on his shoulder, and he dropped his keys. He turned to see who the hand belonged to but the face of the figure that stood behind him was obscured by shadow.

"What do you want?" Niccola asked shakily, to which the figure raised a hand in attack. Niccola reacted by instinct and a blinding light shot out from his palm, it exploded, the force of it pushing his opponent back. In a brief moment, Niccola had seen the face of the figure, but he couldn't believe it, he wouldn't. It looked like Luca, but why would his old friend be attacking him?

"Who are you? Why are you doing this?" Niccola yelled out. He had hoped he had seen wrong, that his old eyes were deceiving him.

"You don't recognize me, old friend? Your mind must be going since you had just seen me only two hours earlier." Luca stepped into sight, a devilish grin spread across his face, eyes dancing with enjoyment. "I see now that after years you still haven't lost your touch."

Niccola let his guard down for a moment, "Are you testing me? You know I can handle myself." But in the blink of an eye, Luca was in front of him, the grin never leaving his face. "What ...?" But Niccola couldn't finish speaking. Pain shot through his body, and he suddenly felt very cold. Luca stared down at him and said, "No, old friend. You have simply outlived your usefulness to me. You shall serve one final use, though. The only use your kind are good for." And with that, Luca slammed his fangs into Niccola's neck. The old man was unable to cry out or fight back. Luca drank greedily and drained Niccola of the blood that hadn't already spilled out of the large chest wound still plugged with Luca's hand.

Niccola's body slumped to the ground, the last of his light draining from his eyes, the gaping hole in his chest crusted over with dry blood. Luca left his body where it fell to serve as a message to any who would oppose him, though none yet would know it was him.

Sanctuary

When they finally landed in Rome, they didn't get any time for sightseeing. A black unmarked car sat on the landing pad, an AVIA agent standing by to escort them to their next destination. Kendra was a bit dismayed to find that the windows were so tinted that you couldn't see in or out of them. There was a tinted shield between the passenger seats and the driver seats blocking them from seeing out the windshield. They were completely encapsulated.

The drive was boring and try as she might, Kendra could not focus on anything outside the windows. Just as she thought she would see something, a blur of colors obscured her vision and gave her a massive headache, much like brain freeze. The windows had been polarized against vampire vision, a feature Kendra didn't think possible, but she was just beginning to understand the complexities of vampire ingenuity.

"I wouldn't bother. You're not going to see anything. Focus on something else. Look, here's some magazines. You're only going to hurt yourself by trying." Rick sat back in his seat, his head leaned back and his eyes closed. She looked over to find the magazines he had mentioned. Kendra picked one up and began to flip through the pages only to find they were written in Italian. Frustrated, she dropped the magazine back into its basket between her and Rick. It was going to be a long ride.

***

Anton stood with his hands in his pockets, looking solemnly at the field before him. Just five days ago, this area was almost covered in blood and carnage. It is still a mystery as to what exactly had happened here, but Anton was told they were sending someone of high regard to investigate further, someone with higher access than himself. He wondered at what kind of man this person was — if this person was indeed even a man — and how much more of a help he could be. Anton was the best at what he does, even some of the strongest vampires didn't have Anton's knack for tracking, which is why they've kept him in the agency.

Anton took a deep breath, trying to pick up some subtle scent left behind, hoping that with the all blood cleaned up, he would have a better chance at finding — anything. The wind picked up, almost like it was trying to aid him in the discovery that may put an end to this case, he pulled as much of it into his nose that he could. Nothing. Whatever scent may have been here it was either cleaned up with the blood or swept away by the forces of nature.

He didn't know how much time had passed while he stood there breathing, trying to get a feeling about the place, doing as much as he could to track down the person responsible. There had to be someone behind it. Ghouls don't gather like that, they don't happen spontaneously enough for this — this atrocity of nature to happen. Anton had certainly never heard of them doing so, nor has it ever been known for them to kidnap people. Of course everyone assumes the ghouls were behind it. There isn't any proof to say someone else was involved, at least not yet.

A black car pulled up behind him, dragging Anton from his thoughts. He turned to watch as two people got out of the car, the man wasn't very striking in his appearance, but, the woman, however, caught his eye. Her bright red hair billowed like silk in the breeze. Her green eyes seemed to catch the light, even where there was none. She was stunning. Anton wasn't sure what it was he felt, but he knew he wanted to know her better. He secretly hoped she was the agent they had sent to help so they would be working more closely together; he would even bet her name was as exotic as she looked.

The man started toward him first and Anton had a sinking feeling he was the agent, which sucked because his feelings were never wrong. With a sigh, he headed up the slight incline to meet him, gritting back his disappointment. The woman walked toward him as well but was a little more cautious, not as sure-footed as the guy. The fact that she was joining them give him some hope that he could get to know her better after all. Anton and the other man met in the middle, with the man at a slightly higher angle than Anton, leaving him at a disadvantage if this meeting were to go sour.

"I'm Richard Blake, class 5 agent, though you can just call me Rick." He extended his hand to shake but quickly thought better of the gesture, it would seem this Richard guy has at least read his file. "And this is Deputy Kendra Hughes, she will be shadowing me during this mission." Rick extended his hand out to aid in her continued descent. She glowered at him and refused, continuing down unaided. Anton's lip twitched in what would have been a smile if he wasn't trying to hold on to his composure. She had an attitude that matched her fiery red hair. Anton liked that in a woman, it only strengthened the growing feelings he had for this woman whom he barely knew.

"I'm Anton Miller, class 3 agent. It's nice to meet you both." Anton said, delighted he would indeed be working with this red-haired goddess. He wanted to kiss her hand but he worried he would not like what he would see, or worse, that the gesture would not be welcome. Anton decided to keep it at that and moved on to business, "Well, I guess since introductions have been made, it's time to get down to it. What do you know about the case?"

"Basically, unusual ghoul activity, lots of carnage, and no other known suspects, though there is believed to be a mastermind behind this." Anton nodded his confirmation, "What you've probably not heard while overseas is that there are also several missing people, their bodies are unaccounted for, most of which are Dhampirs." Rick's brows furrowed. Anton wasn't sure what was going through the man's mind until he spoke again.

"Pure Dhampirs? Dhampirs? How many were taken, and of that, how many weren't Dhampir. Were there any humans involved? These are things I need to know."

Rick wasn't angry but there was definitely some authority in his voice, Anton suddenly got the feeling this man was very old. It wasn't unusual for Anton to be around vampires, though it was sometimes hard to tell. He may feel old, but that didn't mean anything. It was also considered rude for a human to ask.

"Roughly 16 Pure Dhampirs, 3 Dhampirs, one human with telekinetic abilities — no other humans are known to be involved in any way." Anton gave a dark laugh that sounded more like a hiccup. "We don't have any witnesses that could put someone sane at the scene nor do we even have any suspects." Rick snarled and shoved his hands deep into his pockets. Anton scratched the back of his head "It's all really well-coordinated and in a place that is secret to everyone not working within Vampire Agency's, almost like it's …" Anton's eyes met Rick's and an understanding passed between them.

"An inside job," Rick confirmed. Kendra looked between them both, not sure what just happened but trying hard to take in as much information as possible. Anton risked a glance at her and found the half bewildered look on her face strangely adorable. He wasn't much for a girl without brains but she had an intelligent air about her despite the confused expression. There was no doubt now — he was definitely smitten. By the look on Rick's face, he knew as well, and wasn't happy about it.

After a small staring contest between the two, leaving Kendra even more confused, Rick sighed.

"So, a telekinetic, huh? The Council is probably up in arms about this. Those guys are pretty rare. What was the human doing here, visiting a relative?" Anton pulled out a small notebook from an inside pocket of his denim jacket and flipped through a few pages, "Yes, her mother Ms. Silvia Lavern. Unfortunately, she is also counted among the missing. If I had to guess, the perp would want one to control the other and I would put money on the daughter being the main prize."

"Right, well you did well for today. Let's meet up for lunch tomorrow to continue the investigation. I've got someone to see that may be helpful in this before we move forward." Rick turned to leave with Kendra on his heels.

"Wait," Anton called after him, "whether you like it or not, I'm a part of this investigation. I deserve to talk to anyone who you think is relevant in this case." Rick had stopped in his tracks and turned his head to look at Anton.

"You don't want to meet this contact, trust me. He doesn't do well around strangers. He especially doesn't like humans, no matter your lineage. Besides, he is an old friend of mine, he probably already knows I'm coming."

"Well, if he's that dangerous, maybe Kendra should stay here and help me with the investigation on this end." Anton was hopeful that he would be able to spend time alone with her. Rick turned to look at him straight on, and a small smile spread across his face.

"Oh, she should be quite alright with my friend, he just adores the company of females. Besides ..." Rick's arm whipped out and wrapped around Kendra's shoulders, pulling her close to him, "I wouldn't let anything happen to her, anyway. It also helps that she is my fledgling, a young vampire of my blood. She will not be harmed; he may even welcome her as he would a granddaughter." Rick couldn't help but jab at the man's ego a little. He even made a show of holding the door open while she got in. The last look Anton got of Kendra's face told him she wasn't happy with how Rick handled that.

They drove off, leaving Anton wondering about the relationship between Rick and Kendra, wondering if he would even have a chance with her. He knew now she was a vampire, a young vampire just learning about everything he grew up with. Squaring his shoulders, he figured he had just as much of a chance at winning Kendra's heart as Rick did, and with that, continued his sweep of the area to see what, if anything, he could pick up.

***

Kendra was fuming when Rick got back in the car. Rick looked her dead in the face, his smile never fading and with a look of satisfaction that made her want to slap him.

"Did I ever tell you how adorable you are when you're mad at me?" Kendra didn't know how he did it, but he always found some way of disarming her. She had no words. Still angry, however, she huffed and focused her attention at the pane of tinted glass in front of her, paying him no attention. That only seemed to satisfy him more and he settled contentedly in his seat.

After what seemed like forever, she couldn't stand the silence anymore and asked: "So, who is this friend of yours?" Rick didn't look at her, staring at his shoes he answered: "A very dangerous vampire, not as old as I am, but almost as powerful. The Council doesn't bother him and he obeys our laws, but even the most influential of Council members won't cross him. The name he has chosen in this century is Maddox, and some of the rumors that circle around pretty much paint him as a demon." He paused for a long time. Kendra was about to ask another question when Rick continued.

"I met him when I was younger, he was just a boy. No one knew what kind of man he would become being the second son of a king. I saw potential in him, and at the time, I had gained a unique standing with the Ottoman Sultan. When he and his younger brother were taken to fight in the army, I trained him."

Rick sighed, pinching the bridge of his nose. "Such a long time ago — only a little over a century after I had been turned. He is known as Maddox now but when I knew him, he was Vlad Dracula Tepes, a boy who, once a man, would become known as Vlad the Impaler. He refused to give a tribute to the Sultan Mehmet and sought to gain power as a vampire. I refused him. He was angry with me after that, but once he did find a vampire who would turn him, he became a fearsome, bloodthirsty beast. It took about 150 years before we met up again and were able to stand before each other as friends."

Kendra took all of this in slowly. A small panic attack building in her chest. *Vlad the Impaler? I'm about to meet Dracula himself?* A vivid picture of a wooden pike being shoved through her abdomen flashed through her mind. Rick could see the panic in her eyes, "Don't be worried. Vlad, I mean Maddox, would never harm anyone in my company. Plus, his impaling days are behind him, there is very little need for such violence in these times. He usually likes to be left alone, but he also told me once that my somewhat infrequent visits give him a feeling of life back, and my next visit is a bit overdue."

"We aren't going all the way to Transylvania, are we?" Rick chuckled, "First off, please, drop the occult fiction, Vlad is from Wallachia, not Transylvania, though you're not that far off. Both are in Romania. Second, no we are not going as far as Romania. Maddox moved to Viterbo, Italy after the beginnings of Russian occupation in the late 1760's and has pretty much been there ever since. The trip is only a little over an hour from Rome by car. We should be there soon."

***

Over 45 minutes later, they stood before a two-story white house with vines crawling up the sides. Pillars adorned both sides of the entrance going up to the second floor where they also supported a balcony. The house was elegant but the front yard looked as if it hadn't been kept in the last hundred years. The grass came up just above Kendra's waist. The trees looked over-encumbered by invasive vines crawling up their trunks and entwining in their branches, on which some of the vines bore grapes and other fruit. The underbrush grew so thick you couldn't make out individual plants and probably housed a menagerie of critters. Kendra shivered at the idea of what could be living in there, she didn't mind most rodents, but snakes terrified her.

The house lacked a doorbell but had a huge black dragon head door knocker with a ring in its mouth, the base of the ring had a small dragon claw instead of the usual metal ball and was very finely detailed. Kendra admired the workmanship of the door knocker, not quite sure what it was made from, but the details were astonishing. The eyes were red, possibly even had real rubies in the eye settings, and the details in the scales and horns made her think it could have been handcrafted. One thing was true: the door knocker was too good to have been simply poured into a mold; this was definitely made to order.

The loud banging of the metal and wood clashing together as Rick used it to knock woke Kendra from her admiration of the handy work. She couldn't help but think how fitting it was for the "son of the dragon" to have a dragon head for a door knocker. Her nerves, however, brought her back to earth as the door began to open. A man, that seemed not much taller than herself, stood in the doorway. He ran his eyes briefly over Kendra before looking at Rick, he stood straighter and began to beam up at the man that stood over a foot taller than himself.

"Jericho! *Benvenuto vecchio amico*! come, come in and bring your friend!" The three of them entered the house, the entrance was wide with gray speckled tile. A small step separated the entrance from the main part of the house. Light wood floor covered what must have been the living room with a giant beige grand piano gracing the center. The main source of light in the room was a chandelier with candles and a candelabra on top of the piano. It was like walking into the Victorian age. "Jericho?" Kendra whispered, to which Rick waved his hand at her to signify another time.

"Sorry, *bella signora*, I did not catch your name." Kendra peeled her eyes away from the lovely house to look at Maddox.

"Oh, I'm sorry. I'm Kendra." She held out her hand intending to shake his, Maddox grasped it lightly and turned it over, before she could protest, he planted a kiss on the back of her hand. Looking up at her he said, "Pardon, I don't really care for the practice of Faire Le Bise." He stood up straight. "This is much more elegant and shows more respect to a *giovane e belladonna* such as yourself."

Maddox stood with his hands regally folded behind his back. He had a mustache very similar to the one she had seen in history books. His hair didn't seem as long as it was in some of his portraits, though it was hard to tell with it pulled into a ponytail at the nape of his neck. He had a thick "soul patch" going from his bottom lip and disappearing under strong his chin. His dark green eyes were hard and partly in shadow from his pronounced brow ridge and bushy eyebrows. Kendra could sense an air of ferocity with a hint of kindness in those eyes.

"I'm sorry," she blinked, "I don't speak Italian, what does that mean?" Kendra asked a little flustered from the peck on the hand received from this supposedly fearsome man. The short Romanian smiled.

"It means to be in the presence of a rare goddess, young and lovely, a beauty of which time could not touch." Rick laughed.

"Why don't you tell her the truth? Seriously, it does not mean all that. You old show off." Rick continued to laugh as Maddox got red in the face. Kendra wasn't sure if it was embarrassment or anger.

"Simply put, it means 'beautiful young lady' but I am a man of passions and find that small phrases can mean much more," Maddox said, purring the last words as he shot piercing glances at the still laughing Rick.

Maddox ushered them further into the house. "My apologies, mademoiselle, my home is not furnished for company. The only room in this house fit for more than one person is my kitchen." They walked past the grand piano in the living room into a dark room. Kendra heard a gentle click and soft white light bulbs blazed to life, illuminating the room in a soft glow. "*La naiba*! These modern lights!" Maddox spat, shielding his eyes from the light.

"You've modernized your house?" Rick almost sounded astonished. "That's a big change for you, don't tell me you're finally coming into the 20ᵗʰ century!" He exclaimed, clasping a hand on Maddox's shoulder.

"No, nothing as drastic as all that, this invention *du ridicule*. I can't stand this lighting. It's too harsh. I only had my kitchen upgraded to get the Council off my back about being more modernized. *Ezeket a hibákat!* Like I care!" Maddox sighed, twisting a few long hairs on his chin between his thumb and forefinger. "I will not trouble you with my problems, *amico mio*, ah but you do have a reason for coming. Sit, sit, tell me what troubles you." The three of them sat at the dinette in Maddox's kitchen.

"I'm sure you are aware of the influx of seemingly random ghoul attacks lately. Kendra and I are on assignment to investigate and hopefully put an end to them. I had heard recently that this latest attack left in its wake a missing persons list."

Maddox held up a hand to halt Rick's words, "I can already see where this is going. I knew you would be coming here for this purpose. Those hunde in the Council couldn't help but have you on this wild goose hunt, eh?" Maddox laughed throatily. "I'll be honest here, Jericho. I don't know much in regards to narrowing your search. I do, however, know of suspicious active goings-on in the Council." Maddox leaned in close. "A young pup has taken up a secretarial position within the Council, normally that would be a common occurrence, eh? Well, normal if it weren't for the fact that she was given to a Council member and no one knows anything more about her than her name. *Très suspect*, no?"

Rick looked his friend in the eye and asked: "Is that all the suspicious activity you know of?" Maddox huffed.

"'Tis just the tip of the iceberg! The Council member the lassie is attached to is Ilium, and from what I hear, it wasn't by his choice. Wouldn't you say that is a bit unprecedented? Even he is suspicious of her and avoids her at all costs; he won't fire her. Heaven knows I would have, and many think it's due to him not having the capability to do so. Also, there is this new blooded in the senate; he was inaugurated two months ago. His name is Luca Bladimir, a name I know is very much fake. Whelp didn't come from my country and the name is unknown; no family lineage tied to it. He walks around like a peacock with brilliant feathers, yet he is quite humble in the presence of elders. He is on my radar, nothing about him seems genuine; he has no heart, no fire, no passion."

Maddox looked right at Kendra as he spoke those last words, a light danced behind them, like fire in a windy chimney. "Speaking of passion," he continued, "what did you say was your relation to mademoiselle Kendra?" Maddox almost purred, rolling the "R" in her name. Rick's brows furrowed.

"She is my fledgling. Why?" Minuets passed before Maddox broke eye contact to looked at Rick, the fire gone, leaving Kendra feeling self-conscious.

"Curiosity, *amico mio*. You must forgive me — it truly has been some time since I was in the presence of a woman. My thoughts are in the wrong place." With another throaty laugh, Maddox jabbed Rick playfully in his ribs. Kendra blushed but thankfully neither of them noticed. "Anyway, back to business. Instinct isn't the only thing that plays a part in my distrust of the pup. What does have the old gears turning is the fact that he owns several empty warehouses on the outskirts of Roma, and some in the city proper. All of which would, at first glance, seem abandoned. Now, what would he need all that space for, hmmm?"

The room grew silent for a time; Kendra was the first to speak.

"Maybe he's a hoarder. It's quite common for people to rent storage units to put the extra stuff away instead of getting rid of it. Maybe, he's amassed such a collection that he needs a place to store it all, he may even have empty ones to add to later." Maddox sat back in his chair and studied Kendra for a moment longer than she would have liked. The fiery stares were one thing, but the way he was looking at her now made her feel like a specimen trapped in a petri dish, and she squirmed under his gaze.

"A similar thought had crossed my mind, as well, *mon cheri*." Maddox spoke without breaking his stare. "If it weren't for the fact that his presence rubbed me wrong, I would have been happy with that explanation. I did have it investigated, though, thinking he was a spy or terrorist trying to get inside. All of the ones we know of are completely empty — nothing is housed within." He looked over at Rick then, "I would suggest you start with talking to Councilman Ilium. He would at least be friendlier if not amenable." Rick shook his head "It's not going to be easy getting an audience with only one of the Councilmen, even for me."

The Council

Kendra wasn't sure what to expect when meeting the Vampire Council for the first time. She wished Rick would be a little more open about the details, but he seemed to relish her being caught off guard. After they had returned to Rome, Rick had the driver stop in at a restaurant called *Il Vero Alfredo*. The outside was a mix of modern style with classic Italian design, but when they went inside it was almost like stepping back in time.

It was very cozy and inviting. The Maître d greeted them at the door and Kendra assumed he asked about a reservation by the way he spoke. Rick stepped closer to the man and spoke in low Italian, placing a wad of Euros in the man's vest pocket. Rick stepped back and the man placed his hand over the lump and bowed, Kendra could only guess that the man was apologizing. With a couple of menus in hand, he escorted them over to a table for two in the back. He pulled out the seat for both Kendra and then Rick to sit, and placed their menus in front of them. He bowed again, mumbling in Italian and backed away.

The walls were covered in pictures from which many faces looked back at them, some looked familiar, but Kendra couldn't put her place where she had seen them or remember their names. She picked up her menu and was relieved to find English written under the Italian. Looking it over, she wondered how much a Euro was in dollars.

"Pick whatever you like, lunch is on me, but regardless of what you are going to have, you will also try some fettuccini alfredo with me. *Molto delizioso* — best in the world!" After a while, a server arrived to take their order and before Kendra could get a word in, Rick spoke up in brisk Italian, making hand gestures at her and the table. At the end of his list he and the server looked at her, waiting for her order.

Kendra wasn't sure if her pronunciation of the dish she wanted was correct, so she just looked at Rick and said, "I'll have the lasagna," to which Rick laughed and repeated the name in an Italian accent for the server. He then left with their orders leaving Kendra a bit in the dark about what all Rick had on the menu. After a moment of silence, Kendra spoke up.

"I want to learn to speak Italian, can you teach me?" Rick's eyebrows shot up into his hairline, a small smile made his mouth look crooked, and with a small chuckle he said, "Are you sure you want me as an instructor?"

Kendra leaned forward.

"You seem to have a firm grasp on the language, why not you?" She took on a sly smile of her own, "Unless you plan on leading me on in order to make me make a fool of myself. I'd like to think you would have more class than that toward an apt student. If that's the case, though, I could always ask Maddox or Anton — they both seem eager to teach me new things." Rick's smile faded some, not expecting her to bait him the way she did and reminding him that she wasn't as inattentive as she sometimes appeared. Rick looked about to say something just as the server brought out the appetizer Rick had ordered. A platter of meats and cheeses was placed in the middle of the table, a bottle of wine was popped open and poured into their glasses, then left at their table.

The conversation was put on hold while they placed some of the contents of the platter on individual serving dishes in front of them. The meat was very flavorful, the cheese came in variety, and all was presented in an eye-catching display.

"There is no need to ask someone else," Rick spoke around a bite of cheese in his mouth. "I'll teach you and I promise to keep it genuine. However, learning under the stress we will be experiencing on this case will not make for a good learning environment." He finished with a gulp of wine.

Kendra swallowed her bite. "I need to know how to speak Italian for the sake of this investigation. I can't think of a time when I would need it more. If you want me to help you then this is something I need to learn." There was silence for a moment while Rick pondered what had been said. A man pushed a table up to theirs and spoke only a few words before he began to mix fettuccini noodles in a white bowl. Kendra and Rick watched as he made their dishes, tableside style, without speaking. Once the plates were placed in front of them, the man left their table, and Kendra dug into the pile of fettuccini noodles. A man came by their table with an accordion and started singing in Italian. Kendra didn't know why but the song made Rick chuckle as he slurped up his noodles.

The man sang loud enough to prevent any conversation between the two of them. Regardless of its meaning, Kendra still thought the song sounded quite beautiful. Her lasagna came out while he serenaded them, along with a second dish for Rick, which looked kind of like ravioli. They greedily ate up the delicious dishes and when the serenade was over, Rick and Kendra applauded. Rick pulled out few Euros to give to the man to which he bowed slightly, thanking Rick, and left to another table.

"Why did you laugh? The song was beautiful." Kendra finally got the burning question off her chest. Rick looked up at her from his plate of ravioli.

"It was a romance song, implying that the two persons the one was singing to were in love. It's a pretty common serenade to sing when there is a perceived couple sitting down for a romantic meal." He shoved another bite into his mouth. Kendra began to blush.

"Oh, I didn't guess." Rick shrugged.

"I laughed because for the next year we are probably going to be perceived as such. It is defiantly going to be an interesting year." He chuckled, Kendra felt a little peeved at this revelation.

"You're just going to sit back and enjoy this, aren't you? Just laugh it up like it doesn't matter, right?"

"I don't know what your problem is," Rick leaned back, semi amused. "I'm just having a little fun. It's not like I can stop people from thinking a certain way. Why not have some fun with it?" Kendra sighed. He was right, but she was hard-pressed to admit that to him.

"Fine, have your fun. Just don't give them the wrong impression." Rick smiled mischievously.

"Would the impression really be all that incorrect? I mean, I was in your bed" Kendra's face blazed, she was so angry and embarrassed she had no words. If the table wasn't in the way she would have slapped him so hard his mother would have felt it.

Rick only smiled wider at her reaction and seemed quite content with himself. They finished their meals in silence, after which their server brought out two small plates with a small cake that looked like it might be chocolate placed right in the center. The server set the plates down and provided a small dessert fork with which Kendra cut off a small bite to try. It tasted like coffee and custard, and instantly she knew what it was.

"Mmmm, Tiramisù." She cut a bigger bite of the cake, "As much of a jerk as you are, you do make good culinary choices. The food here is amazing, and this dessert is to-die-for." Rick smiled in response and their server came by with the check.

***

After lunch was paid for, they loaded back into the black car. It smelled strongly of McDonald's, giving Kendra the impression that the driver wasn't always outside the restaurant. Kendra buckled her seatbelt.

"Now, what happens?" Rick pulled out his phone, making Kendra snort a little at how old fashioned he was. "That is a very old cell phone, and you make fun of Maddox for not having electricity, shame on you." She giggled. Rick turned the cell phone over in his hand, it was silver with grey trim. It wasn't a flip phone or a touch screen, it had actual buttons, and had probably come out sometime in the early 90's. In cell phone standards, it was quite outdated, but Rick liked that about the phone; that gave it some character.

"I don't see what all the hype is over these new-age cell phones. I've heard the touch screens can be very temperamental, I don't see the point in having a device that can malfunction so easily." Rick pressed a button on the keypad and the screen lit up with the date and time. "We need to head to the Council now. They're probably waiting for us." He said putting the cell phone back in his pocket. "We should have been there over a half-hour ago." Kendra stared at him wide-eyed, "Why then did we get lunch?" With a straight face Rick said "Final meal"

The implication of what he had said hit home, Kendra really didn't know what to expect — what kind of men were on the Vampire Council?

Rick sensed her discomfort and asked, "So, what is so great about the modern phones that you feel the need to mock mine?" And with that Kendra pulled hers out. It wasn't a long trip, but by the end of it, she managed to get Rick hooked on Candy Crush, one of her favorite games.

***

The car stopped off to the side of the street. Rick and Kendra got out, then once their doors were closed, the car left. They walked across the plaza to the building with two flags hanging down over the door. A guard stopped them and Rick spoke quickly in Italian, flashing a badge and motioning toward Kendra. The guard let them by and they continued toward the building. Once they reached the entrance Rick turned toward Kendra and said, "Welcome to the Palazzo Montecitorio, home of the Italian Parliament as well as the Vampire Council. It was built in 1653 after which the Council took up residence here in 1664 and has been here ever since. Now, if you'll follow me, we will enter the building, please keep your hands, feet, and elbows to yourself." He turned and opened the door, holding it so she could pass through.

It was beautiful. Paintings and statues lined the walls, the floor was polished to shine, but before Kendra could take it all in, Rick pushed her passed it all. They turned down a corridor and through several doors that eventually lead to steps going down. Once they reached the bottom it was clear that this part of the building was much older and not as traversed. It was beautiful on its own but had a more dungeon feel to it. The long corridor led them to a double door that was so ornate it stood out from the stone walls like a beacon on the water.

Rick pushed it open and it was as if they had been in a cave until now, they were underground, but the ceiling seemed to go for miles in a dome shape. It looked like what most had imagined the pantheon must have looked like ages ago; it was golden with various carvings and depictions of Gods and cherubs. Various people bustled about in the open space and corridors opened up all around them. A large round desk sat in the middle of it all with about four people behind it, several signs hung in every direction, all had the same word on them: *Informazioni*.

They didn't stop there. Rick lightly grabbed Kendra's elbow and led her to the right, down one of the corridors. They reached a door to the right, through which Rick continued to lead her through. Inside was a small room with benches that kind of reminded Kendra of a courtroom waiting area. They were the only ones in the room, however. They walked up to a lady at a desk and Rick again spoke quickly in Italian, to which the lady replied just as quickly in Italian, motioning with her hand. Rick grumbled; he and Kendra then took a seat close by.

"What's wrong?" Kendra asked, fidgeting on the hard bench. Rick shook his head in disgust.

"The Council has been tied up for the last hour. They're too busy to see us right now. The receptionist said to just wait and see if we can get an audience, they may still see us since they were expecting our arrival." Kendra leaned back with a sigh. They ended up waiting for over an hour before anyone came out of the door offset from the receptionist's desk. The man that stepped out was of average build with long black hair slicked back so that you could see his widows peak. He had bright blue eyes that stood out in stunning contrast to his black hair and pale complexion.

"Ah, Richard. How nice to see you again, my friend." He greeted Rick with a warm smile that didn't seem possible with the grimace he wore moments ago. Rick stood and shook the man's hand with the vigor of close friends. In contrast the dark-haired gentleman stood about a head shorter than Rick and his frame was very slight.

"Ilium, how have you been? You've slimmed down some. Is Council life not suited to you, friend?" They let go of one another, Ilium's hand instinctively going to his face, pressing his forefinger and thumb along the bridge of his nose. Ilium sighed deeply.

"If only it was just the Council, it wouldn't be this bad. These strange cases of ghoul attacks keep cropping up around the country. I can't even imagine what would happen if we couldn't contain it thus far. It's quite maddening." Rick sighed.

"Well, with this rare opportunity, I do have some questions regarding that, if you have the time."

Ilium shook his head. "Not here, friend. Not sure when, but I will get you whatever information you seek — later." Ilium's eyes fell on Kendra, for a moment he hadn't seemed to realize she was even there, and now that her presence was known to him, he looked between her and Rick expectantly. Rick got the message and reached a hand toward her to help her stand from the bench.

"This is Kendra, my newest fledgling. We're here for our evaluation."

"Ah, yes, well, it is very nice to meet you, my dear." He bowed slightly, "And may I be one of the few to welcome you to the fold." The hint of an accent danced in his words and Kendra quite couldn't place it. "I hope you don't mind me asking, but your accent, it's very intriguing, where are you from?" Ilium stood tall.

"I was born in Bulgaria, 1553. Of course this was during Turkish rule, so different dialects were abounded." He looked between her and Rick again and spoke to Rick in a matter of fact tone. "The Council isn't seeing anyone today. I was sent out here to inform you of that fact and I needed to give you this in person." Ilium handed Rick a medium-sized manila envelope. Rick took the envelope,

"What is it, good news?" Ilium shook his head solemnly.

"I'm afraid not, my friend." He nodded in parting to Kendra and with those words, he disappeared back into the door he came.

Rick looked at the envelope in his hands flipping it this way and that, hoping the outside may give a clue as to its contents.

"How about you just open it?" Kendra said, curiously. Rick looked over at her.

"Not here." And with that, he headed out of the building with Kendra in tow.

A Mystery

Rick sat in the seat next to Kendra eyeing the envelope, unsure of what awaited inside. They were back in the black car headed to a destination Rick had indicated in Italian to the driver. The wheels were turning in his head, but it was clear to Kendra he wanted to wait until they had arrived wherever it was they were headed before opening the envelope. She was dying inside. However, curiosity was eating away at her insides. She fidgeted worse than ever, unsure what to do with her hands and how to keep her thoughts away from the possibilities of what information the envelope could hold.

The trip seemed to take forever. Kendra felt as though she was going to explode. By the time they reached their destination, her curiosity was bursting at the seams.

"Aw, come on, open it already, please. I'm dying here!" she gushed, bouncing in her seat. It was a bit out of character for her, but she couldn't stop the whine in her voice. Seeing an opportune moment, Rick sat back his seat, arms folded behind his head.

"Impatient, aren't we? I was going to open it once inside but now I think I'll put it up for, oh, say ten years. You can wait that long, right? I mean, all we have is time." A devilish grin played at the corners of his mouth. She gapped at him, shocked and unsure of how to respond.

"Bu...bu...but you can't" was all she managed. Then, an idea came to her mind, "What if it's important information or instructions from the Council." She smiled "Or AVIA." She added the last part in a rush.

Rick gasped rather overdramatically, "You're right, which means I can wait for about 50 years before they even realize I've not read it, good thinking." He was having way too much fun with this and wondered how much longer he could keep it up. She was bound to catch on, though, the thought of her angry face almost made him chuckle. She began to stutter something in exasperation when he interjected. "Relax, I'm joking. Let's get inside, then we can read it in private." He opened the door and got out of the car.

Kendra stepped out and her eyes grew wide at the beautiful estate that lay before her. It was huge for a house, Kendra guessed about three stories tall, and every light was on so that it shined so bright, Kendra was sure it was visible from space. There were two large water fountains on either side of a wide path leading to the front door. Cherubs danced naked around each fountain, pouring water into the fountain base. The path was lined with pillars covered in creeping vines that, Kendra suspected, were grapevines though they did not yet produce fruit. More, smaller pillars lined the edge of the porch. The front door was wide with chiseled white trim; it was elegant and made Kendra feel like she was walking into a palace.

"Who lives here?" the awe in her voice made the question sound more like a whisper.

"Hm? Oh, you like the house?" Kendra couldn't take her eyes off the detail, swirling patterns were carved into the rounded door frame and the whole porch looked as if it were topped with pure white marble held together with concrete. The house screamed elegance; lit oil lanterns were bolted to the wall on either side of the door, which made the house seem warm and inviting.

"It's like walking into a palace." She said breathlessly. Rick shrugged.

"Hmm, yes, well, it wasn't exactly my idea. I find it rather flashy but that's what I get for letting James talk me into something. I've been debating on selling it for some time." Kendra had stopped staring at everything to stare at Rick,

"This house is yours?" The shock in her voice made Rick take a step back.

"Madam, I would not lie." He said with feigned indignation. "Yes, this estate is mine for the time being. As I have said, I've been thinking about selling it. I don't spend much time here and it's an unnecessary drain to my finances. However, in our time of need, it will serve a purpose. Come, enter my domain." Ending with a cheesy Dracula voice, he opened the door and stepped aside. Bowing slightly and with a dramatic wave of his hand, he motioned for her to enter first.

The house was just as lavish inside, but Kendra's curiosity with the contents of the envelop made that priority number one. It was Rick's house, she could take it in later. Rick seemed to have read her mind as he all but pulled her into a room with a large fireplace already ablaze. He sat in a heavily cushioned love seat and Kendra took a seat in the center of a couch just as cushioned. She sat at the edge of her seat, partly because she too was on edge, and partly because she felt she would fall into the couch, never to be seen again.

Rick picked an ornate letter opener off of the coffee table that stood between them. It glittered in the light of the fire, the only light that was in the room which illuminated everything with a soft glow. The sound of paper tearing as Rick opened the envelope seemed to last forever, Kendra felt that she would soon be sweating. The room was warm but not warm enough for her to feel hot, the tension was reaching its peak and she all but held herself against the urge to snatch the envelope from Rick's hands. He pulled out a plain white piece of paper, it appeared to be the only one, and the contents made Rick's brows furrow into the biggest knot Kendra had ever seen.

"What does it say?" She was twitching in her seat with anticipation. Rick laid the paper on the table in front of him. Kendra had to turn it so she could read it. On the plain white surface of the parchment was the sentence *Don't trust the Council.* A large black *V* encircled with red was stamped on the bottom of the page. Kendra sat back. "Well, that's cryptic." Rick nodded.

"More importantly, we need to find out what this means." He pointed to the strange symbol.

"You're not worried that a Councilman is telling you not to trust the Council? I would be more worried about that!" Kendra felt like Rick was missing the point of the message.

"Honestly, I've never trusted the Council. Sure, it regulates the main population of vampires and dhampirs, but power corrupts. Vampires are easily corrupted; it's our nature. We have a thirst for power stronger than humans. Many believe it's due to us being superior in just about everything. That's no excuse in my mind." Kendra stared at him for a while, a question dancing in her eyes, but she waited to see if he had more to say. When he didn't continue she asked, "What do you believe?"

Rick stared at the fire roaring in the fireplace, but was silent. Kendra was about to ask again, thinking maybe he was lost in thought and didn't hear her.

"I'm not sure what I believe anymore. The world has changed, where once we were feared, now we have disappeared into obscurity. Nobody believes in vampires anymore, calling yourself as such is even cause for ridicule, and those that know we exist either want to be turned or want us dead." He sighed, sitting up, he sat back in his seat and stared hard at Kendra, almost accusingly. "What do you think? Are you the type to be complacent toward a group of monsters who sanctioned you to be forced into this world simply because one old monster didn't want to damn anyone else?"

Kendra squirmed and wondered why he had suddenly become so accusing. She wanted to be angry, but something in his face gave her pause, and she tried a different approach.

"You really do hate them, don't you? The Council, I mean." Rick didn't respond immediately; he sat still as a statue, and stared straight through her into some distant memory. After what seemed like forever, Rick sighed, leaned forward and hung his head almost in defeat.

"The truth is, I don't hate them," he whispered. "At least, *hate* isn't the word for it — it's more like *regret*." He sighed. "Once upon a time, the idea of the Council was just that — an idea. It was a great, radical idea that was concocted by one vamp who was tired of the violence and two others who wanted to see change. Those two are dead now. At the time, it was supposed to help bring vampire kind together, *all* of vampire kind. Now it just serves as a reminder that government in any form has potential to be corrupted. Vampires are not that different from humans with how we think. Though some believe we are very different. The Council wasn't supposed to be this way, so much has changed."

Rick sat back some, staring at the paper on the coffee table, but Kendra wasn't going to let it end there.

"Who is the surviving founder?" She was sure she knew the answer, but she didn't want to assume as much. Rick looked up at her, barely lifting his head, but didn't answer. "Rick, who is the surviving founder?" He lifted his head and looked straight at Kendra, an answer sparkled in his eyes, and she got the confirmation she was looking for. "You? You were the surviving founder?" He shook his head solemnly.

"I'm not the *surviving* founder. I was — am — the only founder. It was my idea. I roped the others in because I knew I couldn't do it alone. I never imagined it would be like this. It's all my fault."

Kendra was rendered speechless; it was kind of hard to believe, and she wasn't sure what her feelings were in this situation. An awkward silence fell as the weird truth settled over them, the last spoken words hung in the air. Rick sat further back into the love seat, surprising Kendra a little that he didn't sink into oblivion. He laid his arms across the back and rested his left ankle on his right knee.

"How about a change of subject — put this Council mess behind us for a while. Why don't you tell me a little about yourself?" Kendra raised an eyebrow, "Didn't the Council give you all of my information beforehand? Or did you not read the file they undoubtedly have on me?"

Rick smirked, *Kendra is perceptive, a good trait for a vampire to have.*

"Yes, they gave me a file and I'll have you know I did read it. However, it's much better to hear a spoken story than to read a second and even third-hand account of certain events in a person's life. Besides, it's incomplete. A report can only capture the event itself, not the emotion. A story is one thing, a cold, distant report of someone is another.

"Fine, how about you tell me briefly what you already know and I'll fill in the blanks. Sound good?" Kendra's compromise intrigued Rick and he conceded to the deal.

"Ok, here is what I know. You were born in 1986 to parents Linda and Kevin Bradley. You graduated high school with honors in 2004 and began attendance at Georgia State University for a degree in nursing the following year. There you met Travis Hughes, a man two years your senior, and you began to date. He graduated in 2008 and began to work as a firefighter to help get you through those last two years.

"After your graduation in 2010, the two of you got married and started a family together, which would have been a happily ever after if not for the accident that stole your prince charming away when your youngest was just about to turn one. Then, roughly a month later, here I come to make things just a little more complicated. Does that about sum things up?" Kendra shrunk a little, hearing her life story laid out in what must have only been a paragraph really struck home. She wasn't all that interesting. Compared to Rick, her life was like a blank canvas, whereas his was a beautiful mosaic full of color, and she was only just starting to take it all in.

"Well, there you go. You know my life story practically by heart. You know, it's strange. You've lived 665 years and I have barely scratched the surface of your story. Yet, here you are, wanting me to tell you what you already know just to include some emotion. My life is nothing to shake a stick at when compared to the man born during the Renaissance, founder of an organization known as the Vampire Council, and best friends with *the* Vlad Dracula. Honestly, I think you're toying with me. You're always toying with me. I'm nothing but a young mouse to an old cat who has nothing better to do than to put his paw on my tail and watch me squirm."

Kendra stood, anger flooded her cheeks, hunger gnawed at her sides. That damned vampire need for blood only seemed to feed her fire. "I'm going for a hunt and I might just get a hotel while I'm out. You have my cell phone number. If not, you shouldn't have any trouble finding it. Call me when the Council is ready to see me. Otherwise, I'd like to be left alone for a while."

Blood

Kendra wasn't sure what got her so mad. His pretentious attitude toward the mundane life Kendra was once fond of or the continuous mind games he likes to play. He was always keeping secrets, waiting around for that epic reveal, only to show he knew what would happen all along, or at least guessed at it. She moved through Rome, too angry to sight see. The lights of a city alive with nightly activities; all of it became nothing but a blur to her. She just kept moving, not caring where she ended up. She briefly pondered whether or not her hunger may have had some effect on her mood, but that thought didn't stick around too long.

After some time, she found herself in the middle of nowhere and began mentally kicking herself for not paying attention to where she was going. It looked like she had wondered into some park, and, taking in her surroundings, she saw that she stood in the middle of a tree-lined walkway. Benches nestled between the trees, no doubt providing a nice resting place to gaze at the foliage. Old fashioned styled lamps dotted the path giving off a soft glow, separating the path from the darker parts of the park. Kendra stood there and, even though it was the middle of the night, she could feel eyes on her. Her gut clenched in the now-familiar pain of bloodthirst, all the while feeling like she was caught in someone's crosshairs.

She felt like she was being hunted. However, this feeling only served to stoke the fire of her anger. She was a vampire, a creature of the night; she was not going to be someone else's plaything anymore. She stood up straighter and sniffed the air, looking for a whiff of anything familiar. She heard a light rustle in the trees behind her, but she wasn't going to give in to her thirst just yet. Whoever it was thought they were going to play with her, they had another thing coming — prey doesn't play with predators.

The rustling came closer and Kendra continued to remain still, playing the bait in her trap. The seconds ticked away agonizingly until finally, the hunter made himself known. Jumping down from a tree behind Kendra, the hunter held a knife to Kendra's throat, the scent of blood and silver wafted to her nose as the cold metal was pressed into her jugular. He spoke quickly and harshly in Italian; his breath smelled of rotting meat. Kendra wanted to gag, but when she didn't respond to whatever he had said he pressed the knife deeper into her flesh, drawing blood.

"I don't speak Italian," she growled as she grabbed the arm around her neck and threw him from off her. He landed on his back about 5 feet away from her with a loud grunt. Kendra knew he wasn't dead as she could still hear his heartbeat, though he continued to lay there, trying not to breathe too hard. She folded her arms at the infantile attempt to fool her into getting closer. "Get up and face me like a man, you coward. You're trying my patience."

After a short pause, the still figure of the hunter began to shake and the sound of low chuckling made its way to Kendra's ears. He began to stand slowly, his chuckle turning into manic laughter. He turned toward her, his face twisted into an ugly sneer, a huge mangled scar ran diagonally from his forehead to his jawline, splitting his face in two. His eyes had a horrible gleam like that of a wild animal, dirt-caked the clothes he wore and a lump of dirt was tangled in his long scraggly hair. Kendra wondered at the state of the man. Were the hunters here in Italy unkempt, wild men, shunned by normal society? Or is this one an exception?

He stood straighter and spoke again, only this time, in English.

"My apologies, signora, I was not expecting a foreign bloodsucker to be out and about on her own. Where might your *scorta* be hiding? Hmmm?" Kendra shifted her weight, "My what?" she asked impatiently. The scraggly man cursed under his breath, "Your maker, Bitch. Where is he? Don't play games with me! I know he is here, you were acting as his bait to lure me out, now it's time for him to show himself!" He spat angrily, saliva running down his chin, his eyes darted around the area, expecting someone to jump out at any moment. Kendra waited for his bout of madness to subside as he continued to rant and rave until his speech reverted back to Italian.

Kendra sighed, "I don't have the patience for this." In an instant, she was on him, one of his arms tucked neatly behind his back, she glared down at him. The knife he wielded glittered as he slowly plunged it into her. She let it come. She wanted him to know it wouldn't work. The knife blade pierced her skin, staining her clothes red. Surprisingly, it barely stung as he pushed for the knife to pierce her heart. His eyes widened as he realized the knife wasn't going to save him, Kendra then sank her fangs into the neck of the old hunter. He struggled in his last moments, panicked and afraid, before dying in her arms.

Kendra drained him dry, the first time she had ever been such a blood glutton, and worried if maybe this would turn her into a rogue of some sort. There was no going back now — all there was left to do was to get rid of the body. His stench hit her nose and she had wondered if he had already started to decay. Kendra dropped his limp body on the ground and surveyed the area carefully. There was a wide-open patch of dirt off to her left, there she thought would be a good place to bury a body.

A twinge of pain came from her knife wound, the knife still stuck in her flesh. She pulled it free, feeling the metal crape across a rib bone. She thought she was going to be sick as it closed up, the sensation more painful than getting hurt in the first place. Now fully healed, the hunter's blood sat heavy in her stomach, making her feel bloated. However, she still had one more task to do. Kendra picked up the body and carried him over her shoulder to the dirt patch. The dull thump of his dead weight hitting the ground was almost as satisfying as watching the fear spread across his face before death, and she wondered about how monstrous she had become. Kendra quickly dug a 6 to 7-foot hole in the ground before dropping his body into the pit. A moment of grief swept over her, not for the dead man in the hole, but for her lost humanity. After all, how could she call herself human now after what she had just done?

She pushed all the dirt back into the hole, then took some time to make the surrounding area look just as disheveled and upturned as the spot where she had buried the crazy old hunter. Once finished, she brushed as much of the dirt off herself as she could, and looking down, she saw the red stain that covered her left breast. Kendra was in no condition to be seen by any human society. She would draw too much attention out on the streets tonight. Before she could panic, she remembered that Rick had said there was some sort of connection between them. Maybe if she focused on that she could pinpoint his location and head that way.

She closed her eyes and focused on finding that connection. The blood of the hunter buzzed in her veins; it was different from the blood of other humans — it had power. She focused on that power, trying to harness it, use it to her advantage. All of a sudden, she could feel energy tingling run through her and in her mind's eye, she could see Rick's house. She knew in what direction and how far she needed to go to be back at his doorstep. She moved so fast, making a beeline for his house. She hated having to go back but she needed his help. He was the only one she could trust right now.

***

Rick sat staring at the dying embers of the fireplace, the pain in his chest was gone now, though he knew Kendra was still alive. She was strong but he still hated himself for not running to her rescue. He knew to some extent what she would say if he had gone. He also knows what she will say when they see each other again. Either way, he was damned if he did and damned if he didn't. He shook his head and took a sip of his brandy, the third glass he had poured after she had left. He wasn't trying to drown any emotion like humans do when they drink; he couldn't get drunk even if he wanted to. Rick just enjoyed the tingling sensation of the alcohol on his tongue.

Hell, brandy wasn't even his first choice. It just happened to be what was stocked in the liquor cabinet, no doubt another one of James' designs. Rick chuckled — that vamp really had some strange tastes in Rick's opinion. He would have preferred bourbon or gin, but the brandy was of good quality. Rick swirled the glass, making the square ice cubes clink against each other, and thought briefly on calling James to see how he was doing. Then, a thought struck him that made him laugh: here he was a 665-year-old vampire and he was feeling lonely. It was so absurd to him that he just about threw himself into a fit of laughter.

With his chuckles dying down, he sipped the last of the brandy from his glass. He got up from the couch and placed the glass down on the bar. An old-style telephone sat at the other end of the bar and the thought crossed his mind again to call James when a movement outside the window caught his eye. In an instant, he was in the foyer and opening the front door so fast that the hinges creaked loudly in protest. He was about to yell something he was sure he would find very absurd later and end up chuckling harder than before when the figure standing in his doorway gave him pause.

"Kendra, you're back!" he said, barely able to contain the surprise in his voice, he had blocked most of the connection he felt in the bond to give her some time alone. She looked at him somewhat shamefaced without saying anything. The expression on her was surprisingly cute to him and with that thought toying with his mind, Rick was lost for words. Kendra, however, looked like she wanted to say a million words but her mouth lacked the motivation to do so. She did eventually break the silence and asked Rick if he was going to let her in. He was still in somewhat of a daze and didn't hear her.

"Hello — Earth to Rick. are we going to stand out here for all eternity or can I come in?" He shook his head as though waking himself from a dream.

"Yeah, yes, sure, I just ... with the way you had left I wasn't sure I'd see you again for some time." He moved to one side to allow her entry as he stammered out his words.

"I got stabbed tonight" Kendra blurted out, she walked into the room where the fire place's dying embers barely lit the room anymore.

"Yes, I felt that" Rick said as he rubbed the spot on his chest that still throbbed with the ghost pain. "Would you like to tell me what happened?" He asked, trying not to pry, but was curious about the night's events. Kendra turned slowly, her red hair dancing in the remaining light, almost as though the fire was again blazing in the fireplace. Her eyes trained on the glass at the bar, a puddle forming under it making the glass slide slightly to the right. A single ice cube clanked into a new space left behind from the melting of its brothers.

"I was going to ask why you didn't show up if you felt my pain, but I see now what kept you company." Her eyes took on a hardness as she stared at the bar glass, the smell of brandy still lingering in the air.

Rick waved half-heartedly at the lonely glass.

"Vampires can't get drunk. Our metabolism is too high, we burn it off almost immediately." Kendra's gaze softened a bit as she nodded her head.

"Good to know" She looked back up at Rick, her eyes dancing with worry; this new expression threw him off. He expected her to be angry, not worried, and what the hell was she worried about, anyway? Despite how long he has lived, how much he now understands about the world, a woman's mind might continue to be a mystery to him. Every time he thinks he has figured women out, there comes one that makes him rethink what he knows.

"Rick, can I ask you something and you not be too judgmental about it?" Yep, that was definitely not what he was expecting.

"Of course, I can guarantee you I won't be judgmental. Now, whether or not I'll laugh or poke fun is another matter entirely." He gave a little wink and to his satisfaction, she gave him a grimace that clearly was an attempt to cover a smile. She turned and walked further into the room where she sat in the same spot she had occupied only hours before. He followed her lead and moved to sit in the spot across from her, the mood shifting back to a serious feel.

***

Kendra squirmed slightly, trying to figure out how she wanted to word the question burning on her tongue. She decided to just continue blurting out what was on her mind, at the very least, it might get a conversation started.

"Rick, has anyone ever killed a hunter before?" Rick stared at her in disbelief. He tried to contain his laughter as he answered her question.

"Kendra, have you forgotten the two hunters you took down before our trip here? Of course hunters have been killed. We didn't recover one of the bodies but the big guy was definitely dead." Kendra sighed.

"That's not what I mean. What I meant to say was, has anyone ever killed a hunter in a way that only a vampire can?" She stumbled a bit in her words. Rick stared at her, the realization of what she was asking dawned on him. He sat forward.

"Do you mean, has anyone drank the blood of a hunter? Is that what you're asking?" His voice was low, almost as if it were a conspiracy of sorts. Kendra nodded, the shame-faced expression returned to her features. Rick sat back, a hand gripped his chin as he pondered her question. "Well, it's not illegal, I know that. Hunter blood has always been considered tainted, so it was often regarded as taboo. If anyone has ever drunk the blood of a hunter, they more than likely never spoke of it. I can't think of any time where it was recorded or the effects afterward that had ever taken place. I am curious, though, as to why you would ask that?"

Kendra bit her lip, "Tonight, while I was out, I ran into a hunter. I hadn't fed yet and he started ranting and raving like a lunatic. I lost patience with him and attacked. He stabbed me with a silver knife and in retaliation, I bit him. Before I knew it, I had drained him of blood and he was dead, limp in my arms. I ... I buried him about 6 feet or so in the ground before coming back here." She spat out her story in a sort of rush, some of her words meshed together and she hoped Rick understood, saving her from having to repeat herself. Rick continued to sit silently, mulling over her brief retelling of her indulgence in hunter blood.

"I have a few questions." He finally broke the agonizing silence. "First of all, how do you feel? Do you notice any differences?" Rick sat forward, a serious tone in his voice, sounding a lot like a psychiatrist. Kendra squirmed a little.

"Not really, no. There was a bit of a tingling sensation after I drank it, but otherwise I feel fine." Rick's brows furrowed, "What kind of tingling? Where did you feel it?" he asked quickly, seeming more intrigued. "I don't know, everywhere. It spread to all parts of my body. The tingling felt kind of like ... do you remember what it was like to have your foot or hand 'go to sleep?'" Rick nodded.

"That can still happen as a vampire, just not as often. Do you mean it felt like your whole body lost circulation?"

"Not exactly." Kendra shook her head, her red hair falling from behind her ears where it had been tucked. "It was more fleeting, but the tingling was similar to that sleeping limb sensation."

"Ok, anything else? How are you feeling right now? think long and hard on it — is there anything that feels out of place?" Kendra sat still, silently taking stock of her condition before answering.

"No, I feel fine. Actually I still feel like I need to feed, but it's not as urgent." Rick sat back with a sigh.

"Maybe it's taboo because it doesn't do much for a vampire and is a wasted effort." He rubbed the bridge of his nose.

"There is one other thing," Kendra added. Rick looked at her through his fingers, waiting. "I feel … more powerful." She spoke the words slowly, trying to convey that this was more than fully feeling her vampire powers, more than a fledgling discovering their potential.

"What do you mean 'more powerful?'" Kendra thought for a moment. She was about to answer when a knock startled them. Neither, of them were paying any attention, so when the second knock came, they both looked at the time wondering who would visit at 3:30 in the morning. When the third knock came, it seemed more urgent, and Rick jumped up to answer it. Kendra followed, staying back some, not wanting to pry but was awfully curious. Rick opened the door and from where Kendra stood, her view was somewhat impaired by Rick's wider frame.

"Well, this is a face I never thought I would see on my doorstep." Rick bolstered "Anton Miller, what brings you here? Isn't it past your bedtime?" The blonde psychic just stood there. Rick's good natured jabs didn't seem to faze him.

"I know it's late, I hope I didn't wake anyone, but this is rather urgent. May I come in so we can speak, you'll want to hear what I have to say." Kendra went around Rick to see the special human she had met not long after arriving in Rome.

"Anton, It's good to see you again." She gave him a bright smile which made him smile in return, he had looked tired but seemed to perk up after seeing Kendra. Rick cleared his throat.

"Yes, come on in Anton and tell us your news, and don't worry, vampires don't sleep."

"Oh, well, I guess, if you don't sleep you wouldn't have a bed in your house then, would you?" He seemed a bit bummed about it and that piqued Kendra's curiosity, but before she could say anything, Rick piped up.

"Oh, vampires do own beds. We just don't use them for sleeping." Rick then walked off with a sly grin and a wink to Kendra as Anton stood blushing slightly in the doorway of the living room. Kendra sighed.

"Why were you asking about beds, anyway? Do you need a place to stay?" Anton stepped into the room, a grim expression on his face.

"Actually, that's only part of the reason why I'm here. I have good reason to believe my place has been compromised and I currently don't trust the Council to relocate me. I just need a place to lay low for a while," he finished in a rush.

"No," came the quick answer from Rick. "Absolutely not." Kendra glared at him.

"Why, Rick? What's wrong with helping out a friend?" Rick glared back at her "One, he's not my friend. We were put on a mission together, that's all. Two, despite his lineage, he's still human. Having him stay here would mean I would be responsible if something happens to him. He's a prized asset to the Council and because of that he's a liability for me. And three, no other dudes in my house. End of story." Rick stomped over to the fireplace and started working on getting a fire going again.

Kendra couldn't believe him, a 6-century-old vampire and he was being utterly childish. She stared at him for a moment before a wicked thought crossed her mind.

"Ok, fine, if that's how you want to be." She looked at Anton. "I've been meaning to go somewhere else anyway, so how about you and me go half on a hotel room. We could save some money that way. As a matter of fact, we can go get one now, you can tell me what's going on and we'll let scrooge here fester. What do you say?"

Anton's eyes were lit with a new fire and the tiredness seemed to vanish from his frame.

"Sounds good to me!" And with that the two of them headed toward the still-open door. The air moved around them as though someone had opened a window and in the blink of an eye Rick was leaning nonchalantly against the now-closed front door. Kendra had, of course, seen it coming, but the sudden movement made Anton flinch.

"Anton, buddy, I was just kidding back there. Of course you can room here." Rick stood from his lean, hands in pockets. "Of course there will be some ground rules." Anton shook his head,.

"No, I don't want to impose, Kendra is right we can see about getting a hotel room." Rick held up his hand.

"No imposition! Besides, those rooms can be pricey, I insist, stay. Me casa es tu casa."

"Well, with that settled, On to business," Kendra interrupted before the pleasantries became more unpleasant. "You said you came here with news, something we needed to hear?" Anton sighed in defeat and Rick was staring hard at Kendra. She looked away from his gaze and moved to sit on the couch in the living room.

"Yes, I'm afraid so." Rick turned on the electric lights rather than fight with the dying fireplace. The soft white bulbs flickered to life, illuminating everything in the room. Anton gasped, with his human eyes now being able to see clearer, he stared at the state of Kendra's clothes. "What happened to you? You look like you were in a war!"

Kendra looked down at herself, half forgetting she had been stabbed earlier that night, but she now saw what Anton was talking about. Dirt was caked under her fingernails, dried blood covered almost half of her light pink blouse, more dirt was streaked down her beige pants and her heels were covered with mud.

"Oh, I had forgotten about this," she stood, "Rick, where are my bags?"

"Hmm? Oh, I had the maid put them in the first bedroom on the left upstairs." Before more was said, Kendra, not wanting to waste time, used her vampiric speed to dash up and change. In minutes, she had changed into a tee-shirt, a pair of jeans, sneakers, and was back in the living room. She sat back down on the couch, the two men staring at her. "Well, you are coming into your vampiric powers nicely," Rick beamed. "That was almost impressive." Anton glared at Rick.

"Almost impressive?" he shook his head, "That was spectacular. At any rate, would you mind telling me how you got into that state in the first place? Though I have a pretty good guess…" he trailed off staring at Rick.

"Hey, don't look at me— she was the one who went off on her own. I had nothing to do it." He waved his hand and moved over to the bar, "Would anyone like a brandy?" Anton shook his head, still staring at Kendra. "None for me either," she said uneasily, "can we please just get on with it?" Anton straightened, pulling out his notepad. Rick sat down next to Kendra, brandy in hand, and sprawled out, taking up half of the loveseat. As Anton looked at them with envy, he began to go over everything he had found out since Rick and Kendra had arrived on the scene that day.

"Let's begin with the physical evidence, shall we? that won't take as long. First off, I found a boot print in some dried mud that looked rather out of place. I took a mold of it and had it examined. According to the forensics team, the footwear that made it was a size 11 and, based on the ridges, was a basic work boot. What made it stand out, however, was the placement". Anton pulled a large manila envelope out from inside his jacket. Then, from the envelope he procured a stack of enlarged pictures, all of which were neatly coded, dated, and marked with a location. "This one shows the print," he laid a picture on the table, "And this one shows the surrounding area." Another picture was placed on the table.

Rick and Kendra leaned over to look at the two photographs. At first nothing really looked out of place.

"Ok, it's a boot print, I'm sure there were a lot of people in that field that night. It could belong to anyone so what makes you think otherwise?" Kendra asked, unsure of where he was going with this revelation. Anton shook his head slightly.

"Remember — I said it's the placement of the print, not the print itself, that I find suspicious." After he had said that, a sharp intake of air made Kendra turn to look at Rick.

"He's right," he said, pointing at one of the pictures. "Look, the print was found outside of the crime scene, almost as if someone was watching the carnage. Which means, either we have a witness to find, or this is our perp."

"Has anyone come forward as a witness?" Kendra turned back to Anton. He shook his head.

"No, unfortunately we aren't that lucky in this investigation. However," He placed another photo on the table, "I did manage to recover this." In the photo was a piece of torn fabric, spattered with blood, and the letters *M A R* embroidered on one end.

"Looks like it's torn," Rick huffed. "And like this investigation, we were left with the scraps. We are holding but a handful of pieces in very large puzzle." Kendra picked up the picture staring at the scrap of cloth.

"Hey, Rick, check this out. Doesn't this look familiar?" Rick looked over at the picture as she pointed to something in the image. "Doesn't that look like…" before she could finish the sentence, Rick got up and walked over to a roll-top desk all but forgotten in the corner of the room. He opened a drawer and carried over the envelope given to him earlier that day. He pulled out the obscure note and dropped it on the table, Kendra followed his lead and placed the picture next to it. Anton looked at the note, eyes wide.

"What is that?" Rick shrugged.

"A note that Ilium gave me at the Council Hall, it's quite vague and tells me to do something I've pretty much been doing for centuries. "However, I believe the real message is this symbol right here." He pointed at the red *V* on the note. "And Kendra found what looks to be a partial of the same symbol on the fabric in this picture." Kendra pointed to the section of the fabric with the partial. Anton studied the two, looking between the picture and the note. "It's very small, are you sure they are the same? I mean, if anything, it could be the tip of the encircled V, but how can you be sure?" Rick shrugged again.

"If the puzzle piece fits …"

Puzzled

The three of them spent hours going over all the evidence, pouring over documents and pictures. In the end the only conclusion they could agree on were these three things, 1) A group tied to a red V-shaped symbol was involved in some way, and it wasn't positive whether they were friend or foe. 2) Someone was definitely behind the attacks and may have ties with the Council. Finally, 3) Ilium knows something and they needed to get an audience with *just* him soon.

Also, Anton's psychic abilities came a little too late, as he had explained he can only read the past as far back as seven hours and no more. It was common knowledge that the attack had happened over seven hours prior to his arrival. Rick had pointed out sometime during the night that it was rather stupid of the Council to send in someone with such a limitation. The most Anton could read was the beginnings of the clean-up and the other events leading up to his arrival. At any rate, his abilities were rather useless in this investigation.

Anton yawned wide for the thirtieth time that night. Kendra watched him stretch and rub his eyes like a tired child. As the sun began to peak over the horizon, she marveled at the fact that she no longer felt the need for sleep, it would seem, though, that that need was replaced with a new one as her hunger rumbled from deep inside her. Twice she found herself hyper-focused on the pulse in his neck and had to snap back to reality. One of those times, he had caught her staring and she was worried he might have gotten the wrong impression. Rick seemed to be oblivious, but Kendra knew better. He was probably enjoying the awkwardness of Kendra's obvious hunger.

It was happening again — her focus on the subtle pounding of his heartbeat, the skin moving ever so slightly over his jugular vein, the phantom taste of blood on her tongue. She couldn't take it anymore. Kendra pushed herself off the couch making both men jump, she knew she had startled Anton, but she suspected Rick jumped for fear she would attack the other man.

"Well, it's been fun and all, but I need to get going." She stammered awkwardly. Rick stared at her with kind of a sad puppy dog face.

"Aww. You're leaving so soon?"

Kendra started inching toward the door.

"Yeah, I have to go …" she looked at Anton and felt ashamed for looking at him like food. "…take care of something. Besides, I told you before, I was looking to get a hotel room and I meant it." Rick stood

"Wait, you're still doing that? I thought we had settled it last night, you and Anton were to stay here." Kendra still backing toward the front door, shook her head.

"No, we had agreed that Anton would stay here. We never discussed me staying as well. Sorry, but I really should be going, you boys play nice now, bye!" With a little wave she was out the door, beginning her day with an early morning hunt.

***

"That tricky little vixen," Rick gripped, "She had planned this all along. I just know it. Of course, I guess it didn't help the fact that she was hungry. Still, that's one hell of a bomb to drop all of a sudden." Anton leaned back on the couch.

"It wasn't much of a 'bomb' if she had told you about it before. Either way, I wouldn't say hunger was much of a motivation, I'm sure she could have found something to eat here." Rick sighed.

"You've been raised around vampires and still you act like you don't know anything. It's wasn't food she was after, you moron." Rick smiled a little. "Unless you had intended to offer yourself as her meal, she had no choice but to go on a hunt." Anton's cheeks flushed bright red in his embarrassment. There was nothing he could say, least of all to Rick.

"Well, I guess I should hit the hay, I won't be any good to anyone while I'm dead on my feet." Rick laughed.

"It's not so hard once you get used to it" he said with a wink. "Come on. I'll show you to your room." Rick headed upstairs; various pieces of obscure art hung on the walls. He barely spent any time in this house anymore and had forgotten how weird James' taste really was. Rick stopped to examine a piece. It was an artificially worn oil painting, dark tones made it hard to see in a darker setting, but being a vampire, James may not have considered that when he placed it in a dark stairway. The painting was of a sleeping woman dressed in Victorian age clothing; her hands folded over her abdomen, and a peaceful expression on her average face.

Anton caught up with him on the staircase. Rick shook his head at the painting, lost in thought. James was much younger than him, so it's a wonder they got along the way they did. Some would say it was because they both loved the same woman, though in different ways, but Rick knew better. He has lived long enough to know connections happen despite the passage of time. Rick briefly wondered again if he should give the man a call and tell him …. what exactly? That he was wrong? That thousands of years won't change his stubbornness? That saving Kendra's children from their fate isn't going to fix what had to be done? That he lied and he was sorry? Would he even believe him?

His head buzzed with all that had transpired between himself and the only real friend he had ever known. Of course, he would never tell him that. Rick would never be able to live it down. A small smile crossed his face as he opened the door to the only prepared room in the house, the one that had been intended for Kendra. Rick stepped in. First, Kendra's bags still sat on the floor at the foot of the bed. One of them sat on the bed, presumably the one that she got her clean set of clothes out of, but otherwise the room hadn't been touched. Rick picked up the bags and put them in the closet and then locked it with a master key.

"That's so you don't get any funny idea's about smelling her clothes. Think of it as me saving you from yourself," Rick said, the mischievous twinkle returning to his eyes.

"Dude, come on. You really think I'm that kind of guy?" Rick shrugged.

"Hard to tell, all I have to go on is your file, and you and I both know that's not enough to know someone's character. At any rate, this is my guest room, you're welcome to use the furniture to your liking but don't break anything, and there is an en suite bathroom through that door." Rick turned to leave "Oh, and no matter what you hear, don't go in the room at the end of the hall, that is, if you value your life." And with that cryptic message, Rick left Anton to sit and wonder.

***

The hotel Kendra found was nice and fairly affordable even with her pay, especially considering the generous amount of money Rick had given her. Thankfully, she was able to obtain 4,000 euros at an ATM in a near-by bank. She felt guilty doing so with the money he had given her, but mainly because she wasn't sure what kind of stunt he was going to pull. Is he going to ask what she spent it on, then give her a disapproving look when she ran down the list of things she had used his money for? Or would he ask for all the money back, cruelly snatching away the gift he gave her and leaving her in debt to him? She hated the idea of being in perpetual fear that she would end up the brunt of Rick's practical jokes, and therefore was nervous to spend too much money.

She walked into the room with a sigh, glad to be away from him for a time. Rick was exhausting to be around all the time and the quiet of the room greeted her like an old friend. She sat her purse down on a desk and flopped on the bed, as tired as she felt having dealt with Rick for over 24 hours, she couldn't sleep. Kendra laid there, wondering what it was that kept vampires from being able to sleep.

It was so weird; physically she still had energy, mentally she was tired and missed the bliss of passing out after a long day. Kendra pondered it a while longer and had an epiphany: *maybe this is why so many vampires commit suicide!* She defiantly felt like she was going to go insane if she had to spend the rest of eternity without any sleep. Feeling like her mind was about to slip away, she jumped up off the bed needing to do something — anything.

Keep busy, that's the key, if I keep busy for the next thousand years, I'm sure I will get used to this no sleep thing. Breakfast! I need food, so I'll go get some breakfast. With dedication on her heart, she walked out the door, leaving the idea of sleep behind forever.

In the hotel main lobby, there was a modest little cut spattered with small tables and chairs. A sign with the words *Colazione Gratuita* stood just outside the small "dining" area. Kendra grimaced. She wished she knew at least some Italian, but instead she was in the dark in most conversations. Kendra made a mental note to pick up an English to Italian dictionary to make it easier. She wanted Rick to teach her but with the way he is she'll probably end up saying something off the wall and not know it.

Kendra browsed the goods on the table, plate in hand. She only knew what a few of the items were by just looking at them. Thankfully, the little label cards had English descriptions on them, so if she didn't know what something was, she could read about it. One thing Kendra noted was the abundance of pastries and grains displayed across the buffet table. She picked up two pastries that looked like croissants but were labeled as "cornetto." some thin sliced meat that looked like salami, and a hard-boiled egg.

They even had a single-serve coffee brewer. Kendra grabbed a coffee cup from a small rack and with some excitement picked out a coffee pod from the near-by tree. She was delighted that they posted instructions on how to use the machine and, trying not to dwell on the fact that the instructions were written *only* in English, she began to brew herself a cup. It took a little longer than she had expected before her cup was ready, but it was definitely better than waiting on a whole pot to finish brewing. She added cream and sugar to her coffee and took a seat at a nearby table.

Kendra ate slowly, savoring the coffee as well as the quiet. She wished she had thought to bring a book to read, but sadly she didn't plan to have any free time. She wasn't entirely sure what would happen while she was here. Hell, she still didn't even know what to expect yet, and Rick wasn't going to give her any clues. She hated being left out of the loop, hated not knowing what the Council had in store for her and her kids. A little girl about Zeke's age ran toward the exit door giggling, her parents in tow, and Kendra had to stop herself from crying. She missed her kids with all her being, but it was too early to call them, considering Italy is six hours ahead of Georgia.

Kendra looked at her watch, an almost outdated thing but still used in her profession. It was only 2:30 am in Georgia. She didn't change the time on her watch, so it made it easier to tell the time difference. Also, she wouldn't have to remember to change it back once she was home. When her watch hits 6 am, she will know her kids are getting ready for school and daycare; she planned on calling them then. She sipped her coffee again, wondering what her children were dreaming of, wondering if they were sleeping well, eating well …

Someone cleared their throat, making Kendra jump out of her reverie. She looked up to see a man standing at the front of her table. He was fairly tall, maybe only somewhat shorter than Rick, he had dark brown hair, light brown eyes and was sporting a warm smile. "May I sit with you?" he asked in perfect English, though with a slight accent that Kendra couldn't place. She looked about wondering if maybe the tables were all taken up. All the tables were empty. They were the only ones in the room. Kendra looked back at him now somewhat suspicious. Before she could answer he switched to Italian and Kendra could only assume he repeated the phrase.

Kendra let out a nervous laugh and said, "No, you had it right the first time. I'm sorry, I'm just a little curious. I don't understand why you would rather sit here. This place is pretty open, you could have a table all to yourself."

The stranger laughed, "I figured that would be obvious, the real question here is why would I want to sit alone when I could sit with a pretty lady?" He winked, never loosing that inviting smile.

Kendra chuckled, "How brazen of you, sir. However, flattery won't get you as far as you might think." The stranger straightened.

"I think I'm up for the challenge, do you mind if I try to win the fair lady's heart," He said slightly, mocking the tone Kendra had taken with him.

"Whoa there, Romeo, who said anything about winning hearts? How about we start with a name and then go from there?" Kendra spoke light-heartedly, a small smile on her face.

"I understand. I'm sorry, I didn't mean to be so rude. My name is Aluin Dubois. It just pained me to see you sitting alone. Are you vacationing with anyone?" Aluin took a seat in front of Kendra, his question being a thinly veiled inquiry into her relationship status.

"I'm Kendra Hughes and I wouldn't exactly call this a vacation. It's more like a business trip." She answered him, purposefully avoiding the whole relationship question. It's been almost two months since she had buried Travis, it's hard thinking of herself as a single woman again. Their marriage was short but sweet, lasting only six years, and it still felt like Travis was there with her. As she absentmindedly played with the ring still on her left hand, she still found it difficult to believe that he was truly gone.

She hadn't worn it since she got it back from the jeweler the day Travis died. He had it sent in to be cleaned and, as a late anniversary present, had it engraved with the words *My Beloved* on the inside of the band. She found it among her belongings back at Rick's place and couldn't help but wear it now, feeling naked without it on her finger. Aluin noticed her toying with the ring and his tone changed.

"I find it hard to believe a man would let such a beautiful wife go so far away, all alone. Isn't he afraid she would be snatched away by some charming local?" Kendra stood from the table.

"Excuse me, what business is it of yours, anyway? Sorry, but I must be going." She picked up her dishes and left the table; her emotions swirling inside her. As she was placing her dishes on the return rack Kendra heard Aluin say, "Try not to get snatched up, little lamb." She continued out the double doors, looking back only to see Aluin still reclining in the chair she had left him in, a smug expression on his face. *What was his problem?* When she turned back, she slammed into something hard like a brick wall, only to find it wasn't a something but a someone. Kendra looked up at the person to apologize and found a familiar face looking back.

***

Rick sat in the living room of his overly lavish house, a cup of coffee steaming beside him on the end table. His sensitive ears picked up every sound in the house, from Anton's snoring in the guest bedroom, to the scurrying of mice in the attic. His senses reached through the connection, telling him Kendra was fine. He could sense she was on the move but couldn't pinpoint where. *She can take care of herself*— a thought that kept playing over and over in his head. He was reminded of his last fledgling, a young man named Joseph Crowe, who was a few years younger than Kendra when Rick had turned him.

Rick felt some regret with the memory being that he had lied to Kendra when he told her he was only ten years past due for a new fledgling.

It had actually been 100 years since he had blooded Joseph and the regret he felt was more than just the lie. Remembering the young man brought with it a pain Rick will never forget. Despite how many he had watched die, how many were killed by his hand, Rick would never forget the feeling of losing a fledgling.

New movement in the house pulled Rick from his reverie — Anton was waking up. Rick sighed, 7 in the morning, only 2 hours after sunrise. He didn't sleep very long. A scream rang through the house, deep and bellowing. It echoed through the walls. In moments Rick was in his guest bedroom staring at the half-naked form of his unwanted house guest. Anton lay on the bed, eyes wide, seeing something Rick wasn't and it only took him half a second to realize Anton was having a vision.

His hands and feet twitched, his face had the look of pure fear, pale and sweating. He screamed more and gripped the bed. Rick felt helpless, something he wasn't accustomed to, as he watched the man live for a time in whatever future he was seeing. Rick grabbed the chair from the desk and sat down to wait it out, too curious of what he saw. After about five minutes, Anton settled down before coming to his senses. He sat bolt up in bed ready for a fight once the vision let go of him. Rick held him back trying to calm the psychic down, careful not to touch him directly. If memory served, Rick was sure Anton would be too in tune to the future to be able to handle physical contact.

"Easy there, it's ok. Whatever you just saw is gone now. Relax." Rick coaxed the man into calmness, Anton's pupils were extremely dilated, despite all the light in the room, and Rick watched as they shrunk down to the size of a pinhole.

"Rick? Where am I? Ugh! My head!" Anton flopped back down on the bed and covered his eyes.

"Anton, do you remember what you saw?" He didn't answer right away. When he spoke, his voice was small; all he was able to manage was a whisper. If Rick hadn't been a vampire, he might not have heard what was being said.

"Death, lots of it. It was like a war zone, lots of people, ghouls, mostly, but in the fray were members of Death's Hand. I don't know why *they* were there. I do know, however, it all took place in the US." Rick's face hardened at the mention of Death's Hand. He despised that organization. They were supposed to be a Council secret, working in the shadows to take care of the Council's dirtiest of jobs and a large part of their job description was assassination. They were formed sometime in the late 18th century, while Rick was serving as a Council member, right under his nose. He had only found out about it within the last century and has been at odds with the Council ever since.

"How do you know this takes place in the US?" Rick leaned forward, needing to hear the details as it pertained to the strange ghoul activity they were investigating. Anton sighed.

"I was on a street I'm familiar with. My cousin lives nearby the location." Rick nodded.

"What is the area? Did you see the street name?" Anton groaned out, "Yeah, it was Samaritan Drive, the residential part of it anyways, lots of houses." Rick jumped up, glaring hard at Anton.

"Did you see a house with light blue paneling and white trim?" Rick asked, barely controlling the level of his voice. After all, it wasn't Anton's fault this was happening. Anton shook his head in misery

"I could only get so much detail. I was lucky to see the street name." Rick pulled out his phone and started dialing a number he has been meaning to save in his phone's address book. "Who are you calling" Anton looked up at him, his eyes were very bloodshot now. Rick hit the send button.

"Kendra, she lives on Samaritan — she needs to know."

Visions

"James? What are you doing here?" James looked at her, confusion and surprise played on his face.

"Kendra? Well, I wasn't expecting you to be here, although I was looking for you. I came here to book a room and what luck that I'd run into you in the process. Listen, there is something we must talk about, something I must tell you, but not here." He started looking around nervously, as though afraid of being overheard. "I know this is sudden and not something a gentleman should ever ask a respectable young woman, but would you mind if we spoke in your hotel room? I'm assuming, that is, that you are a patron of this establishment, yes?"

Kendra noticed that James' accent was more noticeable now, but didn't want to make him self-conscious about it, so instead answered his question.

"Sure, we can go there and talk, I don't mind, it's a different era than when you were growing up so it's fine." She gave him a smile that said she was only teasing him. James harrumphed anyway.

"Yes, indeed it is. Well, shall we then." Going back into the lobby of the hotel, Kendra noticed Aluin was no longer around. Wondering where the creep had wandering off to, she led James up to her room. They were quiet as the elevator steadily climbed to the 3rd floor, nothing was said as Kendra slid her key card through the slot to open the door.

James walked in behind her and started checking every nook and cranny in the tiny hotel room. Kendra was about to say something but James pressed his finger to his lips, signaling for silence. He moved slowly and deliberately, looking under lampshades, tracing the edges of the furniture, and all but pulled her bed apart. Kendra realized he must have been looking for hidden cameras and microphones. She wrapped her arms around herself, thinking that she couldn't have had the room long enough for someone to tap it, right? *Then again, anything is possible these days.*

Once he finished his sweep of the room, James looked earnestly at Kendra. "Have you spoken with the Council yet?" Curiosity bubbled inside Kendra as she shook her head no. James sagged with relief "Good, good. Then there is still time" He walked over to Kendra and put his hand on her shoulder. "James, what's wrong?" He stared at her intensely, his light blue eyes seemed to darken, and he smelled strongly of dirt, ash, and cigarettes. "Kendra, we need to get you out of this country as soon as possible, your kids are …"

His words were cut off by Kendra's cell phone going off. She reached in her pocket and saw a number she didn't recognize. She hit the deny button and looked back up at James.

"I'm sorry about that, what was it you were saying?" James's hand had dropped down to his side, but he still kept the dark look in his eyes, "I'm sorry to be the bearer of bad news. I really had hoped Rick would have come to his senses by now." Kendra's phone rang again, the display showing the same number as before. Again she hit the deny button and looked up at James, "What are you talking about? What's wrong with Rick and didn't you say something about my kids earlier?"

"Nothing is wrong with Rick, unless you count his morals and deplorable since of humor. But that is neither here nor there, Kendra … I … Oh, answer that damn thing would you!" Kendra picked up her phone and saw the same number still trying to call her. Baffled by it she hit the send button and put the phone to her ear. Before she could even say hello, Rick's voice boomed from her phone's speaker.

"It's about damn time you answered your phone, what the hell have you been doing that you need the luxury of silence?" Kendra went to speak, but Rick interrupted her.

"Never mind, it's not important. Where are you?"

"Why, what's going on?" Kendra looked at James, who was miming something, he pointed to himself and then slashing across his neck. Kendra took it to mean he doesn't want Rick to know he was here with her. "Kendra it's urgent, we need to talk, please tell me where you are." Kendra's brows furrowed.

"Can't you find me through the bond?" She remembered how she had found his house last night by following the bond. "What? No, of course not, not unless you're in danger, that's when the bond is at its strongest. Kendra, please tell me where you are."

Rick was starting to sound irritated and Kendra wondered how much she still didn't know about this bond.

"I'm at a hotel, I don't know the name, it has a boutique across the way in a large brown building that I believe also serves as apartments." Looking out the window, Kendra told him the name of the boutique and the name of the street both the boutique and hotel were on.

"Alright, I know where you are now I'll be there in about five minutes." Kendra turned back to talk to James, but he was already gone. She had heard a door open and close but thought nothing of it. A note lay on her desk she knew had to be from James.

Kendra picked up the note and was surprised he had time to write as much. The note was written in longhand and had some semblance of calligraphy. It read, *Kendra, I'm sorry to have run out as fast as I did, Rick and I aren't on speaking terms right now, so please excuse my rudeness. What I was trying to tell you before was this, you and your children are in danger. Most of the Council members are ruthless and will stop at nothing to get what they want, don't trust them. You are part of a bigger plan and the Council will try to rule your life, don't let them. They are law keepers only. They are not our Kings and Queens. Be wary, young one, this is a world we all must face. Until next time, Your friend J.*

***

Rick got out of the car. Anton struggled to open his door but still managed to get out of the passenger side of Rick's vintage Lamborghini. When Anton shut the door Rick spun around and snapped, "Hey, don't slam her door like that!" Anton held up his hands and stammered, "Sorry, I didn't mean to. I mean, damn, what is so special about this car, anyway?" Rick snarled "*This car* is not only a classic but was a gift from a friend a

102

long time ago. He's dead now and the model of this car is extremely hard to find, not to mention that particular shade of orange isn't easy to copy."

"No fooling? Who gave you such an expensive ride?" Rick turned away and nonchalantly said, "Frank Sinatra, he left it to me in his will" as he walked away, leaving Anton steeping in his shock. Anton bolted after him, through the hotels' front doors.

"*The* Frank Sinatra?" he yelled after Rick.

"The one and the same" Rick said, a smile playing on the corners of his mouth. Anton was about to start gushing over the deceased artist when he spotted Kendra, and, to Rick's disappointment, the subject was dropped.

"There you two are. I've been pacing the floor waiting for you. What is so important you couldn't tell me over the phone?" Rick didn't exactly know why, but Kendra seemed a little more agitated than she should have been. The scowl plastered on her face seemed a touch out of place on her naturally somber features. Usually, she was rather laid back, that is until you pissed her off. She started tapping her foot impatiently, "Well? Spill, what's going on?" Rick scanned the lobby and dining area quickly.

"Not here, where is your room? We'll go there." For a moment, it seemed she was going to protest. When her internal struggle was over, she sighed, "Fine, I'm sure the hotel staff will be gossiping about this later. Come on."

She led the two men to the elevators and in moments, they were in her room. Rick nodded to Anton, being the superior officer in this investigation, Rick was in charge. Anton began a full sweep of the room, inspecting all corners and crevices. Again, Kendra seemed like she was going to protest, but instead kept quiet about the minor invasion of privacy. Anton settled into a desk chair, sitting in it backward for some strange reason. Rick sat in the cushioned armchair that was nestled catty-corner in the room.

"I'm sorry I couldn't tell you this over the phone, I wasn't sure how you would react to the news." Rick sighed, "We can't leave the country until our business with the Council is over, which I'm sure you'll want to after you hear what I have to say."

Kendra sat down on the edge of the bed, tensed but calm.

"Well, spill it, Rick. I haven't got all day." Rick suppressed an amused chuckle at the irony, now was not the time for laughter.

"Anton had a vision. There will be a ghoul attack in the US. We know the where, we just don't know the when. As far as we know, the ghoul problem hasn't left Italy. It's been well managed here." Kendra held up her hand.

"Rick, stop. I doubt you would have come all this way for a mission report. It sounded urgent on the phone, so what aren't you telling me." Rick sighed

"Kendra, promise me you're not going to do anything rash. This is going to require some planning if everyone is going to make it out of this alive." Kendra nodded.

"Rick, I promise I won't do anything stupid, now get to the point, please." Rick stared at the floor.

"It's about the location. We know where they are going to attack. You're not going to like it ..." Kendra couldn't stand it anymore. She shot up out of frustration, "God damn it Rick! Where?" He stood to face her, at least, as much as his 6-foot plus frame would allow. Rick looked into her deep green eyes and said, "Samaritan Drive, in the residential area. Quite possibly, very near your house."

Kendra sat down, not quite sure what to make of this information.

"My children are with their aunt. It's nearly across town, they should be safe." She absentmindedly mumbled, Rick could almost see the wheels in her head turning.

"Kendra, this isn't happening now." Anton pipped up. Rick would have forgotten he was there if not for the pungent cologne the man insisted on wearing. "I was there in my vision. I only ever see what I will personally witness. I wouldn't know if a plane is going down if I'm not due to be on that plane or be in the area where it will crash. It's not happening now because I'm not there, nor do I currently have any orders to go to the US. There is still time to figure this out."

"Have you ever "seen" something that didn't happen or that you could prevent?" Kendra asked almost sheepishly. He hung his head unwilling to answer her and seemed content to let his eyes follow the patterns on the floor. That was all the answer she needed.

"There is something else you need to know," Rick said, a grim look on his face. "There were more than ghouls there in the fray. Anton says he saw some Death's Hand members. If they are involved, it means something bad is about to happen in the meeting with the Council." Kendra looked up at Rick, her gaze still somewhat far away.

"What is Death's Hand?" Rick's phone buzzed but he ignored it.

"Death's Hand is the Council's lap dog. They're thieves, murderers, scumbags. The Council uses them to do what they can't due to our laws and morals. They live in secrecy, train in secrecy. I, myself, had found out about them roughly 80 years ago, they are ruthless.

"More than likely, if Death's Hand is involved, they have been given orders to assassinate someone, and they are not above going after children. We need to think rationally ..." Before Rick could finish his sentence, he noticed Kendra get up and head for the door; she was moving so quick that Anton couldn't have seen her. He saw her face, rage had taken over her soft features, a rage he had never seen in another person, let alone Kendra. He moved faster, caught her by the arm, she tried to break free, but he held her. She attacked him, blind fury driving her — her children were in danger and her maternal instincts were kicking in.

Rick felt her fangs dig deep into the flesh of his arm. Not wanting to hurt her, he tried to wrench free. When that didn't work, he yanked her by the hair. She let go of him blood dripping from her mouth. She lunged at him.

"Rick, let me go I'll kill them." he knew he had to get her under control and did the one thing he didn't want to do. He grabbed her by the throat and slammed her against the wall. She struggled against him, the drywall crumbling around her. A gasp and an "Oh My God" that came from Anton, who didn't know what had just happened, made them both look in his direction. He had a hard time keeping up with the fight with them moving so fast, and now that Rick had subdued Kendra, their movement has slowed.

Boy, they must have been a sight to see, and, by all intents and purposes, it might have looked like Kendra was the victim.

"What the hell, man? Did you have to hurt her?" Anton wasn't sure what to make of this and his human mind jumped right to Rick being the bad guy. Kendra settled down and the inhuman glow of her eyes dimmed down. Rick set her back on the floor gently, staying close to use his body as a shield should she try something like that again.

"It's ok Anton. I'm not hurt, I am a bit shaken, though. It was like I had no control, what happened to me, Rick?"

Rick leaned in closer, bracing himself against the broken wall, he stared into Kendra's eyes. He was looking for a sign of the rage he had seen earlier, something to indicate any instability. His scrutiny came to an end, though, when he noticed Kendra's face flush at the close encounter, a sudden waft of perfume and feminine musk hit him like a brick wall as she began to perspire. It was almost too intoxicating and it took all his will power to back away. He went and sat back down in the chair he had occupied earlier. It was only then that he noticed the now very jealous Anton glaring at him. That, however, wasn't his fault; the man was easy to forget.

"What you went through just now is called blood rage. It's common in vampires that are still bonded with their sire, though, it becomes a problem when it occurs after the bond fades." Rick said matter-of-factly. "You can usually tell if a vampire is in blood rage when their eyes light up — I saw that in you just a moment ago. It's fueled by strong emotions but doesn't really set in until blood is spilled, usually in a vicious manner like our little squabble. Which is why I was staring at your eyes just now — I wanted to be sure you weren't in danger of raging out again."

"But there wasn't any blood spilled," Anton stood, furious. "I didn't see any of this, so how do I know you weren't just being an abusive prick?" Rick wasn't fazed by the man's words, though, he felt he had to defend himself. Rick pulled his shirt sleeve back, slowly rolling it up. It was tattered where Kendra's fangs had shredded the fabric, though, that wasn't enough to prove to this man that blood had been drawn. Once the sleeve was back and the bite fully exposed, did Anton realize his mistake in accusing Rick of wanting to fight for the sake of fighting.

Kendra gaped at the fresh bite marks with what seemed like a mixture of shame and awe. Though the wounds were no longer bleeding and looked as if he had already had a few days to heal, there were still visible marks in his skin.

"These will be visible for a while longer. They're the equivalent of scars for humans. They could last for another hour," Rick informed them. Anton sat down in his chair, facing the right way this time, seeming somewhat defeated. Rick's phone buzzed again and, in the silence, he figured he would check his messages.

***

Kendra sat at the edge of her hotel bed staring at the two men. Both of them were upset for different reasons. Kendra wasn't exactly calm either as she pondered what had just happened, she didn't just get angry just now, she had lost control. Most of it was a blur but in the end she knew what Rick had said was true. At first she was just pissed and for some strange reason she thought she would be able to go give the Council a piece of her mind, but when Rick grabbed her … she didn't remember much else after that … the taste of blood, maybe. She ran her tongue over her teeth and there it was — that pungent, tangy, and only slightly metallic taste of blood that mocked her as it clung to her gums.

Rick's blood tasted different from human's blood and Kendra began to compare that with the blood of hunters as well. Vampire blood was more potent tasting, almost like comparing milk to vodka. There was something stronger, deeper in vampire blood, and unlike milk, didn't seem to be very nourishing. Whereas human blood didn't have this added quality, it wasn't overpowered.; it wasn't exotic; it was just nourishing, like milk. Then you have hunter blood — not gross, but not tasty either, kind of like if you had mixed just milk and vodka, while not bad, just not appealing.

As the blood taste faded, a realization hit her: if she could lose control over simply getting angry, what would happen if left with disciplining her children? The gravity of the implications weighed heavy on her. Could she still be a mother after becoming this monster? Is the real threat to her children's lives their own mother? The horror of Kendra's thoughts didn't even have time to set in before Rick interrupted the slow spin into cold darkness.

"We have to go, I've received a message, the Council is ready to see us now."

Secrets

Back outside the Palazzo Montecitorio, Kendra stepped aside, asking for a bit of privacy. Anton was going to object but Rick stopped him. Kendra stood by the fence surrounding a large obelisk just out front of the building. She pulled out her phone, scrolled through her contacts, and hit send. The other end rang four times before she heard the familiar voice of her sister-in-law. Kendra didn't get much time to speak with her kids or Janet before they had to go. They were already running late to school and all Kendra could do was assure Janet that all was well. She told Zeke she would be home soon and to give his sisters big hugs for her, then, with a tear in her eye, she hung up the phone.

She couldn't help but miss her kids dearly as she reunited with the two men waiting by the door. They walked in the same way Rick had taken Kendra last time, and, as they walked, Kendra's mind began to wonder. Could she still be a mother to her children, is that even possible? The vampire laws prohibit non-special humans to know of their existence. There are some exceptions to this rule, but could her kids be the exception? No, she would have to keep this a secret until they're adults and then what? Could she turn her own children? Would the Council even let her?

Her thoughts were interrupted when someone started shouting. Looking across the council hall, the three of them spotted a woman with brunette hair wearing a light gray pants suit and a pink blouse waving at them. She was yelling out Anton's name and waving him over. He didn't seem to want to leave and tried to get her to come over to us but she refused. Shrugging his shoulders, he uttered a quick goodbye and reluctantly ran over to see what she wanted.

Rick and Kendra went up to the same receptionist as last time and she directed them to a small conference room down one of the halls. Once inside, she closed the door with a promise that someone would be with them shortly. A long, brown, oval-shaped table took up most of the room, there were at least ten chairs surrounding it and a platter of sweets sat in its middle. Coffee permeated the air. Kendra looked around and in the corner of the room was a small square table with a coffee pot.

Kendra grabbed a Styrofoam cup and began to make herself a cup of coffee, with cream and lots of sugar. Rick paced by the door anxiously, making Kendra nervous and more than a little worried.

"Rick, why don't you sit down? You're making my feet hurt watching you." Without stopping Rick said, "Then stop watching." Kendra gaped at him, "Well, you don't have to be rude. I sure there isn't anything to be worried about. If anything I should be the nervous one, right?" Rick stopped and looked at her.

"Yes, you should be. Why aren't you?" Kendra shrugged and Rick went back to pacing.

"Rick, did I do something wrong? Is that why you're worried? Are you afraid the Council won't approve?" He continued pacing, ignoring her for a time, before he stopped. He sighed heavily.

"No, that's not it at all. Look, Kendra, there is something I have to tell you and you're not going to like it." He sat down next to her, a guilty look on his face, his mouth opened and he was about to speak when the back door of the room swung open. Two people stepped into the room, a woman with long black hair, wearing a pair of black slacks and a forest green blouse. Her green eyes were a stark contrast to her light milk chocolate skin.

The other person was Ilium, dressed in a black suit with a dark red undershirt that looked like he was wearing blood made into fabric. Kendra and Rick stood at their entrance. The woman offered her hand to Kendra.

"Hi, I'm Meeka. I'm one of the Council members who will be

overseeing your inspection today." Her bright smile warmed Kendra as they shook hands.

"Hello, it's nice to meet you. I'm Kendra." Meeka beamed, "I know, I've heard a lot about you."

Kendra went to speak when Ilium said, "We needed to speak with you two as soon as possible. Sorry about the summons, I hope it wasn't at a bad time. The Council has you scheduled to stand before them in an hour, so we have a moment. I would like to get to business, nonetheless." Rick nodded and all four of them took a seat at the big table with Meeka and Ilium across from Kendra and Rick. "As I'm sure you have figured out by now, Rick, this isn't about the upcoming inspection. Anything that is said in this room stays in this room, is that clear?" Ilium looked around as everyone else nodded in agreement.

"Fine. Do you mind explaining that note you gave me yesterday? Its hidden meaning is driving me crazy," Rick began.

"Note? Ah, yes, I have no clue." Ilium pondered, "It was left on my desk with instructions to make sure it landed safely in your hands. I haven't got a clue what it was about. I figured it was some AVIA business." Rick blinked.

"Well, that's not very helpful." Ilium rubbed his chin.

"Why what did it say?" Rick mumbled, "Not very much, its infuriatingly vague, to use Kendra's words. I'll talk to you more about it later. Let's just try to wrap this mess up first."

"Ok, to begin, Rick, I received your request for an audience to discuss the ghoul insurrection. I have some information on that, but this will have to be off the books. I have a secretary whom I don't trust and can't seem to get away from. This is one of the few moments I'll have away from her. I also suspect her to be a spy, but I can't get any info on her." Rick's ears seemed to perk up.

"What do you mean a spy? For who and why?" Ilium nodded.

"Those are the right questions and ones I want answered. I don't believe she's a special human and I think she has allegiance to someone other than me. I hope you're the man for the job."

Rick leaned back in his chair, "Ok, I'll look into it, what about the info on the insurrection you mentioned?" This time Meeka spoke up.

"That's where I come in. I've got someone working on the connections

between the ghoul problem and our newest Councilman, Luca Bladimir."
Rick sat up.

"I had heard he was a senator. How did he become a councilman?"
Meeka's face dropped at the question.

"Well, as you know, Rick, there weren't any new positions open for the
Council. Most of us are in the middle of our terms with Ilium being the
only one almost done. Last week, however, Councilman Alannah White
was pronounced dead.

"We didn't find her body, but we found a suicide letter and her
residence here in Italy was burnt to the ground. So far, no foul play has
been suspected. It's simply being ruled as a suicide. I know better. I knew
Alannah — she wasn't depressed about being immortal— she had a thirst
for life." Meeka shook her head, she seemed to be holding back tears for
her lost friend, "She was murdered, Rick. I know it, I just can't prove it,
not yet. I almost have everything I need and I'm almost certain that if Luca
isn't behind it, he had a hand in it and is just as guilty."

Rick sat back, taking in all that he had heard. Kendra couldn't stand
the quiet and had questions burning a hole in her tongue.

"How do you know it's Luca? What makes you think he had anything
to do with it?" Meeka frowned.

"Because he managed to get voted into the Council before she was
pronounced dead. It was made official two days ago, and all without
Ilium and I voting. Council member votes must be done when all current
members are accounted for. We weren't even at the meeting!" She was
shouting now and Ilium patted her on the back, her eyes welled with tears
of frustration.

It is as she has said, once more, it was his idea to have all twelve
Council members at your inspection today." Rick shot up from his chair.

"What!" he bellowed so loud Kendra was sure that others could hear
him through the soundproof walls. "That is absurd and unnecessary. It's
only supposed to take three at most. That's what was agreed on in 1615
between me and Bodiccius. It's one of the things I had to agree on to get
the stubborn ass to join me in building the Council. This Luca person is
taking things way too far." Kendra was pulling at Rick's arm.

"Rick, please sit down, there isn't much we can do right now. We should probably see if they have something else to say." Rick continued to stand but was quiet and Ilium just shrugged his shoulders.

"That's all you really need to know, well, save for one thing. My head secretary, Susan Dunski, she should be in her office doing some paperwork." Ilium stood from his chair. "I'm sure she would be a mountain of information if someone could get her to talk, alone." With a coy wink, Ilium left the room, Meeka trailing after him. "Bye, Kendra. It was nice meeting you." She waved and was out the door. Rick looked at his watch, then headed for the door. Kendra tried to follow but Rick turned.

"No, I need you to stay here. I have to do this alone. I don't have time to explain why, just trust me, ok?"

"Well, what am I supposed to do? Just sit in this room until you get back, how boring. Please let me go with you, I won't get in the way." Rick shook his head. "Here." He reached into his inner coat pocket. "Read this while I'm gone," and he tossed her a small book called *Wallthumping* by Ally Cameron. Curiosity gave her pause long enough for Rick to make his escape.

***

In the back of his mind, Rick wished he could have seen her face as she read the "good" parts of the book, but he didn't have time for such luxuries right now. He dashed down the hallways rounded a couple of corners and dodged several people headed to meetings and pushing mail carts full of paperwork. After having to stop for directions, he finally came to the door he was searching for. *Secretary Susan Dunski* was embossed in gold lettering on the clouded glass window of her door. Rick knocked on her door and waited, but there was no answer. He knocked again, this time louder, but there was still no answer. Rick checked his watch. He was running out of time. In frustration he grabbed the door handle and opened the door.

"Ms. Dunski, I'm sorry for the intrusion ..." he began, but the room was empty. Rick looked around at the hallway and snuck into the office. He started rifling through her drawers and sifting through mounds of paperwork. He was looking in her filing cabinet when he came across a folder that was unmarked in a sea of carefully organized files. It was fairly thick and tucked near the back of the cabinet drawer. Rick pulled it out and opened it up, inside were case files of crime scenes; red marker was used to make notations. One of the files didn't seem to match, though. It wasn't of the ghoul attacks like the others. It was a file of the recent death in the Council. There was another closer to the back of the folder that didn't match either. It was a case file of the death of a Niccola Francesco, a special human working in the Vatican.

Were these cases related somehow? Rick looked around the room, there was a printer with a photocopier top he could use to copy all these papers, but he wasn't sure he would have time for that. Then he had remembered he had spotted a camera in one of the drawers he had pulled out. Grabbing the camera, he started snapping pictures of the files, getting close-ups when needed. Rick pulled the memory chip from the camera and placed the camera back in its drawer, then chip tucked away in his inner pocket. Rick quickly put the room back together and was just about to head out the door when someone opened it and stepped through.

A woman about four heads shorter than him blinked behind her square-shaped glasses. Her light brown hair was pulled back into a messy bun with a few strands outlining her heart-shaped face. A look of confusion wrinkled her forehead as she tried to figure out who was standing in front of her.

"Who are you and what are you doing here?" Rick wasn't sure what kind of woman Susan was, or *what* she was, for that matter. Dhampirs can fight a vampire's hypnosis, but weak-minded ones can fall prey to it. Pure dhampirs rarely fall under its spell, same as vampires. Special humans, however, seem to have a natural immunity to it which is one reason why the Council keeps them close. If he can hypnotize her, it'll be proof enough that she doesn't belong here.

Rick walked up to her and closed the door behind her, the door latch gently clicking into place.

"I've been waiting for you. I figured I could meet you here rather than in the noisy hallway." His closeness pressed her against the door

"Waiting for me? Why, what do you want?" she asked, her heart rate speeding up, practically pounding in his ears; he could smell her perspiration. She looked away from him, trying to avoid his eyes, but that wasn't enough he had to know.

"Susan, look at me," he purred. She shook her head, unable to speak now. Rick cupped his hand under her chin and lifted her head up to look into his eyes.

She squeezed her eyes shut with all her might. Rick sighed; he knew he was going to have to do something drastic. He could feel Susan begin to shake. Though, whether or not it was from fear, he didn't know. It was now or never. He wrapped one arm around the small of her back, then in one motion he pulled her to him and planted his lips on hers. Just as he had planned, her eyes flew open in shock, their gazes locked and he knew he had her as her eyes glazed over. He set her down gently and took a step back.

"Now, Susan. Could you tell me if you have a tape recorder anywhere in this room and where I might find it?" When Susan spoke, it was almost robotic, "In the bottom drawer to the left, under some papers." Rick went around the desk and opened the drawer. He pulled out the recorder and checked to make sure it worked. Once he had it recording, he came back around to Susan and said, "Ok, Susan. I have some questions for you and you will answer them to the best of your ability. Is that clear?" Once the robotic *yes* came from Susan the questioning began.

***

Kendra was debating on reading *Wallthumping*, the book Rick had loaned her, but the picture on the cover made her think otherwise. She had just hidden the offensive looking reading material in her purse when someone came into the room. She looked up expecting to see Rick, but instead a tall man with dark black hair came in. At first she thought, she thought it was Ilium, but this man was taller and had more angled features than Ilium. Also, he smelled different. She looked over at the odd man and said, "Can I help you?" He smiled a toothy grin and asked, "Are you Kendra Hughes?" She kept her face as blank as possible and asked, "Who wants to know?"

His smiled widened and he stepped forward, shutting the door behind him. All of Kendra's instincts were screaming at her that this man was bad news; she worked hard to keep calm, not wanting him to know he caused such a stir in her. The strange man came over to Kendra's side of the table and extended his hand.

"It's nice to meet you. I'm a member of the Council, I'll be one of a few presiding over your case." Kendra grudgingly shook the man's hand. "I wanted to meet you beforehand, but I was told you were in a meeting with a couple of other Councilmen. Would you mind telling me what it was about?" Kendra could feel some kind of mental pull to tell him all the details of her recent meeting, but she was able to easily ignore it. *Was he trying to hypnotize me?*

"I'm not at liberty to say, sorry. If you want to know, you'll just have to wait for the report like everyone else." The man looked a bit taken back but didn't seem to be perturbed by her defiance.

"Well, in that case, would you mind if I asked a few more questions?" Kendra shrugged, "Ask away, can't guarantee you'll like the answers, though." He smiled a crooked grin, then pulled out the chair next to Kendra, and sat down awfully close to her. With him being this close, Kendra could smell something awful coming off of him; it was a smell she didn't recognize, but it was strong enough to make her gag.

Kendra pulled herself together and did her best to ignore the smell as the man asked her the first question.

"Now, Kendra, I want you to answer me honestly," *There's that pull again. Can he not control himself?* "Your sire, Mr. Richard Blake, would you say he's … trustworthy?" Kendra couldn't figure out what he was getting at, but when she went to answer, she realized she really didn't know. He was pretty upfront about most things. She knew he was hiding some things, but for the most part, he hasn't lead her astray. She sat up a little before giving her answer, "I trust him. For me, that's enough."

He had a slightly smug expression as he nodded his head.

"Alright. What if I told you he wasn't telling you everything? That he was keeping secrets?" Now that was intriguing. It was true that Kendra knew very little about Rick; his life before being a vampire was a complete mystery. But did it really matter? His life isn't some big secret and she was sure, given enough time, she'd learn more about him. He is her sire after all, and they have nothing but time. Her mind set, she again answered his question.

"So what? We all have secrets, don't we? It's none of my business what he has hidden in his closets. When he's ready to tell me, he will." The strange man got closer.

"It is your business if it pertains to you." His breath was awful. She could hardly think over her queasy stomach; breakfast was trying to make an encore. "There are things he isn't telling you, important things about what you have become, how to gain power." He was whispering in her ear now and it wasn't just his breath that stinks. Kendra was fighting a losing battle with the bile in the back of her throat. "I can show you everything you need to know. I won't keep secrets from you, Kendra. You'll know true power, true strength if you choose the right side — if you choose me."

He backed away from her. Kendra's head was spinning from more than his words. He was just about to open the door to leave when she said, "Wait, I didn't catch your name." He chuckled.

"Choose wisely and you'll have all the answers you're looking for and more." Once he was out of the room, Kendra officially lost her battle in one of the tin trash cans sitting next to the coffee maker. She was in a frazzled state when Rick entered the room.

"Oh, man, Kendra, you didn't ..." Rick ran his fingers through his hair. "Don't tell me you did *that* in here. Talk about risqué" he said, shaking his head, a slight smile on his face.

"What are you talking about? It's not like I could help it. It just happened, I couldn't hold it back anymore." Rick sauntered over to her.

"Well, if I had known you needed it that badly I would have ..." he paused and sniffed the air. "What the hell is that smell?" he crinkled his nose, "That smells awful!" Kendra hung her head shamefully, "That was me. I threw up in that trashcan." She pointed to the tin can by the wall, "No, I don't believe that is what I'm smelling. I can now smell both and your upchucked breakfast isn't what has me gagging. It smells worse than a decaying corpse in here, what happened while I was gone?" Kendra coughed.

"Oh, that's probably that guy that came by. He smelled like that. That smell is the reason I threw up."

"Guy? What guy?" Rick was trying not to breath in too much.

"I'm not sure. He wouldn't give me a name. He was really strange though. He said he was on the Council, but that was as much as I could get out of him." Rick nodded.

"Ok, well, what did he want?" Kendra shrugged.

"To ask me questions. They were weird, too. He asked me if I thought you were trustworthy. I told him I trusted you and that's all I needed." Rick gently took Kendra by the arm and moved her over to the other side of the room, away from the smell.

"Look, Kendra, there is something I've been meaning to tell you and I'm afraid I've run out of time."

"What is it, Rick?" Rick's hazel eye's looked into hers with sadness.

"I've been keeping something from you, something important. I didn't have much of a choice in the matter. I'm risking a lot, but I feel you should know. The Council … the Council isn't going to let you keep your children." Kendra ripped her arm away from Rick, fury bubbled in her green eyes as she shrieked "*What?!*" Rick tried to put his hands on her shoulders but she backed away. "I wanted to lessen the blow by telling you what to expect. It's out of my control, Kendra." Her jade eyes hardened.

"Like hell it is, Rick! You of all people would let them walk all over you? Whether or not I keep my children will be my decision!"

"I'm afraid that's not how this works, Kendra. You'll be given a choice and an arrangement will be made on how they will be dealt with." Kendra turned away from him.

"What if I don't agree to anything? What if I don't want to give them up?" She thought back to how she doubted whether she could still be a good mother, and wondered if it was possible. She couldn't stand to be away from her children this long. How could she deal with eternity? Tears slid down her cheeks. The truth was she couldn't, they were her babies, and the last thing she had left of Travis.

Remembering her lost love gave her heart the fire it needed, she would fight, she had to, for him as much as for herself. She wiped her tears away and turned toward Rick, "Is there any way to fight this? Do I get to have a lawyer? What are the rules of this?" Rick shook his head.

"No lawyer. The Council sets down the rules, and if you fight it you could potentially be confined." Her heart sank. What was she going to do? Just then a knock sounded at the door and the receptionist poked her head into the room.

"They're ready for you"

Ultimatum

The blonde receptionist led them to a set of double doors. She pushed one side open and held it as Rick and Kendra walked in. The room was already packed full of people, a sea of faces turned to gawk at them, none of which Kendra recognized. A uniformed guard led them to the podiums in the front of the gawkers. The back of the room had twelve desks neatly placed in a semicircle below a short wall, the top of which had twelve ornate seats. The wall came high enough to obscure the sight of the throne-like seating, but the backs were beautifully carved and painted white.

Rick was instructed to stand behind one podium facing the Council's seating and Kendra was directed to the podium on the opposite side of the aisle from him, like plaintiff and defendant. Kendra looked down at her assigned podium to gather her thoughts. She had to fight this, for her kids' sake, she had to win, the question was how? Like a prayer being answered, there on the podium lay an envelope, with her name written on it. Is it an answer to her problem? Will this be helpful to her? There was only one way to find out. As discreetly as she could, she opened the envelope and pulled out the paper it contained.

It was a handwritten note that read, *Kendra, I really liked the talk we had earlier, and I hope you have thought about my proposal. I know what is to come and I can save your children. All you have to do is join me. Just use the code word "Jaybird" during the hearing and I will make this whole mess go away. Sincerely, Luca.* Kendra's hands shook. She felt like she was being backed into a corner. What was she going to do? Could she trust Luca to save her children? And what exactly did he want with her?

There wasn't much time left to ponder it; the court-like proceedings were beginning. First a line of people came out and sat down at a desk that lined the bottom of the wall. Their names and titles were announced as the took their sets. Most of it was in Italian, but some of the names were of different languages. It became clear that all of them were the head secretaries for the Councilmen when a familiar name came up. The one who sat for the name Susan Dunski looked like a frail, mousey woman. She was easily the shortest one there and seemed a bit nervous. When she looked over at Rick sitting in his podium, she blushed then seemed confused before looking away. Kendra's nervous mind mulled over that strange reaction, trying to find something to distract herself from the harsh reality.

Once they were seated, the line of Councilmen started to walk out from a door hidden behind the left side of the wall. The same protocol was taken as with the secretaries. They were named in order of appearance and once name and title was announced, they took their seat. Ilium was off to the right side, one of the first to emerge. The man Kendra now knew as Luca sat more central, with Meeka bringing taking up the last seat. The guard who announced the arrival of all twenty-four people continued to speak, announcing the lead Councilmen in the case of the fledgling Kendra Hughes to be Seraphine Dunbrook. She stood and gave a curt bow before sitting back down.

She was a pretty woman, the vampire blood keeping her from showing how old she really was. She had a hunter's lithe in her movements and her eyes shined with a glint of perceptiveness unheard of in humans. Her light brown hair was tucked up in a high ponytail making her cheekbones seem more prominent. You could tell she was an intelligent woman by the way she carefully scanned the room. Once everything fell silent, she began to speak with an interesting accent in Italian which made placing it harder. Kendra had no idea what was going on. She didn't understand Italian and was afraid she wasn't going to have a say in anything.

Panic set in, a sense of hopelessness made her nearly collapse. Then she heard Rick speak up; his voice rang in her ears as he spoke in fluent Italian.

She didn't know what he said, but the look on his face was reassuring, Councilman Seraphine nodded her head toward the guard who then disappeared through a door. When he emerged once again, he brought with him a man of short stature, with a small bald spot on the back of his head, and some reading glasses hanging around his neck.

The man was ushered into the far-right corner of the room. He sat in a chair while a microphone was placed in front of him, looking a bit nervous, but ready for the task he was given. When Councilman Seraphine spoke again, it was directed at Kendra and she spoke in clear English.

"Mrs. Hughes, you stand in front of the Council of Vampires for a mandatory Fledgling Evaluation. I will make it known that you were picked at random for a bloodening due to your sire's lack of interest in upholding the law and continuing the species." There was a pause for the interpreter to finish speaking in Italian for the portion of the room that didn't speak English.

In that time, Kendra noticed the sideways glare Councilman Seraphine was giving Rick. It was clear she had some resentment toward Kendra's sire, though, as to why, Kendra could only speculate. Rick didn't seem fazed by it, though there really isn't any telling with him. "I have to ask, now for all to hear, how has your transition been? Are you coping well to your new life? And I ask this because a forced bloodening isn't always carried out with care." She waited for Kendra to answer. However it felt like she had been put on the spot.

Kendra squirmed, feeling a little self-conscious before giving an answer.

"Fine, I guess. I don't know how these things normally go so I can't really compare it to anything else. He did make breakfast afterwards, so bonus points, I guess." Kendra giggled nervously, trying to ease the tension and maybe even win this woman over some. *Maybe I can sweet talk my way into a beneficial agreement.* The Councilman smiled slightly. A few chuckles came from the audience behind Kendra; then it became serious again.

"Good. So, now we move on to more important matters. Mrs. Hughes I have been made aware that you are the mother of three human children conceived before your bloodening. Is that correct?" Kendra's throat was dry, she found it hard to speak, so instead, she just nodded. "Mrs. Hughes, we need you to speak your answers for documentation purposes, please."

Kendra swallowed hard before giving a meek "Yes." Councilman Seraphine sifted through some papers she had in front of her, apparently the top of the wall also served as a desk of sorts. She pulled out a yellow piece of paper before speaking again "Ah, yes, here it is, the section regarding humans. The law states in subsection B1 that, with the exception of special humans, vampires are not to share their home with humans, unless shown that these humans are guaranteed to never discover the vampire's true nature.

"It is my experience that human children are rather curious creatures. Will you contest the fact that one day they may discover your true nature?" Kendra thought hard, could it be possible to keep this secret from her children? Then with more confidence than she felt Kendra straightened.

"Yes, Councilman Seraphine, I am sure I can raise my children without them discovering my identity." Luca moved forward in his seat.

"Seraphine, I have a question or two for the fledgling Kendra. May I?"

Seraphine nodded and Luca continued, "Mrs. Hughes, are you saying you want to keep your children, that you wouldn't be willing to give them up?" Kendra answered with a strong "Yes." Luca started to grin a little, "But, what about the temptation of their blood? It's pretty well known that children's blood is rather enticing to some. Is it that way for you?" Kendra gasped and wasn't alone in her shock, several gasps from the audience, as well as a few from the Council, could also be heard. Councilman Seraphine seemed content to allow the question, but Kendra stood her ground.

"No Councilman Luca it is not that way for me. They are my children I would not allow harm to come to them."

"Mrs. Hughes, be that as it may, the law is the law." Councilman Seraphine continued. "It is to be upheld — if we allow everyone to get away with not abiding by it, we invite calamity." Kendra sighed.

"I am aware of that Councilman, I only ask for an exception. My children are young. Their memories aren't fully developed — they won't know any different. I don't want to lose them. They are … all I have." Kendra's voice broke and she couldn't continue.

Some murmuring could be heard as the audience talked amongst themselves. A few of the Councilmen whispered back and forth with one another and when silence fell again, Councilman Seraphine spoke.

"We have heard your plea, Mrs. Hughes. The Council of Vampires will adjourn to discuss this matter amongst ourselves and differ to the laws. We will send word when we shall pick this back up. It is advised that all who must attend remain in the building." All the Council members stood and began to leave, followed by their secretaries.

***

Kendra met up with Rick in the hallway. He seemed to be beaming with pride, which seemed to contradict the feeling Kendra had toward him. She walked right up to him and full-on, no holding back, and slapped his stupid grin off his face. The sound reverberated off every wall in the Council Hall. It seemed every head turned in their direction even if they couldn't quite see what was going on. Rick lifted his head from the awkward angle Kendra's slap had sent it. The grin was gone but the beaming in his eyes was still there, which only seemed to infuriate Kendra more.

"Ow, glad I'm not human, that might have killed me."

Kendra huffed, "You'd better be glad that's all I did. Why didn't you tell me? I could have been better prepared!"

"I did tell you!" Kendra glared at him.

"Yeah, at the last possible minute!" Rick sighed.

"Look I wanted to, but it was considered top secret information. I wasn't even supposed to know." Kendra threw her hands up.

"Top secret? Really? Why was that top secret? I'm nothing special, so why me?" Rick shook his head.

"It's not because it's about you, it's insider Council knowledge, everything they talk about is top secret until it's made known to the general public. It's just basic protocol to prevent panic in dire situations and they use it with everything until they feel it can be revealed. I didn't want them to know I knew anything because if they found out about their little leak, I lose precious insider info."

Kendra scoffed, "Well, if you're so hung up on the information, then why not run for Councilman in the next election." Rick rolled his eyes.

"I said I wanted info, not be hidden away in a closet debating over laws that, for the most part I wrote, with some two-century-old child who thinks they know what was going on in *my* head some 400 years ago. I would rather have a stroke." Kendra rolled her eyes.

"You don't have to be so dramatic" Just then, she spotted Anton headed in their direction and for some reason he didn't look too happy.

"Hey guys, bad news, my assignment has changed. This is happening faster than I had expected. I have to head for the airport in a few days. My flight has already been scheduled. They're sending me to Georgia."

"So soon? What's the rush?" Kendra asked, hoping she would have at least one friendly face in the audience this time, but Anton only shook his head,.

"Hey, before you go, take these with you," Rick said as he pulled the smallest manila envelope that Kendra had ever seen from his pocket and handed it to the other man. It may have been big enough to hold a prescription pill bottle in it and there were some bulges at the edges. Both Kendra and Anton were curious about its contents, but neither had the time to ask. "Bring it to the AVIA branch in Georgia and have them put it under lock and key till I get there." Anton nodded, tucked the envelope away in a pocket, then turned around and left with a quick goodbye.

"Rick, what are you not telling me?" Kendra asked offhandedly. She wasn't expecting a straight answer.

"A lot of things, baby, a lot of things," he said with a wink. "But in regards to this situation, let's just say I met with Susan Dunski and she had an amazing singing voice, just like a bird." With that, he walked back toward the Council room. Kendra stood there in the middle of the large Council hall staring at the painted walls. Angels and Demons battled overhead, the painting on the ceiling representing the heavens in turmoil; the sight filled Kendra with a sense of trepidation. She then headed back to the Council hall to await her fate.

***

The wait was longer than most had expected, the audience murmured amongst themselves, some even milled around talking to others in different seating areas. Though Anton wasn't able to be there, it was nice to still be greeted with a familiar face in the crowd. James had tucked himself away in the far right corner of the audience side of the room, silently offering his support. Kendra sat in the chair behind her podium, staring at the envelope that had been left unmolested on the slanted surface. Guilt consumed her thoughts, should she have told Rick about the letter? She couldn't get angry at him for not telling her his secrets when she was keeping some herself.

She wasn't sure how long she spent on mulling over her guilt when the Council room began to stir with a new movement. The proceedings were about to begin again and Kendra was mortified that she wasn't thinking about how she was going to save her children. It was too late, she was out of options, and the note sat there mocking her as she walked up to the podium. Should she risk it? The secretaries and the Councilmen filled into the room once again in their usual orderly fashion. The announcements were made once again as they took their seats. The balding man from before scurried over to his chair, trying not to be noticed, and once all was settled, Councilman Seraphine stood to address the room.

She spoke in Italian the opening speech before sitting in her seat. Then, looking at Kendra, she slipped into English flawlessly.

"We have come to a verdict after much debate. I wouldn't say our vote was unanimous. However, it was in greater favor among my colleagues and I. First, Mrs. Hughes, I must ask, will you not recant your last statement of refusal to abide by our laws?" Kendra panicked, *It's a trap, they are trying to make me seem like the bad guy here. What do I say?* The room grew silent and Kendra could feel the tension in the room.

"And which laws is she refusing to abide by?" Rick's voice was like a light at the end of the tunnel.

"Mr. Blake, you above anyone else should know the laws best. Don't pretend ignorance to buy time. Our decision has already been made." Councilman Seraphine scoffed at him and Kendra could tell he wasn't about to give up.

"Don't talk down to me, Seraphine. Yes, I know the laws. It is within these laws for a plea of exception and an exemption to be allowed. Kendra wants to keep her children, and why wouldn't she? It's not her fault that you people pulled her number out of a hat. Why is she made to suffer when more outrageous pleas for exception have been made and granted in the past?"

Councilman Seraphine stood, anger flared her nostrils.

"Mr. Blake, if you do not stop, I will have you removed from this Council room." Rick glared at her silently and when it seemed he had no more to say, she sat back down. "Mrs. Hughes, do you wish for me to repeat the question or are you ready to give an answer?" Kendra looked at everyone on the Council. She wasn't sure how this would turn out, but Rick's outburst gave her new fuel to push on.

"I will not recant, I would like the Council to further discuss my plea for exception in the case of my children staying right where they are, with me."

Councilman Seraphine nodded "Very well, then let it be known that the Council has convened and denied your plea for exception under the law Human Interactions subsection b1. You have proven you are incapable of removing your children from your home, and as such, the Council shall take full responsibility to do so on your behalf. The execution date will be decided by this Council on the morrow. The meeting has now come to an end."

The verdict had been set. They were going to kill Kendra's children and she couldn't stop them. She glared at Rick. He stood at his podium, head hung like a beaten dog, and she was furious. The voices of the Council members trailed off as reality sank in, she desperately looked for a face that would help her. Ilium sat with a grimace on his face, he could do nothing, and she knew it. James hung back, lurking in the shadows, he wore a strange expression, but he wasn't looking at her. Kendra followed his gaze until she was looking back at Rick. Something in his face had changed, his eyes looked wilder, a grin was slowly spreading, making him look feral. One of his fangs poked over his bottom lip, his shoulders shook, and the room became quiet. Rick's laughter was the only thing heard; he was more maniacal than ever.

"You guys are pathetic! You just about had me fooled." His head came up slowly. "Don't get me wrong, I commend the effort, it's not easy to fool an old monster. Bravo, bravo!" Everyone was stunned into silence as he began to clap. When his strange applause stopped, Rick sighed. "But you are forgetting one teensy detail." He then leaped over the podium and landed with cat-like grace. With one hand in his pocket, the other pushing his hair out of his face, he walked closer to where the Council sat. The line of secretaries, seated in front of their respective council members, stood and backed away. The smell of fear filled the room. Some of the secretaries were special humans, the rest were dhampirs and they all knew power when they saw it.

"I made you what you are today." Rick continued unfazed, "I am the reason you sit here, talking to me the way you are, like I'm a child who needs scolding. If you ask me, it's you who needs scolding. Look at this mess, you people can't even keep your own members in line. How truly pathetic!" He stopped where the secretaries had been backed against the wall. "Don't judge me and my fledgling with the same incompetence that led us down this road. You have done nothing for me. I have given everything to *this!*" He swept his arm, gesturing to the Council members. Rick sighed again. "Actually, that's not true, you were the ones who chose my next fledgling for me, so I have you idiots to thank for me having Kendra."

A loud bang interrupted Rick's speech. Councilman Seraphine laid her gavel down and looked down at Rick with contempt.

"You are out of line, Richard. I don't care if you are the founder — you will respect our authority." Rick chuckled.

"Lady, you have no authority here. You think you have me in a corner, but you're wrong, I have options. For example, ..." Rick grabbed one of the secretaries standing in front of him, Susan Dunski, the one the Council had saddled Ilium with. She screamed before Rick put a hand over her mouth, her glasses fell to the floor. "I could go on about how corrupt your little group has become. I could tell you all to fuck off and dare you to try me. It would all work out in my favor in the end, but I've decided I like this alternative better." He practically waved Susan at them. "I refuse to follow the leadership of people so blind that they allow spies in their midst!"

With that, Rick did something no one expected him to do. He bit deeply into Susan's neck and it was clear he intended to kill her. The Council sat stunned, though not for long, Four of them started calling for the guards. Ilium, Luca, and Meeka sat quietly, watching the chaos unfold. Different expressions played on all three of their faces. The rest of them were in so much shock they couldn't speak. The room quickly became bombarded with armed vampires and dhampirs. Kendra leaped over her podium much like Rick had done before. From the corner of her eye, Kendra could see James moving in much the same manner as her. An understanding passed between them as their eyes met, then they stood between Rick and the coming barrage of guards. Rick was vulnerable so long as he was feeding. Kendra and James worked to keep the other vampires off of him.

The Council members were moved single file out of the room for their safety. Kendra and James were over encumbered with guards and were quickly losing the battle. Finally, Susan's body fell lifeless to the floor. Rick turned around, the blood of his kill blazed in his hazel eyes, they almost seemed to glow red.

"Rick, whenever you're ready to help, we're waiting!" James yelled as he batted off one of the guards. Rick stomped his foot on the floor, ice trailed and branched off, freezing solid everything it touched.

The room had grown so cold that Kendra and James were beginning to shiver. Several of the guards turned into solid ice. Some managed to break free. A small stampede broke out as guards began running away from Rick. Rick moved at lightning speed, braking the solid forms of the guards, effectively killing them. He didn't stop with them either. Blood splattered the walls of the council room, screams bouncing off the vaulted ceiling, the room became a blood bath. It was clear Rick was on a rampage.

Kendra feared that her sire was going rogue; the look he had said he was on the verge of doing just that. James patted her shoulder.

"Don't you worry about Rick," he said, seeming to read her mind. "He has lived for so long his chances of going rogue are minimal. Age isn't really much of a factor, but you can't live for six centuries without some tolerance for living." Kendra looked up at James.

"What can we do, how do we stop him, isn't he going too far?" James sighed.

"Yeah, I suppose he has, though, I believe he's just trying to leave a message, a show of power if you will. They won't mess with him after this, and in turn, they may even leave you alone — if they know what's good for them anyway. Come on. It's not safe. We have to get out of here."

James gently grabbed Kendra's arm and led her to a side door. Kendra panicked and turned to yell at Rick to follow them so they could all get out. What she saw made her stop dead in her tracks, blood covered everything from the marble tiles on the floor to the angelic mosaics on the ceiling. There was something profoundly disturbing about a panted angel's face covered in dripping blood that had her feeling nauseous. The smell of it was so strong that, given her vampirism, was still making her feel ill. Rick began to walk toward them. He was moving too slow, though. She began wondering why he was moving so casually. Rick was even saying something that sounded important but she couldn't hear him.

Then the room turned black and strange thoughts took over her mind. *This is what I have become. I really am a monster now, aren't I? And a monster couldn't possibly be a mother, could it? That would be unthinkable. This is my destiny. I'm to become the killer of man. Isn't that right, Travis? You left me here and now I shall kill everything — the ender of worlds.* A scream broke through the mad ranting in her head, and after a few minutes she realized the one screaming was her. Before she could stop herself, the room that had just come back into focus began to spin. This time she really was swooning. Then everything turned black once again; only now it was silent.

Unknown

Kendra woke slowly. Her mind immediately began to wander. For a while, she felt as if she had just awoken from a long dream and hoped that everything she had experienced was just that, a dream. She lay there with her eyes closed, thinking that she was in her own bed, she was still human, and that vampires didn't really exist. Kendra didn't want to open her eyes because she knew it would break the spell, she wanted to believe for as long as possible that she was safe at home. She wanted with all her heart to continue living out the fantasy that she was still living her old life, her human life.

"I know you're awake, you faker, now get up." The voice sounded familiar. She knew the person who was speaking to her, but she couldn't quite place who it was. She searched her memory for a name, if she was indeed still human then who's voice was this. It was a male voice, but it couldn't be her brother-in-law; Marcus's voice was deeper than this.

Then Kendra smiled; she knew this voice, and the person who had it filled her with so much joy inside.

"Travis, what time is it?" she mumbled sleepily.

"Ha, figures," came the voice again, only it wasn't Travis that spoke. Kendra opened her eyes in shock. The voice came from right next to her. She looked over at the man lying in bed next to her. "Of course, it's just my luck that I would be in bed with a woman and she'd call out someone else's name," Rick said with a smirk. He lay on the bed propped up on his elbow, fully clothed, and laying on top of the blankets. Kendra was so startled to see him so close that she fell out of the bed, trying to push herself away from him. She landed with such a thud that in moments James was standing in the doorway. He had a worried look on his face until he observed the situation; the confused look that he wore after was mixed with irritation.

"What the hell is going on in here?" James asked, almost sounding like a scolding mother. Rick shrugged and Kendra looked around confused, then stammered out, "I'm not sure, where am I, what happened after …?" She held her head; a huge headache came over her and then it was gone just as fast as it had come. James sighed.

"You just woke up, didn't you, Kendra? You had us all worried." Rick sat at the edge of the bed.

"Actually, she's been awake for about ten minutes. She was refusing to get up, though, so I just gave her a little nudge." James looked at him in shock while helping Kendra stand.

"So you pushed her off the bed?" Rick looked at him, mockingly mirroring James's shock.

"You'd believe I would do such a thing? Well, excuse me," he scoffed "The fact is she did that to herself, I just gave her a mental nudge."

"Um," Kendra interrupted the men's bickering. "What am I wearing?" she asked looking down at herself, "And more importantly, who dressed me?" Rick grinned wide.

"I did of course!" Kendra stared at him wide-eyed.

"Don't believe him, dear, he wasn't the one that changed your clothes. He's just trying to goad you." Rick chuckled, James glared at him before continuing "The fact of the matter is, when you fainted, you fell right in a puddle of blood. We both tried to catch you, but we weren't prepared for your fainting spell. We very well couldn't leave the country covered in blood with an unconscious woman. So, we fled, used a few contacts to find a safe house, and now we're here. The lady of the house is the one who cleaned you up and dressed you. Unfortunately though, she couldn't save your outfit. So, what you are currently wearing is the lady's daughter's most comfortable clothing, seeing as they didn't have any nightwear handy."

Someone cleared their throat and everyone in the room turned to look at the woman that now stood in the doorway. She wasn't very tall, but her posture was regal, like someone who was used to commanding attention from a crowd. She had somewhat angular features though not so that it would make her seem unattractive. In fact, she was quite beautiful. Her slender frame hid nothing about her grace as she carried herself like royalty, even as she meekly stood in the doorway. She pushed back her dark hair and stared at Kendra with her light brown eyes, smiling warmly.

"Oh good, you're awake. My name is Yvonne Rosenfeld, but you can just call me Evie. Everyone else does." She spoke with something of an accent almost rolling the *R* in her name, though it came out sounding more like an *H*. "Is there anything I can get for you, dear?"

"Oh, I don't …" Kendra began to protest when a sharp pain in her gums stopped her. Her vampiric hunger had become so great that her fangs extended to their full length, threatening to reveal her true nature. She didn't know if the hostess of the house was aware of the dangers she had brought upon herself in unknowingly inviting monsters into her home. Kendra gently clasped her hand over her mouth, finding it a bit hard to speak just then, as her senses became hyper-aware of Evie's beating heart and thundering pulse points. Rick walked over to Kendra and pulled her face up to meet his. His sudden scrutiny made Kendra blush. She felt shameful that she couldn't control herself.

"Evie, could you send up Robert, please," Rick said, still calmly examining Kendra's pained expression. Without another word Evie left, closing the door behind her; silence dominating the room. With Evie gone, Kendra's need subsided some, though not enough for her teeth to fully recede. She ran her tongue over her gums, trying in vain to massage away the pounding hunger.

"How long have I been out?" Rick walked over to the dresser. He shrugged his shoulders.

"About eight hours, it's been nearly a day and a half since you fed last, if that's what you're wondering. You shouldn't feel this hungry right now, but you have been under a lot of pressure lately, so the stress could be pushing your metabolism into overdrive." Rick tossed her some plastic bags from the top drawer of the dresser. They contained brand new clothes with price tags still intact, all of them were in her size. "You might want to get dressed before Robert comes in." Rick said cryptically before he and James walked out of the room.

"We'll talk later, I promise," James said before shutting the door behind him. It was but mere moments after she had slipped on the last article of clothing with tags, stickers, and plastic fasteners all removed, that someone knocked on the door. Kendra ran her fingers through her hair, trying to make herself presentable for this Robert person. She wasn't sure what his role was going to be in all this, but she didn't want to seem disheveled, nonetheless.

"Come in," she called while awkwardly standing in the middle of the room, unsure of what was about to happen. A blond man of average height with slight Germanic features stepped into the room. Instantly the hunger threatened to give her away, his smell was stronger than Evie's and much more alluring, it took all of her will power to not attack this man. Then she realized why, this man was human, pure and simple. Rick had sent him into what essentially was the lion's den, he was doing this on purpose and that thought just about enraged Kendra. If it wasn't for the fact that Robert was standing in front of her just then Kendra would have stormed out of the room and gave Rick an earful.

"You must be Kendra, it's nice to meet you. I saw you when you were carried in by the big guy. Rick, I think his name was. Anyway I'm Robert, Evie sent me up here to help you." Kendra swallowed hard, she wasn't even sure she would be able to speak, the idea of even opening her mouth painted images of closing it on his jugular. She looked away from him, finding it easier to focus on the conversation when she wasn't focused on his pounding heartbeat.

"Yes, I'm Kendra, it's nice to meet you, too. What exactly did Evie say I needed help with?" Kendra was surprised her voice hadn't cracked like a teenager.

"What else would a vampire need help with?" Robert asked with a casual shrug. Kendra felt a twinge of fear and then shock as she realized that he knew what she was. Her shock quickly turned to horror as Robert pulled out a small dagger. It was sheathed with an ornamental bat on the hilt, and Kendra couldn't help but think it was fitting for what she foresaw him doing with it. "If you need a little help, I don't mind. I'm told you're a fledgling and still not accustomed to our world. This should make it easier." Kendra was frozen in shock as he unsheathed the dagger and raked it across his neck. Was he committing suicide right in front of her? Kendra yelled but the damage had been done, she now stood face to face with him, blood dripping from the wound on his neck. She ignored her need, ignored the blood — her medical training kicked in, Kendra looked desperately around for first aid material. She could work with just about anything in this room but she didn't want to leave his side in case he passed out. She was terrified this man was going to die.

A hand grabbed her arm. It wasn't strong, but it was firm and it gave her pause. Kendra realized her imagination must have gotten away from her, Robert's wound wasn't very big, it wasn't even lethal, and he was gently leading her to it. Some new instincts kicked in, ancient and primal, addressing a need she had neglected. The blood dripping down his neck was enticing; she lost herself in its pull, and gently licked it away. She pressed her mouth against the wound and drew deeply of his blood, it wasn't flowing fast enough for her, so she used her fangs to break open the wound some more.

Robert gasped, whether from pain or surprise she didn't know nor care. The absurdity of the situation wasn't lost on her, though, as she drank. Here she was, a nurse by trade, dedicated to saving lives, and if she wasn't careful this man will die in her arms all for her needs, not his. The blood flowed over her tongue, and she tried to figure out what about it she craved. Medically speaking, there really wasn't anything in blood that could nourish the body, yet there are animals in nature that feed off animal blood. Maybe if she could understand the need she could control herself better.

She wasn't completely sated when she let go of Robert, but if she had continued, she very well could have killed him. He wasn't very steady as it was, so she helped him to a chair. He tried to protest but was almost too weak to fight her insistence.

"So, you knew about me being a vampire?" Kendra began, no point beating around the bush by this point. Robert nodded "Everyone here does. We're a small town. Most of us are dhampir, and as I'm sure you already know, I am human." This information shouldn't surprise Kendra, but she still felt a little surprised anyway. "How do you fit in here if everyone else is dhampir?" Robert chuckled.

"I'm not the only human here, there are more of us. We call ourselves Council rejects, special humans with abilities the council can't find a use for. I am an empath, someone who can control emotions through touch."

"Really? So that just then was you?" Kendra didn't know how she felt being manipulated like that, though she knew she didn't have much room to judge. Robert chuckled again, "Oh, no, that was all you. My power doesn't work on anyone of the vampire variety. Hence the reason I am here and not the Council's lapdog." Kendra frowned.

"But why wouldn't they want an empath that can control humans?" Robert's expression turned dark.

"Because there are other empaths that are better than me. Empaths that can influence vampires. There is a rumor that one of the empaths the Council has can change the mood of an entire room without touching anyone." Robert got up then and started toward the door. "I didn't mean to upset you. You need to rest. I won't ask any more questions, I promise."

Robert waved his hand.

"No, no it's not you, I tend to get pretty sour when I'm tired, and a feeding really takes it out of me. I'll just go lay down for a bit. I'm happy to have helped you, Kendra." Then he left the room. Kendra couldn't help but feel a bit confused about the whole scene. She shuttered at the thought of losing her control like that again. *What if it happens around my kids? What do I do?* Kendra straightened, there was only one thing she could do. She left the room with a resolve in her heart. She wasn't going to let this vampire thing take over her whole life. She knew that if she was going to protect her kids from them — from her kind — she had to learn how to protect them from *her* first.

The hallway outside of the room was dark but it didn't stop her. It wasn't hard getting used to being able to see in near blackness. It was everything else that was a strain. There were pictures of various people hanging on the walls, none of them looked like they were related in the slightest; some were of better quality while others looked like they should be in a museum. There were even a few paintings here and there of yet more people, Kendra wondered what they all had in common, it certainly didn't look like genes were a factor, but she could be wrong.

Kendra could hear Rick and James talking from downstairs. She could also hear the voice of Evie and what sounded like two other guys. At first she hesitated, the two unknown people were a factor she hadn't counted on, but her resolve was strong. She made no attempt to hide her footsteps, allowing for her presence to be known, as she marched down the stairs and into the room where everyone was talking. Turns out it was the kitchen, its bright lights all but blinded her as she pushed through the swinging door.

She briefly looked around the room before spotting Rick leaning against a counter with a glass of clear liquid in his hand, she knew it wasn't water and by the smell of the room, everyone was drinking. Kendra found it strange for a creature that she knew couldn't get drunk, to be drinking alcohol pretty consistently. He gave her one of his mischievous grins before waving her further into the room. Kendra shook her head and motioned for him to follow her out on to the back porch. He expertly slipped away still holding his alcoholic drink.

"Is something wrong?" He asked after shutting the sliding door. The moonlight lit up his light brown hair, washing it out. The result was actually kind of attractive in a bad boy kind of way. Kendra had never been into the bad boy type but could understand the appeal. She had to shake herself to focus on the task at hand. She managed to find the confidence to say what she needed to say. Kendra stared into Rick's eyes, determination burning in her heart with a fire she never knew she harbored. The images of her kids passed through her mind's eye, like an unspoken prayer. She needs Rick in more ways than she ever had needed anyone, but she wasn't sure if she could convey to him just how much he already meant to her.

"Rick, don't say anything until I'm done. I have a lot to say, a lot to get off my chest, so please let me talk and then you can have your say." Rick nodded and to her relief said nothing. She sighed and continued, "There is so much to say. I have a thousand questions and not enough answers. I want to scream at you for constantly putting me in weird situations with nothing more than a sly remark. I want to thank you for all your guidance in the past months. I want to kill you for turning my life upside down in the blink of an eye. I want to keep you close because I'm afraid if I don't it could mean my life, and in turn, my children will be left unguarded.

"These are only a few things I struggle with. My emotions are haywire and my world has become a roller coaster ride I never wanted to get on. It is one I am becoming accustomed to and I am working to acclimate to this new life. I feel sometimes that the world is against me, that it has been since Travis died, that I never truly got to grieve. Maybe I haven't yet, but one thing is for sure, if anyone had to come and turn my world on its head, I'm glad it was you.

"Which is why I need to ask a favor of you. You're the only one I feel I can trust, and I thought who better for this than my centuries-old sire?" Kendra breathed in deeply. Rick's face was shadowed but he was still listening. "Rick, I need you to coach me — I need to be stronger. I want to learn how to fight. So far, I've only been running on instinct, but I need training, I don't want to walk into a battlefield and just wing it. Moreover, I have to know how to better my control. I … I don't want … to lose control of myself again … I need to be able to hold back even when I'm hungry … I don't want to hurt or kill anyone unless it is a conscious act on my part."

Silence filled the air between them, that last part was hard for Kendra, the fear that she's going to seriously hurt her children was like a solid mass in the pit of her stomach, weighing her down. The wind blew between them as the silence grew and seemingly took on a life of its own, Kendra wondered if it was possible that she had bored the oldest vampire she knew to sleep. Her irritation became almost as palpable as the silence groaning around them. When the silence finally broke, Kendra was almost surprised by the sudden sound. It started with a grunt and then sniffing like someone had a cold, followed by the clinking of ice in Rick's glass.

Rick cleared his throat and then looked at Kendra, his eyes glinting unnaturally in the waning moonlight.

"Damn, Kendra." He finally said. "You really are full of surprises, aren't you?" He bent and set his cup on the concrete porch. Rick stood, hands now in his pockets, and smiled warmly at Kendra. It was a shock seeing that smile. It was a smile that touched his eyes and lit his face, even in the shadowed porch. Kendra found herself breathless for time, unable to speak or move. Rick pushed his fingers through his hair. "I want you to know that in all my years I have never had a fledgling more interesting than you. It's positively entertaining. I want you to understand, I consider myself a bit of a strategist. I'm usually pretty good at predicting what people will do. You, however, throw me off." He shook his head, chuckling lightly. "I wasn't expecting this little speech of yours. If anything, I was expecting you to slap the shit out of me for not explaining the situation with Robert. Honestly, it's so fun just trying to figure you out that I feel like I might stick around for another 600 years."

He began to laugh then, it wasn't a "from-the-gut" kind of laugh, but a light-hearted one; he genuinely was having the time of his life. As much as Kendra wanted to be mad at him, she just smiled — damn it, his laugh was almost contagious. Almost, although she didn't laugh, she was feeling happier than she had been, but it didn't stop what came next. When her hand connected with flesh, the sound was like a thunderclap in the night sky. She straightened herself still smiling brightly into the confused eyes of her sire.

Kendra blew on her hand to relieve the light sting and shrugged her shoulders.

"What?" she asked innocently, "Don't deny that you've had that one coming for a long time." She walked past him, her hand landed on the door knob as he chuckled again. "I guess I did deserve that" Kendra chuckle some herself and replied "Yes, you most certainly did" as she walked back into the house.

Others

The morning brought a flurry of activity. It pulled Kendra's attention from the book she had borrowed from Evie after her little heart to heart with Rick last night. Well, it was more like the whole library that Kendra had borrowed, she sat in the biggest chair, in a small office with large floor to ceiling bookcases. There weren't many, but the cases were all overflowing with a rather impressive personal collection. Kendra hadn't stepped foot outside of this room after Evie had escorted her here, she didn't think a simple request for a book to keep her company would lead to her having complete access to Evie's immense collection.

Now, the house was abuzz with movement and it was distracting enough that Kendra had to put the book down. She had read a small portion of the books in this room and wanted nothing more than to keep reading, but the noise going on in the rest of the house had piqued her curiosity. She opened the door that led from the little office to the main living area, immediately several figures rushed past her. She stepped out and closed the door behind her, about five or so people were in the room talking rapidly in Italian. Kendra cursed herself for not knowing the language and was even more regretful for not picking up that dictionary as well.

Thankfully, a familiar voice led her into the adjoining kitchen.

Standing under the bright fluorescent lights and surrounded by five guys Kendra didn't recognize, was Evie. Kendra couldn't understand how this house had turned into a giant clown car, let alone what all these people were doing here. She walked over to Evie and the conversation ended abruptly as her presence was known. The five guys all varied in appearance, but the look they were now giving Kendra was identical on each face. It made her feel like she was suddenly under a microscope as they studied her with an unnerving intensity.

Kendra shook herself and decided to ignore them. She looked over at Evie and was greeted with a warm, patient smile.

"Good morning, Kendra. I'm terribly sorry for all the noise. My home isn't often so busy. I only hope we didn't disturb you." Kendra smiled back at her. She was such a warm person Kendra couldn't help but be infected by her charm.

"Oh, no it's ok, I was just wondering what all the commotion was. Maybe I could be of some use instead of laying around reading books all day — if you need the help, of course." Evie laughed warmly.

"Help? I afraid there isn't anything you could do, dear. I appreciate the offer, though, there really isn't anything that comes to mind. You see, these men," She gestured to the hulking figures around her, "and their associates running around are my eyes and ears. They help me keep tabs on nearly all of Europe. We are currently working to find you and your companions a safe route out of Italy." Kendra blinked, the implications of what she was saying started to sink in.

"So, all of this … is for us?" Evie giggle almost like a schoolgirl and said, "Oh, don't you worry, dear. Rick and I go way back, I owe him for more than I can repay, so this little act is only a drop in the bucket for me. Besides, any fledgling of Rick's is welcome in my home. Here you are family, so think nothing of it."

Kendra was weak with gratitude. She had no words for Evie's generosity and she certainly didn't feel she had done anything to deserve it. She struggled for composure with every intent to thank Evie from the bottom of her heart, when a small-statured young man came flying into the room. He didn't look any older than sixteen and seemed a bit out of place in the room. After a moment to catch his breath, he looked past everyone else and stammered out: "Sorry to interrupt ma'am, Dominic is here, he has news you should hear and requests your immediate presence in the foyer."

"Thank you very much, Michael. You are dismissed." As the youth left, Evie said, "Kendra, walk with me, would you?" Kendra nodded and followed Evie into a hallway leading straight to the front of the house. Evie pushed through the door at the end of the hall and Kendra followed her into a large, dimly lit entrance hall. The front double doors being the only source of light as the morning sun shone through stained glass, giving the room a strange hue. Blues, reds, and purples danced across darker wood tones and sparse furnishing.

A few people milled about talking to newcomers, some dressed in service uniforms and taking coats. One person stood by himself, however, off to the side in a shadowed corner of the room. He simply observed and didn't interact with anyone. Likewise, the rest of them seemed content to just ignore him, even those whose job it was to greet. He wasn't overly tall but his façade was an imposing one. Even so, Kendra could sense the man's discomfort at being in the room. He didn't seem to be able to relax; the slightest movement was followed with a precision that could have only come from broken trust and betrayal.

Evie walked through the meandering stragglers with Kendra in tow, the man's quick eyes spotted the hostess of the house immediately and ignored everyone else in the room. His eyes were piercing, though they lacked the shine seen in most vampire eyes, it didn't take away the sharpness of his stare. There were a few people who Kendra met that was at least of vampire descent but lacked the preternatural shine and she made a mental note to ask Rick about it. It's not overly apparent but if you know what you're looking for, a vampire's eyes are almost a dead giveaway. She had noticed Ilium's eyes were rather lackluster compared to others of their kind, it could be due to workplace stress, though she doubted that was even possible.

As they drew closer, Kendra's sharp nose picked up on a strange smell. It kind of reminded her of a wet dog, but there was something more to it. She couldn't quite put her finger on it, but something was definitely off about the smell; It wasn't terribly offensive; though it also wasn't pleasant. His mood seemed to shift, though not into a more welcoming one; it was almost as if he braced himself for something as she and Evie drew closer.

"Dominic, it's good to see you again. How long has it been since you last graced my doorway?"

He stood then to his full height and grunted: "Not nearly a year," Came his gruff response, to which Evie replied, "Oh, has it really been that long? That's a shame. You really should visit me more often." She tsked and then sighed heavily, "Oh, well, on to business, I suppose. Dom, sweetie, I'd like you to meet Kendra. She is one of my closest friends' newest additions to the family. Kendra, this is Dominic Jones, one of my more obscure friends and colleague." Dominic looked at Kendra with obvious curiosity, not even trying to hide it on his features.

"Kendra, huh? Tell me girl, who is your sire?" Kendra's brows furrowed, she didn't like the tone of his voice but couldn't place why.

"Why do you want to know?" she asked, staring into his eyes, hoping that maybe they would give way to some deeper understanding of his inner workings. His dark amber eyes were complimented by his dark chocolate brown hair giving him a wild kind of charm. He smirked at her almost like he could read her mind and Kendra did everything in her power not to blush.

"Not very trusting are you? That's good. Trust can get you killed." He said glancing at Evie "Don't worry girl, I'm simply interested in your lineage. In my line of work, knowing is living. Vampires are strange creatures and sometimes that translates into their choice of offspring. Knowing who your sire is will give me an idea of how much trouble you'll be in the future."

"Oh, really? And what exactly is your line of work, Mr. Jones?" Kendra asked with a raised eyebrow. Dominic stared her down, the smirk never leaving his face. "I think I'm beginning to like you. I'll have you know, your diversion tactics won't work on me. You answer my question and then I'll answer yours." Kendra couldn't help but feel like she had been pushed into a corner. She sighed her defeat and answered his question

"Fine, if you want to know so badly, then the name of my sire is Richard Blake. Happy now?" Dominic chuckled then "Oh, he finally went and did it, did he? I was wondering how long it would take for the Council to brake him. I have to say, I think he found himself a winner here. Definitely better than the last one that's for sure."

"If you must know, I didn't pick her." Rick's voice sliced through the room, everyone still hanging around turned to see him standing in the archway leading into the dining room. "She was the name the council pulled out of their hat." He shrugged "It was in poor choosing but I don't think they realized how much potential she really had when they made the choice." Dominic stood straighter, his face hardened as he looked over at Kendra's sire.

"Nice of you to join us, leech," Dominic said through gritted teeth. Rick began walking toward them.

"Wouldn't miss it for the world, mutt," he bit back.

"Parasite."

"Hairball."

"Blood whore."

"I'd call you a dog but I bet you can't even lick yourself."

"Go suck a tampon, ass hat."

"Guys! That's enough. We have more important matters to discuss. If you can't deal with each other like adults, then you can leave!" Evie was so furious her face had turned a bright red. With every insult thrown the color had deepened and the closer the two men were to each other. The two of them stood face to face, staring the other down, with Rick being the taller of the two. Kendra looked around at the room and found that everyone else had cleared out, just the four of them were left standing in the foyer.

Rick and Dominic stepped back from each other simultaneously, they looked everywhere but at each other or at Evie. They refused to apologize but didn't say anything more to each other. Evie cleared her throat and seemed to regain her composure.

"Rick, I had requested your presence here because I felt you needed to hear what Dom has to say. I've had him on a very important mission. I'm assuming that since he is standing in my foyer, the mission was a success?"

Dominic adjusted his posture and said, "Yes, however I have good news and bad. The good news is that the Council is struggling to regain control after the incident. A lot of their troops are still not accounted for. That gives us options for getting our wards out safely and discretely. The bad news is they had already taken into consideration that they would be fleeing the country and have made several exit points their main objective. That leaves only one guaranteed way out, only one that will see them to safety. I've already made the arrangements. We leave at sundown."

"Hold on," Rick piped up. "What do you mean *we*? You're not coming!" Dominic scoffed, "Oh, yes I am Mr. Blake. I'm your ticket out of here." Rick grunted, "I don't fly coach, especially with a mongrel." Dominic rounded on him.

"Ooo, the big bad bat doesn't wanna fly coach when fleeing from one of the world's most powerful organizations. I'm so sorry for the inconvenience, sir. Would you like free blood martinis during your trip as compensation?" Dominic mocked him. Rick turned, staring him down once more.

"You offering yourself up, fur face? Well, no thank you, the last thing I wanna do is catch mange."

Evie sighed while the guys bickered and stared daggers at each other.

"I don't envy you, Kendra dear. Those two are going to be a handful." She rubbed the bridge of her nose as Kendra fidgeted nervously.

"Why are they fighting like that?" Evie snorted,

"There has always been animosity between vampires and werewolves. Theirs however, has continuously been more of a sibling rivalry. They are too much like each other for their own good. If their roles had been reversed, I doubt that there would be much difference between them."

"Werewolves?" Kendra mulled it over in her head. "I guess I shouldn't be surprised after everything I've already been through, though that does explain the smell." Evie cocked her head to one side.

"What smell?" Kendra stared at her.

"You can't smell that?" Evie giggled some.

"I'm not a vampire, dear. I can't smell the things you can." Kendra blinked in confusion.

"So, are you a dhampir?" Evie shook her head.

"No, silly, but my kind are related to vampires. I'm a succubus." That did shock her, Kendra had no words. Kendra is a vampire so the existence of werewolves was a given, but the idea of demons was just beyond that assumption. "Oh, don't give me that look" Evie giggled, "It's not like I'm a demon or anything" repeating Kendra's thoughts.

"You're not?" Evie shook her head.

"That's a misconception. I'm no more demonic than you are the walking dead. It comes from the long years of humans demonizing sex, Succubi and Incubi are related to vampires, but it's not blood we feed on."

Evie giggled again. "I guess you could call us energy vampires, our bread and butter is sexual energy, hence the reason I tend to surround myself with good looking men." She wagged her eyebrows suggestively at Kendra. Meanwhile, the arguing seemed to be coming to a close. Rick stomped away like a child and Dominic looked a little too proud of himself.

"Honestly, Dom, couldn't you at least try to be a bit more civilized?" Evie walked past him, throwing her hair over her shoulder, following the path of a raging Rick.

"What? What did I do?" he asked her, though she pointedly ignored him. Dominic tsked, "Women. Is it really too much to ask for a little cooperation?" He muttered, forgetting for a time that Kendra was still standing in the room. Kendra wasn't sure what she should do, she really needed to get home to her kids, but how will she handle traveling with an enraged vampire and a battle-ready werewolf? This whole thing was getting more out of hand than it was before.

"Hey, don't take this the wrong way, but your sire is an asshole." Dominic hadn't turned around but it wasn't like she was trying to hide her presence. She laughed nervously.

"Yeah, he can be, but he must see something he likes in you, you'd be dead otherwise." Dominic rubbed the back of his neck, "I s'pose. He has definitely had plenty of opportunity to do so, and I can't say I haven't given him enough reason. You'd think I'd learn not to poke the bear by now, especially after what I saw today." He shrugged. "Anyhow, sorry if I bored you with my ramblings, I need to get going though, I have some prep work to do."

Dominic walked out the front door before Kendra could get another word out, leaving her alone in the foyer. The house had settled down and a strong aroma of cooking food tingled her nose. The smell would have been enough to lure her into the kitchen but her stomach growling was the nail in the proverbial coffin.

Conflict

The house never truly settled down; various individuals came and went. Most were new faces and some were faces Kendra had seen before throughout the house. There was a handful that never left the property and Kendra was inherently aware of a patrol on the grounds. They kept an odd schedule but were still pretty consistent, nonetheless. Evie was almost always surround by people. Most were men but there were various women that came and went. Kendra figured there was more to it than what Evie had told her that morning.

It almost seemed like she had a constant guard around her, like they were protecting her. She noticed that some were vampires, and some were most definitely werewolves; the wet dog smell seemed to be a common scent among them with individual variation. The rest of her ever-changing guards were of questionable lineage. Some had a weird smell and others had almost no scent at all. There were those that sneered at Kendra as she walked past while others only dipped their head to her. Kendra found the procession weird each time she saw it, though Evie always looked to be in high spirits.

Kendra didn't want to dwell on the reasons why these men hung around Evie like a lifeline. After what Evie had said, it was hard to keep the thought from her mind. She shook herself for what seemed like the hundredth time that day and, checking the clock, Kendra figured it was time to slip away. She grabbed her cell phone and walked out the back sliding door. She stood on the concrete slab that served as a back porch, in the spot Rick had stood when they talked. Smiling at the memory, Kendra pushed the button to call her sister-in-law; before the dial tone could even sound, her phone was snatched away and the call was ended. Rick stood in front of her, holding her cell phone in hand as he held down the power bottom effectively turning the phone off.

"I should have taken this from you sooner, but I figured you'd be smarter than this." Rick pocketed her cell phone, the anger practically flowing from him.

"What are you doing? That's my phone, Rick, give it back!" Rick shook his head.

"I can't do that Kendra. I know you want to check in with your kids but it's too dangerous. Do you not know how close you just came to getting yourself killed?" Kendra stared at him hard, now she was angry, it wasn't his place.

"One phone call won't kill me, Rick. You're being ridiculous!"

"Am I, Kendra?" he was shouting now. "Pay attention, woman. The Council is always watching! Do you really think they wouldn't be listening in? They've tapped the phone. They'll know where you are the instant a phone call is dialed out." He grabbed her shoulders "Think, Kendra. Have you seen anyone else using a phone?" Kendra shook her head, tears flowing down her cheeks.

"You can't know that, they've only been looking for us for a little while. There's no way ..." Rick gave her a hard shake.

"Goddamnit, Kendra. Think! They picked you. I know I've joked about them pulling your name from a lotto, but it's a joke. The Council is more organized than that! They've been watching you from the very beginning!" He let go of her then. Kendra had never seen Rick this frustrated before.

"Do you really think they've tapped my phone?" she asked eyeing his pocket like it was a bomb about to go off. Rick laughed darkly.

"I don't think, darlin', I know. They like to think they can pull the wool over my eyes, but I've kept tabs on all the inner workings ever since I started the damned Council. I know all their dirty little tricks."

"What about my kids? I told Janet I would check in, they're expecting me to call." Rick sighed and reached into his pocket, "Here, you can use my phone — it's protected. It's one of the reasons I haven't upgraded in a while; the layers of protection on this thing are a pain in the ass to replicate in the new tech." Kendra took the Nokia from Rick with shaking hands. "Kendra, I'm sorry I flew off the handle, but you must know that putting yourself in danger like that will only leave your children vulnerable. You can't protect them if you get yourself caught or worse."

Kendra nodded then dialed Janet's house. It took calling twice before Janet picked up with an unsure "Hello."

"Hey, Jan, it's me. Just calling to see how you and the kids are doing." There was a sigh on the other side then Janet's voice crackled through the earpiece, "Oh, Kendra, it's you. Why are you calling on a blocked number?" Kendra hesitated.

"My cell died. The number is blocked?" she eyed Rick for help. He mouthed the word "hotel" as Janet relayed again that the number was blocked, "Oh, I guess the hotel I'm staying in has their numbers blocked, might just be a safety measure for guests." Rick gave her a thumbs up, Kendra wasn't sure her lie would be believable but it seemed Janet had bought it.

"Oh, ok. I guess that makes sense. Do you want to give me the number for your room so I can call if there is an emergency?" Kendra watched as Rick mimed putting a chord into her cell and was grateful for all the charades her family use to play.

"I don't think that'll be necessary. My phone is on the charger now. Besides, I'm only in the hotel room at night, so it wouldn't be very helpful." Rick gave her a silent applause and Kendra felt like her lying must be improving. She wasn't sure, however, if that was a good thing. "Do you mind if I get to talk to my little ones before I have to let you go. I miss them terribly." Kendra said quickly to change the subject. Janet chuckled.

"Of course, they were just getting ready for their day." There was some crackling and a whispered *"It's Mommy"* before Zeke's voice came over the line.

"Hi, Mommy!" the little boy's excitement was infectious. Kendra couldn't help but smile from ear to ear.

"Hey, kiddo, how's my little man doing? Staying out of trouble I hope." There was a moment of silence before he spoke again.

"Well ... I pushed Sasha down today." Kendra gave an exaggerated gasp.

"Why?" Silence followed, "Ezekiel, why did you push your sister down?" Kendra said, using her "mom voice."

"Because she wouldn't ... she took my toy and I was playing with it," came the whinny answer.

"Zeke, you are bigger than her, you could have hurt her really bad. You have plenty of other toys you could have played with. You should have just got another one." Kendra could almost hear him pouting on the other end.

"But I wanted to play with that one. It's my favorite!" Kendra sighed.

"Zeke, sweetie. It's not nice to hurt your sister. Do you understand me, young man? I don't care what she is doing. If she is being mean then you tell an adult and we will deal with it, ok?"

"Ok, Mommy. When are you coming home?" Kendra swallowed her sadness and replied, "Soon, I love you, Zeke, and I'll see you soon. Now, hand the phone back to your auntie and give your sisters love for me, ok." Zeke sighed.

"Ok, Mommy, I will. I love you, too." Then Kendra heard more shuffling before Janet came back on the line.

"We have to get going in a bit, but I figured you ought to know what Zeke has been up to. Otherwise, he's been a good kid, no bad reports from school either."

"That's good to hear. I'm hoping to get out of here a little earlier than planned but I don't know. I'll give you a call once I know when I'll be leaving." Janet laughed.

"Don't rush it too much, I know it's for work but this is the closest thing you've had to a vacation. Live a little, I've got the kids. They've actually got Marcus talking about starting a family. Finally, right?" Kendra chuckled, "I'm not going to touch on that subject. I'll let you get going though, talk to you later." Kendra hung up with Janet and handed the phone to Rick. He tucked it back into his pocket and said, "You can use it anytime you need, just ask. In the meantime, I'm going to see if I can't get your phone an *update*."

"Thanks, but won't that be hard now — with everything going on?" Rick shrugged.

"Not really. Just because I'm enemy number one doesn't mean I'm out of contacts" he said with a wink. "Besides, I've been needing an upgrade myself. Ever since you got me hooked on that game, I haven't been able to get it out of my mind." They laughed for a time, it giving way to silence as they enjoyed their surroundings. When Kendra looked back at Rick, he was staring right back at her. She looked away and asked him why he was staring at her.

He shrugged. "You're a good mom, Kendra. I was admiring how much your children mean to you. Just talking with one for a short time makes you glow." Kendra blushed.

"You're picking on me again, aren't you?" Rick chuckled.

"No, not this time." She picked at the hem of her shirt and refused to look at him.

"Did you ever have kids, Rick?" He cocked his head slightly to one side.

"When I was human, or after I was turned?" Kendra shrugged.

"At any point in your life. You said vampires can still have children biologically, right? I don't see how it would matter if it had happened before or after."

"Point taken." He paused for a while, still staring at Kendra. It was almost like he was pondering over how much he wanted her to know. Kendra felt like she should be angry that he even had to think it over but figured it was for the best that he be comfortable telling her. "I had one child that I know of," he finally said, breaking through her revere. "I was turned at 18. I had plenty of opportunities to become a father both before and after I was turned. I don't know how many of my escapades ended in a child, but I do know of one that was most certainly mine.

"Her name was Vivian, born in 1710. Though she looked a lot like her mother, the girl had a lot of my charm. There weren't any paternity tests back then, but the time scale from conception to birth added up to me being the father. I was with her mother when she conceived, but I wasn't there when Vivian was born. I wasn't even aware Emma had conceived." Rick stopped; he seemed lost in his thoughts.

"What happened to her?" Rick blinked. At first it didn't seem he had heard her but then he regained himself.

"She was a dhampir. Furthermore she didn't like using her abilities, so when *they* came for her ..."

Rick didn't seem to want to finish his sentence. He didn't have to, Kendra understood.

"I'm so sorry." She whispered, not sure what else to say. The pain of losing a child had to be greater than the pain of losing a spouse. She didn't even want to go down that dark road. "What was she like?" Kendra asked softly, resting her hand on his shoulder.

"She was like an angel." She jumped away when she realized the reply came from behind them. James stood in the shadow of the doorway, a glum look on his face, almost like someone had stolen all his happiness away.

"Yeah," Rick didn't turn around. "That she was. Vivian was just too kindhearted for our world." James didn't approach but his presence seemed to become overwhelming.

"You don't have the right to talk about her, Rick. You stood back and did nothing." Rick shook his head.

"What was I supposed to do, James? She wasn't my fledgling so we didn't have a bond. There was no way for me to know she was in danger." Kendra looked between them, putting the pieces together.

"You loved her, didn't you?" She asked James.

He looked hard at her then, "She was my wife, the mother of my child. Of course I loved her." He gritted his teeth as he spoke.

"Don't get angry at her — she didn't know." James quickly turned his attention back to Rick.

"Shut up! At least I did something! What did you do, Rick? You! Her father!" Rick turned around to face his coworker and son-in-law, his face grim.

"I didn't go chasing after shadows to try to sate a pointless revenge. I didn't drag my daughter into the heart of danger looking for the one who shot her down. James, I've done all I can. You and I both know the hunters wouldn't be as formidable as they are if we could easily track them." James shook his head.

"You never loved her like I did. You never cared for her like I did." Rick sighed.

"You also met her before I did." He shrugged, "Besides, I could have never loved her the way you did, that's a type of love that's generally taboo between father and daughter. Look, we had come to an agreement over thirty years ago — it's all water under the bridge. Her case went cold. We have no new leads. You've gotta let it go." James seemed like he wanted to keep arguing forever, then his shoulders sagged in defeat.

"You're right, Rick. Please excuse my behavior. It wasn't called for. I'm most likely just stressed out over this whole debacle."

"Consider yourself forgiven," Rick said. "Now, was there something you needed?" James walked toward them, "Actually, yes. I came to tell you I'm not going with you tonight. I spoke with a few of my contacts in the Senate. I'm staying here so you and Kendra will have a contact on the inside. Which reminds me." James pulled a large white envelope from inside his jacket pocket. "This was hand-delivered earlier by Sarah. She wanted to make sure we got it — says it's very important." Rick took the envelope from James.

"Sarah, huh? So, let me guess, you caught her up on the latest misadventure, right?"

"Oh yeah," James chuckled. "She had heard what happened with the Council and wanted to know everything." Rick beamed.

"Good. It's always good to have strong family on our side." Kendra cleared her throat.

"Sorry to interrupt, but who is Sarah?" James stood straighter.

"My daughter and an amazing AVIA agent." Kendra gasped softly.

"Oh, ok. That makes sense. So that would make her..." she turned to a still beaming Rick.

"My granddaughter, hence the reason I said 'strong family.'" James shook his head.

"Rick, she's only a pure dhampir, don't drag her into this."

"Doesn't matter," Rick countered, "She's genetically related to me. Sarah is strong and you know it. I'm not going to drag her into anything, James, but keep in mind she's a target now. They may go after her." James nodded

"She's aware, Rick. She has told AVIA she is going dark and is currently in hiding. Only I know how to reach her if we need her, but Rick, I don't want her involved, if possible." Rick clapped his hand down on James' shoulder,

"And I hope it doesn't have to come to that, my friend."

The sound of someone clapping slowly drifted toward them and in unison they turned to look in the sound's direction. From the outcrop of vegetation that surrounded Evie's property stepped Dominic. Though his form was in shadow, there was no doubt in Kendra's mind who that scent belonged to. He walked toward them, his clapping done.

"Well, now that that spectacular performance is done, how about we head inside. We have matters to discuss." The afternoon sunlight drove away the shadows as he moved closer to them. His short, brown hair practically danced in the wind, giving it life.

Kendra noticed that something was different about him; somehow his eyes were changed. Where once they were a clear amber Dominic's eyes were now a shade of black so dark it rivaled a moonless night sky. A ferocity Kendra hadn't noticed before seemed to sparkle on the edges of that blackness like a star circling the event horizon of a black hole. He looked her way and she couldn't find the will turn her gaze. Their eyes met and for a moment Kendra seemed to be swept into the dark void of his stare. A chill ran down her back just before he released her from his hold.

She wasn't sure if she had imagined it all, but she got the strangest of feelings from his eyes. It was almost like a primal urge, pulling her to do … what? She wasn't sure. The feeling left her faster than she could grasp it. Finally, it was gone, leaving her with a strange sense of *Deja vu*. The more she thought about it the more she was lost to it, what was it that drew her to his eyes? What was that feeling? Why was it … familiar?

"Earth to Kendra. Come in, Kendra." A voice pulled her back from the strangeness, she blinked and looked for where the voice came from.

It was Evie. She was staring at her with a somewhat annoyed look. "I'm sorry, did I miss something?" they were back in Evie's kitchen. Kendra stood among a small circle of people with Rick, James, Dominic, Evie and two out of four of her current entourage and they were all staring at her as well. Kendra couldn't remember how she got there. The last thing she could recall was staring into Dominic's eyes just out back. She looked around at them. It seemed an important conversation had been happening but she couldn't remember a lick of it.

Rick shrugged. "What was the last thing you heard and we can fill you in." Kendra blushed a deep red and shakily answered: "I don't remember any of it, to be honest, the last thing I remember is Dominic coming out of the foliage outside. I'm not sure what came over me." She was about at her ends. How could she have lost that time?

"Are you kidding me, Kendra? How could you have just space cadet'd that entire time?" Kendra shook her head.

"I don't know, Rick, I don't know what had happened."

"It's ok, Kendra. Calm down." Evie said, "You've been through a lot, it might just be an internal way of coping. Rick just explain what we talked about and stop being an ass, please." Evie had wrapped her arm around Kendra, the other woman was a bit shorter than Kendra, so it was a little awkward as well as comforting.

Rick pinched the bridge of his nose. "Fine." He sighed heavily "I'll start from the beginning. The mutt has arranged a caravan, in a matter of speaking. We are currently on the outskirts of Terni from which his group will escort us out. We need to travel to the port of Livorno and from there we can take a ship to France. I'll have my private jet waiting for us there, seeing as the Council has locked up all flights leaving Italy, that is our best option." Evie whimpered "I still don't like it, Porto di Livorno is a very big port, something could go wrong. There are many other, smaller ports on the coast, some of which are closer. You could cut your travel time in half if you chose one of them." Dominic shook his head

"Evie, I know you're worried, but this is the best course of action. The smaller ports can be monitored easier by the Council, Porto di Livorno is large and bustling with activity. Your friends can hide better in a crowd." Evie sighed "I suppose it's for the best." She sighed again, "Rick, have you figured out what caused Kendra's fainting spell? That's not supposed to happen with a vampire, is it?" Rick shook his head.

"I've had no luck with it, my best guess is it's the handy work of a special human, but I have no proof." He shrugged, "Until I know more we'll just have to keep an eye on her."

Kendra cleared her throat, "I'm right here. You don't have to talk about me like I'm not." Rick looked right at her.

"Is there anything you can tell us about what happened? Did you notice anything different before you blacked out?" Kendra sighed. *He's just going to gloss right over that, isn't he?* She thought about it, the memory was fuzzy but she could just barely remember what happened to her.

"I do remember the room going black before I heard a strange voice, in my head. It said something about me being a monster, that I could never be a mother to my children. The memory isn't clear, but it mentioned something about Travis."

Rick leaned back, lost in thought. Meanwhile Evie looked around at the room slightly confused.

"I'm sorry, am I missing something here?" No one answered; her guard was clueless. Everyone else, even Dominic, were silent. "Why is a vampire's memory so vague? That's impossible, isn't it? And who is Travis?" Evie really seemed to be in the dark on this, *was it really that strange that a memory could be hazy? Or maybe it's because vampire memories are perfect? No that's impossible ... right?* James spoke then.

"Travis is Kendra's late husband. He was a firefighter and died while on the job. You are correct, Evie, vampire memories are usually pristine unless tampered with."

Coffins

Everyone was on edge. A lot had happened with nothing to show for it; there just aren't enough answers. Once on home turf, Rick said he could get word to AVIA, while they do work for the Council, AVIA is an authority on their own. They needed to solve the mystery of who was really pulling the strings on the Council, only then would they have a hope for an exception to be made in the case of Kendra's children. It wasn't foolproof by a long shot, but it was the best plan they had; if it failed there was no plan B, nothing to fall back on.

Kendra walked over to Rick, where the van was being loaded with supplies. Evie's barely used garage was littered with boxes filled with various medical gadgets; Kendra recognized many of them as she passed. Men and women were pilling boxes into a black van with a medical symbol decal on the sides. In the center of the van lay two coffins, the sight of which made Kendra feel uneasy. The supplies were being piled around them leaving enough space for the intended occupants to slip into the foreboding boxes.

"Rick, do we really have to travel in those things? They give me the willies." Rick chewed on the nail of his middle finger; he didn't seem too happy about it either.

"It's that flea-bitten mongrel's idea. Trust me, I hate having to get into that thing just as much as you do, it wouldn't have been my first choice.

Look, Kendra, whatever happens in there, just remember to breathe, ok? These damned things were used to trap our kind for centuries. The fear you'll feel once inside is justified, believe me." Rick refused to look at her as he spoke; whether it was from shame or fear, Kendra couldn't be sure.

"What do you mean, Rick? How was anyone able to trap a vampire in a wooden box?" Kendra tried not to snicker, but she couldn't stop from sounding incredulous. Rick looked back at her then, his eyes dark.

"Kendra, a lot of what we do requires some momentum, which is hard to gain in tight quarters. Sure, you could claw your way out, but even for us it would take a while. By the time you would get anywhere with that, your enemies would have had enough time to figure out a way to subdue you further. Most vampires don't like to make it a habit of being vulnerable and being trapped in a box just barely big enough for your body is like tying yourself up for the execution."

Kendra looked at the coffins with a new understanding. Somehow they now looked more formidable than any enemy she was soon to face. With a chill running down her spine, she turned back to Rick.

"Rick, do you remember when I had said I still had questions?" Rick stared back at her,.

"I do." She swallowed and faced him head-on, determination burning in her green eyes.

"There has been something I have been worrying about since before we left on this little excursion. The manila envelope you had left on my coffee table — it had a bank card in it with my name. All that money, I don't believe ... I can't understand why. Why would you just give me that money? There isn't a chance in hell I could pay you back so, why?"

Rick began to chuckle. He hadn't expected that; of course she wouldn't understand. He had never actually gotten around to explaining it before. She had been so angry with him he just wanted to get out of there. He hadn't thought ahead enough to write down the purpose of the money, just a teasing note with an old cliché. His chuckles weren't helping matters and Kendra turned to stomp away, but he caught her upper arm before she could leave.

"I'm finished, I promise." Rick straightened up, "The money is yours. It's your inheritance — from me."

Kendra was shocked. "What do you mean it's my inheritance? Rick, you're not thinking of ..." She couldn't finish the sentence. Rick clasped his hands behind his back.

"Oh, I'm thinking about it, alright. I believe I've lived long enough, life truly has gotten very boring." Rick's eyes looked very sad and Kendra was totally lost for words. She felt like she was going to be sick. How long did she have with her sire, when did he plan on killing himself? More importantly, if she hadn't brought it up, would he have even told her? Kendra felt like going on a tirade and at the same time like she was going to pass out, though neither happened.

A familiar laugh broke through her spiral into darkness, the empty void filling with a new emotion. With every chuckle that came out of Rick's mouth, a rage like Kendra had never known filled her being.

"I'm not going to off myself, Kendra. That's just crazy talk," he chuckled, all the while Kendra began to see red. "It's tradition to give a newly turned fledgling an inheritance to ensure their survival, nothing more." Rick continued to talk but Kendra didn't hear a word of it. She channeled all of her anger into energy, he had finally pushed her too far.

In the blink of an eye, Kendra had landed a punch so hard and so fast Rick barely had time to register it. As Rick went flying through the garage wall, nearly decimating it in his wake, Kendra was delighted in her power. Her delight was ruined due to his survival rate of that attack, but she didn't care. She turned and stomped past all the gawkers. *Let them stare, he had it coming.*

***

Rick pulled himself from the rubble; the garage was barely standing after the loss of its sidewall. It seemed the whole structure was only standing because two of the supports in that wall were left intact. Rick stood brushing bits of drywall and wood splinters off his clothes. He wanted to be mad at his fledgling. However, he couldn't help but feel a strong surge of pride. He rubbed his jaw where her fist made contact. She had left a bruise he was sure, even though he could feel it healing that was still rather impressive for a fledgling.

Rick stepped out of the pile of destroyed wall and sighed.

"Evie isn't going to be happy about this." Despite his best efforts he couldn't stop himself from chuckling. *Damn, I really am a glutton for punishment, aren't I?* Rick stopped laughing when he ran into a very shocked James

"Rick, what happened? We're totally exposed …" Rick held up his hand for silence.

"It was just a bad joke gone wrong." James stared after him as he passed, the shock never leaving his face.

"A bad joke? A wall was blown apart over a bad joke? What the fuck, Rick? Don't tell me you were fighting with Dominic again."

"Ha! There is no way that fur face sent me flying through a wall. As far as I know, he isn't even here right now." Rick said, a smile still plastered on his face.

"No, you're right, he was not. However, he has just arrived." Evie interrupted, an entourage of dhampirs escorting her out to speak with Rick; her tone was less than pleased. Rick had expected this, what had caught him off guard, though, was Kendra walking arm in arm with Evie. The entourage stopped but Evie didn't. She pulled Kendra out of the gaggle of men and stood with her full 5 feet to meet Rick as head-on as she could manage.

"Richard Blake, you owe Kendra and I an apology each for the sheer rudeness you've displayed and destruction of property." Rick sighed.

"Kendra, I can't believe you'd go running to Evie like a tattletale." Kendra looked down.

"I didn't exactly go running to her, Rick. She caught me on my way in the house. She asked me what was wrong and I figured the least I could do was tell her about the property damage." Evie sighed.

"Rick, you don't have to act like a cornered child. All I'm asking for is an apology, mainly for Kendra." Rick scoffed, "What? It's not like I hurt her…"

"Richard Lane Blake, I am not playing with you. You will apologize to Kendra or so help me I will make your life a living hell for as long as either of us live." She didn't yell, but her voice got loud enough to make everyone in a close enough radius to stop what they are doing. Evie's entourage seemed to back away from her at least a step or two, a very bad omen. Rick wasn't going to give in at first but with the use of his allusive middle name he knew Evie meant business. The air around them seemed to grow cold and it wasn't even his doing this time.

Rick's ability was to control ice and the manifestation of it causes the air to drop in temperature just before he wields the power. This was different. It was the feeling of a battle brewing on the horizon, the change in ozone just before a storm. Everyone was gearing up for a fight and it wasn't between Rick and Evie; it was between everyone determined to protect Evie and Rick, and it wasn't going to end well. Rick sighed.

"I guess I have been a jerk to Kendra, but a lot of it is just me trying to prepare her. In this day and age, a vampire rarely has need of their powers. Some fledglings don't even realize they have an ability until much later on or when it's too late. Kendra, you are stronger than you know and I don't want you to find that out in the heat of the battle. I want you to be prepared." Evie sniffed.

"Oh Rick, that was beautiful. I can only imagine what kind of apology you will give me. I can almost forgive you on that alone." Rick was confused. He couldn't understand how Evie could be ready for war one minute and then on the verge of tears the next. *I swear I'll never understand women.* He sighed.

"I'm not the one who needs to apologize about that, Kendra is the one who sent me flying through the wall." Evie straighten.

"Is it the fault of the bear for mauling the man, or is it the fault of the man for poking the bear?"

Rick was starting to get irritated, but before he could say anything, Dominic slammed the backdoor and strode out toward them.

"We're out of time. We leave now. You two, into the coffins you go." Rick pushed past Kendra and Evie.

"What happened? We weren't due to leave for another two hours, what changed?" Dominic turned to Rick.

"Everything has changed, Luca is taking over the Council. If we are going to get you two out of here, we need to leave — now!"

***

Kendra laid down in the open coffin; the bags she had brought with her from home and were able to recover from Rick's house in Rome surrounded her personal death trap. She could feel the panic attack coming as the lid came down to encapsulate her, locking her away. She closed her eyes and began the breathing techniques she would coach her patients through when this happened to them. Kendra had never personally experienced a panic attack, but in the ER she saw many people come and go. Several of them would have some form of panic attack. She had to learn really quick how to settle a patient down so the doctor could work on them. Most of the time they would have to resort to medicating them.

Kendra worked to keep her calm, the tight space was hard to move in and what Rick had said proved true. She couldn't just bust out of this thing if she wanted and that worked against her survival instincts. The panic started to seep in again and Kendra worked to force it back, to ignore the rising need to get out and fast. She did her deep breathing exercises and focused on the sounds outside of her close confines. Kendra could hear the black drape being pulled from the back of the van over her and Rick's coffins. The sound of Rick's heavy, deliberate breathing was strangely comforting. She knew he was telling the truth that this was going to be hard on him too.

The rest of the boxes were quickly being piled on top of and around them to conceal them. The trick was to make it look like a huge haul off medical supplies was being shipped from one hospital to another, more in need hospital. Kendra was told these were pretty routine to get the supplies to more remote regions, so it should go smoothly. The boxes were piled so that it gave Kendra the impression of being buried alive and that only served to stoke the fires of panic once again. It quickly became a real struggle to keep composure and the walls felt like they were closing in on her. Not only was she going to be trapped forever but she might spend that eternity on the brink of being crushed.

"Kendra, can you hear me?" It was Rick, his voice was coming from beside her from his coffin. "Yes," She managed to squeak out just before the back of the van closed and the feeling of being trapped forever slammed into Kendra's lungs making it hard to breathe. She needed to breathe, even if just for the comfort of feeling the air move as she exhaled. The panic threatened to eat her alive as she began to silently scream and claw at the lid of her entrapment.

"Kendra! Listen to me!" came the demand of her sire. It was enough to settle her for a time, but the panic wouldn't be satisfied until she was freed. "Kendra, breathe! In through your nose and out through your mouth. You can do this, fight the panic. We need to be calm so as to get through the checkpoint. We're beginning to move, listen to the engine as a distraction if you have to, but don't stop breathing even for a second." Kendra did as she was told and was able to gain control of herself again. She focused on the roar of the engine, the movements of the van as it was driven off Evie's property. She thought of how angry the little succubi was at Rick, but somehow, while everyone's back was turned, he had managed to sweet-talk her into forgiving him.

Kendra didn't understand the relationship Rick had with the enigmatic hostess and even given a hundred years or more, she may never discover the connection they share. He had written her a check for the damages before they climbed into the coffins, though Evie protested; Rick wasn't taking no for an answer. A large bump startled Kendra, reality came back and brought the claustrophobia with it. She deepened her breathing again, focusing on the sounds outside. She heard Dominic at the front of the van. He was sitting in the passenger seat talking with the driver.

Kendra had only met the man once before they loaded up the van. He wasn't very talkative, but he smelled human. She found out later from Evie that he was going to be the driver. She said it was due to his ability. When Kendra asked what his ability was, Evie shushed her and told her it was considered rude to ask. The van picked up speed as they hit the highway, the sounds changed as other cars near them picked up speed as well.

A loud bang sounded from beside her.

"Hey, we're on the autostrada. It's virtually a straight shot from here," Dominic hollered and Kendra could only assume he had hit a box on top of Rick's coffin. The profanity that came from Rick only confirmed it as Dominic laughed without fear. Kendra was starting to acclimate to her small confines. There were other noises now that kept her attention. A horn blared as it's driver rudely passed them. A couple argued in Italian before getting off at a junction. Noise from another vehicle assaulted Kendra's ears. Its rhythm hinted at it possibly being music.

She lost herself to the cacophony of the road; what should have been a few hours felt like a few minutes. She wasn't completely free of the anxiety of being trapped, but everything else had overpowered it, made it easier to cope. Before she knew it, they were at the first checkpoint, a toll booth doubling as a roadblock, Dominic described it for them so they would know to be extra still. Dominic opened one of the bottles of 91% isopropyl alcohol and began splashing the insides of the van. The overpowering aroma would be overlooked in a medical transport vehicle and temporarily cover their scent.

They pulled up to the toll booth. Kendra could hear the sounds of police radios and officers talking with people. There were many other sounds, but Kendra focused on the ones that mattered, keeping an ear open for the first sign of trouble. After a while she could hear the approach of an officer, the dangling of keys and scrambled sound of a hand radio gave away his presence as he drew closer. He knocked on the window, the driver rolled down the automatic window and spoke to the officer in Italian. Kendra kicked herself again for not grabbing that damn dictionary, but she figured it was too late to worry about it now. She was hopefully on her way out of Italy and didn't think she would be in need of one.

The driver got out of the van and walked around the back of the van with the officer. Kendra's heart began to pound as the back doors opened, Rick silently shushed from his coffin and then fell silent. She could hear them chatting casually and relaxed some, the sound of opening boxes and sniffing gave Kendra an idea. She took slow, deep, quiet breaths through her nose, thankfully the wind was on her side and she instantly got enough of a scent from the officer.

To her surprise, he was human. He didn't even seem like a Council pet; just an ordinary, everyday Joe. The doors closed and the driver returned to his seat, the office said a few words before allowing the van to pass. After the toll was paid, Dominic leaned back in his seat with a heavy sigh.

"Alright, boys and girls. That was the first of many toll booths on this journey, one of a few on this route that will have armed forces. We're not quite home free yet, but this was a big step forward. Tuck in, hang tight — Porto di Livorno here we come."

Exodus

Ilium stalked through the halls, marching with determination to Meeting Room B. What Rick did was an outrage but it wasn't anything less than any vampire would have done to protect their fledgling. The Council should have known better. Their founder has always been volatile, this isn't something new. Something strange was afoot and Ilium was adamant about finding out what. As he approached, he used his scry ability to count the bodies in the room. All seemed to be present. Unfortunately, that meant *he* would be there as well. He pushed past a human that smelled lightly of the newly turned Kendra and stopped.

Ilium grabbed the man and turned him around to face him. Instantly, the man looked like he was in pain and Ilium knew exactly who the man was.

"Mr. Miller." Ilium let go of the special human, "I don't care what you just saw in my future. I am, however, curious as to why you smell like the fledgling Kendra." Ilium straightened. Anton Miller blinked at the pure dhampir.

"I smell like her?" he asked, a bit dazed from the sudden contact.

"Vaguely, as though you had had minimal contact, but yes. You smell more like her than any of the others in this room. What was your relationship to this fledgling and don't lie to me, human. I'll smell it on you."

Anton wondered briefly what else the dhampir could smell. *Damn their sense of smell.*

"We were colleagues working on the ghoul case." Ilium pondered that for a while.

"I see. Well, let me ask you, Mr. Miller. If I was to give you a message for Kendra, do you think you could get it to her?" Anton suddenly felt like a mouse trapped in a corner. On the one hand he didn't want Kendra to get hurt and on the other, he knew he couldn't get away with lying to this man. Anton knew it would be a gamble, but he cared for Kendra, so it was worth it to him.

"No, Councilman Ilium, I don't have any way of contacting her," Anton said, hoping he sounded more confident than he felt. Ilium lifted one eyebrow and it was clear he didn't buy it.

"You don't have to lie to me Mr. Miller. I'm an ally in this. If you truly want to protect them, you will relay this message to them as soon as you are able. It is crucial to their survival." Anton didn't feel like he had much of a choice in this, but he agreed to at least hear the message.

After the special human ran off with Ilium's message, he continued down the corridor to the conference room. Once in the room, the true task now was trying to convince these ancient buffoons that they were wrong. It was going to take a lot of tact and even more diplomacy to try to turn this around. *Damnit Rick, what the hell have you got me into now?* He took a deep breath, straightened his clothes, and walked through the door. The room was large with the same Roman décor on the walls as the rest of the Council Hall. Ilium sighed. *Being a pure dhampir is hard enough, what made me think I was cut out for this?*

Every eye in the room turned to look at the latecomer. Ilium straightened.

"Please excuse my tardiness, I was wrapping up a few loose ends." Meeka beamed back at him, "I'm sure I'm not the only one here who would agree that your absence is excused." She didn't bother looking around the room. Most stared back at Ilium with sympathetic looks. It took him a moment to realize they thought he was upset at the loss of that spy posing as a secretary — all except Meeka and Seraphine, who simply smiled and Luca, who ignored everyone else in favor of examining his own nails.

Ilium sat in the only open chair and faced his colleges.

"We need to call off this hunt. It will do us no good to chase down Rick. If we keep this up, we will lose more people than we can replace." Seraphine lifted her hand.

"I understand, Ilium. I know as well as you the trouble we have wrought. The problem is the fledgling is willing to break the law for the sake of a few humans. It can't be allowed." Meeka scoffed, "Just because you were never a mother doesn't mean you can take that away from women who already are. Those 'few humans' are her kids, Seraphine. You can't expect her to just walk away …"

"Enough," Seraphine interjected. "Meeka, please. My lack of offspring has nothing to do with this and you know that." Meeka rounded on the other woman.

"Do I, Seraphine? Do I, really? Tell me more about what I know." Luca stood.

"Ladies, please, this is not the time for petty squabbles, yes? We are here to discuss the latest events, not bicker about lost opportunities." Another of the Councilmen stood as Luca sat back down.

"That is correct, Luca. So on that note, I have dispatched all available AVIA units in Rome to search for the fugitives. We have a few leads that we are working on, but as of now we don't have an idea where they may be."

"Thank you, Markus," Luca said. "Do we have plans on what to do with them once apprehended?" another Councilman spoke "Yes, we have acquired and distributed Serum X among the officers looking for Richard Blake and his fledgling." Seraphine slammed her hands on the table.

"Serum X? Are you insane? That has been banned for decades. Who authorized this?" Luca stared back at her, cool and calculating,

"I did, Councilman Seraphine." Ilium glowered at Luca,

"Do you realize what you have done, you stupid whelp. You have broken an unwritten law. Serum X is a devastating narcotic — it's made from an extinct species of wolf's bane."

Meeka shook her head.

"How did you even get a hold of enough of that stuff? Our labs only had a small amount for testing. The plants themselves were eradicated over 30 years ago." Luca chuckled, "Oh, how little you know Meeka. The Vampire Council may have ordered the extinction of an entire plant species, but it doesn't help to only destroy the wild plants and not the domestic." Seraphine stared hard at him.,

"There were no domestic strains — you're lying." Luca smiled wide.

"Are you so sure about that, Councilman? Maybe you need a history lesson." Luca snapped his fingers and the back door opened through which two figures walked into the room. Ilium had felt their presence and realized just in time that the threat was greater than he had expected. Ilium slipped out the door pulling Meeka with him, but Seraphine was too far away. He closed the door just as a dart landed in the middle of Seraphine's chest and two more were embedded in the wooden door. Ilium and Meeka quickly escaped before anyone could stop them, what was supposed to be routine was now turning into a war.

Luca laughed as the pure dhampir scum and blooded whore escaped into the corridor.

"Should we pursue, Mr. Bladimir?" Luca waved his hand toward the hunter.

"Leave them, Phaze. We have other business to attend to." Luca stood and walked over to the unconscious Seraphine. He lifted her head by her hair and looked at her sleeping face. "Prudish bitch, it's about time you learned your place. Maybe my colleagues will give you a much-needed lesson in New World etiquette, hmm? Phaze, Cobra — take her to the Undertaker for me, would you?"

The two hunters holstered their weapons and moved to comply. One of the Councilmen stood slowly.

"She won't be harmed, will she?" Luca looked over at her.

"Don't worry, Bellona, she's in good hands. Do you doubt me?" Bellona looked up at him and their eyes met.

"No, Luca, you know what's best. For all of us," she said breathlessly.

***

It took several hours before they arrived at Porto di Livorno. The other toll booths were unguarded save for one. The officer that checked the van there didn't even look in the back, he just waved them through. When Kendra finally got to stretch her legs again, they were greeted with the sight of one of the largest ports in Italy: Porto di Livorno. The sea air hit Kendra first, followed closely by the smell of fish and burning gas. Boats sounded their foghorns as they left port as a signal of goodbye, people milled about, and forklifts transported large crates. The bustle of activity was almost overwhelming; the sights and sounds threatened to swallow her alive.

"Kendra, are you ok?" Dominic grabbed her shoulder, making her face him. "Focus, kid, don't lose yourself on me, ok?" Kendra shook herself.

"I'm not a kid. I'm still getting used to my heightened senses. I'm fine." Dominic gave her grunt.

"Fair enough, but I need you to focus. It's a big place. If you get lost I'm not coming to look for you and I can't stop the boat from leaving on schedule." The nameless driver waved goodbye after they unloaded they're belongings and readjusted his cargo.

"Where is he going now?" Kendra asked.

"Well, the medical supplies weren't just for show, there is a facility further north that is in need of them." Kendra gasped.

"We didn't delay him did we?" Dominic laughed.

"No, he left early with his shipment so as to get us here on time. He'll probably arrive a day sooner than expected." They began making their way toward the loading docks, "Hey, Fido, what kind of ship are we looking for?" Dominic chuckled. "Don't worry, Tick, you'll know her when you see her." And with that they pushed on. Dominic led them through the crowded docks, past tons of smaller boats, some with people making adjustments or other activities, while others were empty.

As they advanced on the docks, the smaller boats gave way to larger ones until they came across a three-story cruise ship. Dominic stopped at the bow of the boat and turned to face them.

"Welcome to the *Stella Cadente*, the ship that will take you to freedom. Captain Bellucci, no relation to the actress, will be joining us soon. You can hand your bags off to those men over there," Dominic pointed to a small group of men near the middle of the ship. "And then join me on board. here are your boarding passes."

They watched Dominic leave to stand in line for boarding and walked over to the men loading luggage on to the deck of the ship called *Stella Cadente*. Rick handled the Italian as usual, as they handed over their luggage. Some of the men looked around like they were about to be in trouble.

"What's up with them?" Kendra whispered, Rick peaked over at the deckhands and shrugged.

"It's probably because they're worried about their jobs, this isn't the usual way you board a ship in this day and age."

"Really? I wouldn't know, I've never been on a ship like this before." Rick gave her an inquisitive look.

"You've never been on a ship like this? You mean like on open water?" Kendra shook her head, "Nope." Rick smiled wickedly.

"So what you're saying is this is your maiden voyage?" Kendra rolled her eyes

"Don't break open the champagne, yet. We still have to get on the damn boat." Kendra passed the last of the luggage to the deckhands and turned back to Rick, "Why are we getting the special treatment? If this isn't the process you usually board a cruise ship, then why aren't we following protocol?"

Rick shrugged again, "Fur Face probably fast-tracked us through. It's smart thinking, really. Too much opportunity to be spotted and this way the Council is left guessing. Most of the security cameras are too far away to get a good look at us, so tracking our movements just became that much harder." They walked over to the diminishing boarding line and waited their turn. Rick nudged Kendra, "Here you'll need this, it's the ID that matches your boarding pass. I took it from your luggage in order to have Dog Breath get these passes." Kendra gave him a side look.

"Invasion of privacy much?"

As Rick chuckled next to her, Kendra looked at the ID and boarding pass. Apparently her name was now Naomi Williams. That was something she was going to have to remember. As Kendra pondered her new ID, the line moved up the gangway. She realized there was a card with the cruise ships name on it attached to the boarding pass, Kendra tapped Rick and pointed at it.

"What is this for?" Rick reached over and peeled it off her pass.

"It's your Key Card. You'll use it for various things on the ship. One of which is being our cabin key."

"*Our?*" Rick smiled.

"Of course Mrs. Williams ours. Oh, don't give me that look, the cruise was almost booked when we got these things. Besides, It's not like we are going to be sleeping together." They reached the top of the gangway and one of the crewmembers glanced at their boarding passes and IDs before ushering them into the main atrium of the ship. The bustle of activity was almost as overwhelming as first pulling into the port. The atrium was huge with balconies from the other floors looking over the open area her and Rick were standing in. The noise level was so overpowering that Kendra just wanted to run right off the ship and find another way home.

Rick pulled Kendra closer to him and reached into his pocket. He pulled out two skin toned, squishy nubs and put them in her hand. Kendra looked at them curiously and watched as Rick mimed putting something in his ears. She followed his example and the relief was almost instant. She could still hear very well but the sound was dulled to a comfortable hum.

"Better?" Rick asked. Kendra nodded.

"How come you don't need these?" Rick laughed.

"You've only been a vampire for, what? A month? You haven't learned how to hone your senses. While we're here, I'll teach you how to block it out, so you can move about in a crowded area without needing the earplugs. Until then, don't leave the cabin without them, ok?"

"Why don't you just tell her the truth?" Dominic asked as he walked up to them, a smirk on his face. "You're a sick, perverted bastard who gets off by plugging innocent women's ears with something flesh-colored." Kendra turned beat red, she knew he was goading Rick, but she still wondered why they were colored that way. He glowered at Dominic as he spoke;.

"They are that color so people don't question why she is wearing earplugs. Furthermore, if they notice her wearing them, they look like hearing aids, which, for a vampire her age, they are. There's nothing perverted about them, you mangy mutt." Dominic laughed.

"I was just trying to get a rise out of her. I didn't get to see her send you flying through a wall. Can you blame me for wanting an encore?" Dominic shrugged, Rick snarled lightly.

"Guys, can we please get through this without the loss of human life? I'm sure you boys can put aside this childish feud until we get to where we're going." Rick huffed, "It's not my fault the pup has a death wish." Dominic snorted, "As if. Like I'd let someone like you take me down." This time Kendra snarled, "Geez, get a room, you two."

She stomped off to what looked like an information desk. There were three people standing behind a crescent-shaped desk. Three short lines stretched out from them, Kendra got in the shortest of the three. The line moved just a little when a pair of hands grabbed her by the shoulders. She was about to yell at Rick when hot breath hit the skin of her ear and a whispered voice said, "I told you to be careful and not get snatched up, little lamb, now you're mine." Someone snorted behind them, making Aluin squeeze her tighter.

"Yeah right, I'd like to see you try and take her, little man. You'll be lucky if you only ended up through a wall."

The pressure of his hands was ripped away, and Kendra turned to see Dominic holding Aluin by the scruff of his neck like a puppy who had been caught chewing something it shouldn't have. Kendra crossed her arms over her chest.

"Aluin Dubois, what are you doing here?" The man smirked. He definitely had balls to be so cocky in the clutches of a werewolf. Even if he didn't know, Dominic was an imposing force; it still took guts.

"Call off your pet here and we can talk, hmm?" Dominic snarled "Why you little piss ant …" Kendra laid her hand on Dominic's shoulder.

"Let him speak."

Dominic grunted and let the man go. Aluin straightened his clothes and after adjusting the collar of his shirt he looked at Kendra.

"I knew there was something special about you when we first met. Most can't help but fall prey to my charms. I must apologize, though. When my ability didn't work on you, I was rather sour. Imagine my surprise when I hear that Evie was trying to find someone to get the fledgling Kendra out of the country? I volunteered to escort you out but the wolf here already had a plan, so I was over looked. I'm here on my own. I wanted to make sure you guys had a solid plan, I have a back-up in case this one falls short."

He smiled crookedly. "Let me formally introduce myself. I'm Aluin Dubois, a special human. My ability is Charm, at your service." He took a bow in front of Kendra making a lot of people look at them as they passed. When he straightened back up, he had a devilish grin on his face, "I haven't forgotten that you lied to me, miss Kendra." She blinked, confused.

"What? No, I didn't" Aluin tilted his head.

"Yes you did. You said you were in Italy alone on business. While Council summons are business, you were in Italy with your sire, not alone." Kendra inhaled.

"Oh, that. well, It's not like that, it was … at the hotel …I had a room there by myself …" Kendra sighed, "It's complicated." Aluin nodded.

"No doubt. All is forgiven. Anyway, my cabin number is 23 if you guys need anything. I suspect the two you travel with may have not planned for your fledgling feeding habits, so if you are in need, you can always come to me." Aluin wagged his eyebrows at Kendra. Dominic snorted again making him jump.

"Come on, man. don't kid yourself. Just go. If we need, you we know where to find you." Aluin shrugged and then walked off.

Kendra watched him leave and noticed that she would soon be next in line.

"Dominic, where's Rick?" He huffed.

"That asshole stormed off mumbling to himself." Kendra sighed heavily. She wasn't surprised; for a vampire of his age, he really was very immature. It was both endearing and tiring.

"Hey Dominic, you never did answer my question." Dominic smiled.

"Caught on to that, did ya?" he chuckled "Well to be fair, you did answer mine, so I'll tell you. I'm a porter. My job is to transport people and sometimes goods under the radar. If I'm porting people, I get their travel papers and set up the means to get where they are going. If It's goods, well, there really isn't anything different there, now that I think about it." Kendra nodded.

"Makes sense — It's what you're doing for us. How do you get paid for that?" Dominic shrugged.

"I have set prices. It's kind of a self-employment. As to who pays, that depends. For you guys, Evie has funded most for this endeavor. Rick has contributed as well. The rest came from interested parties that work with Evie. My guess would be some have debts to pay off, but that's not any of my business. You shouldn't have anything to worry about." But Kendra was worrying about it.

"It took that many people to pay for this? How much do you charge?"

"Well, a lot of it goes toward the necessary preparations, like paying for transportation, paperwork, paying people off to keep quiet or hiring a freelance vampire to wipe a few memories. In the end, my take-home is roughly 40% of the whole deal unless I do more of the footwork. I wanted to hire someone to escort you two out of the country, but I couldn't find anyone reliable enough to take on the job. I take pride in what I do, finding people a safe route out of a sticky situation is my lot in life, so if I have to be there in person to get the job done right, I will be. At any rate, I think you're next in line. I'll see you later, Kendra."

France

The trip on the *Stella Cadente* took almost a week to reach France, but that was due to it being a cruise ship. Most of the time was spent being out at sea. The ship made port a few times, but for the most part it was at a leisurely speed that they traveled. Rick spent the time mostly grumbling that Dominic had found the slowest possible way to get them out of Italy and Dominic spent most of his time gripping that Rick was being a big baby. Kendra spent her time mostly on the other end of the ship, away from them.

She saw Aluin from time to time. At one point, they got a couple of drinks at the bar and talked for a while, but for the most part they didn't spend much time together. Kendra enjoyed a lot of what the ship had to offer but still spent more time than she wanted separating Dominic and Rick when things got heated. It was a big boat and still those two always found each other and began bickering. Whenever she went to the cabin, if Rick wasn't there moping, he was sure to be somewhere bickering at Dominic. While it was true that she didn't need to sleep, she still ended up having to use the cabin to wash, change and hang out to at least appear to sleep at some point.

She called to check in with Janet and the kids when Rick's cell had signal, but most of the time, she was lucky to get any reception. Kendra missed her kids terribly and, while alone, was plagued by memories. Their first words, first steps, when Zeke started school — she tried hard to not let it affect her, to keep her mind off of it. The pain was still there, nonetheless. The distractions of the ship sometimes kept her mind occupied but the bursts of forced quiet in the cabin often brought on more emotional pain.

Kendra struggled with being a mother and a vampire. She spent all of the nights she had on that boat weighing the consequences. Technically, she wasn't even the same species as her children anymore, which was a weird concept on its own. Considering the nature of what she has become, it was surprising she still had any nurture left in her. She only wants what is best for them, but is she still what is best for them; would they be better off in the care of others? The more she thought about it, the more she wanted to cry. She couldn't bear losing them; it was all she could do to press on.

There wasn't any real issue on the ship; the trip went off without a hitch, and Kendra felt Dominic had held up to Rick's expectations. As they neared France, Rick laid off of Dominic more and more. The bickering didn't stop, but Rick at least didn't go looking for a fight. Kendra had noticed the tight undercover security Dominic had on the ship, every floor had at least two guards at all times, either disguised as a guest or staff. When France finally came into view, the ship's captain announced the end of their trip and that some of the staff members would be relieved at shore.

Similar to how they boarded the ship, they took the unconventional way of disembarking. They carried their bags off the ship at Port De Nice, walked with the crowd of people, before slipping away to a nearby parking lot. Dominic led them to an all-black minivan, its driver side door opened and a tall man, with broad shoulders, wearing a black suit stepped out. Complete with sunglasses darker than night, clean-cut hair and chiseled features, he looked like he worked for the CIA or some other government office, putting both Kendra and Rick on edge. The man looked over at Dominic and nodded at him, Dominic relaxed some and so did Rick and Kendra. Mr. Tall, Dark, and Silent opened the doors for all of them and took their bags.

Even the ride was silent, with the exception of Rick every so often trying to get a rise out of the man whom he had taken to calling "Tiny." Relief flooded Kendra when they finally got to the busy airport. It wasn't a terribly long car ride, but the endless silence and Rick's bad jokes made it feel like an eternity. The scenery was divine though, they drove mostly along the coast and the sea was magnificent. If it wasn't for the fact they had spent several days on a boat, Kendra would have had her window down, taking in the salty sea air.

Tiny, again, helped them with their doors and luggage before driving off to whatever hole he crawled out of, as they headed inside the building. Rick asked around before leading them to a terminal meant for privet jets, there he checked with the steward and flashed one of his many ids. They walked through the door and down the runway to the familiar privet jet that had brought Kendra to Italy. Dominic hung back and watched as Rick talked with the steward. Kendra walked up to him.

"Well, I guess this is goodbye, huh?" Dominic shrugged.

"For now, I suppose it is. You're gonna live a long ass time, so I'm sure I'll see you around." Kendra nodded.

"Yeah, that's true. I hope you don't mind me asking, how long do werewolves live?" Dominic grumbled "That depends on the werewolf, Mrs. Hughes." And with that, he turned to leave. Confused, Kendra went back to Rick and boarded the jet. A pair of arms ensnared Kendra as she stepped into the cabin.

"Oh, thank goddess, you two are alright. Ilium and I were worried something awful had happened to you," Meeka gushed. Ilium grumbled from somewhere behind the veil of straightened black hair.

"'Maybe you were worried. I know Rick, he wouldn't let anything happen to his fledgling."

"Are you two here on Council business?" By the tone in his voice, Kendra could tell Rick was on edge. It was a slight change in his usually steady voice, but it was enough, and Kendra was sure she wasn't the only one who noticed. Ilium huffed, "Seeing as how I don't have a death wish, that would be a 'no.'" Meeka let go of Kendra.

"It was awful, Rick. The Council as we know it is no more." Ilium sat in a nearby seat.

"Don't be so dramatic, Meekayla. Though I will admit it is pretty bad, the Council isn't done for as of yet."

"Would it really be so bad if it was?" Rick spoke low and with a heavy sigh took a seat in front of Ilium. "Alright tell me what happened, from the beginning if you please." The door to the jet closed and the two women took seats close by. Ilium leaned forward, fingers laced together.

"As you know, Luca had moved unprecedentedly fast up our ranks and become a Councilman. He had just taken that seat the day you had first arrived at the Council. For some reason, it seemed imperative for him to do so before Kendra's inspection.

"After your display of power, a meeting was called, and I was on my way to said meeting when I ran into the human, Anton Miller. He was on his way out with his briefcase, and I had asked him to pass a message on to you, Kendra. That's a moot point now that I am here. I had my suspicions about Luca from the very beginning and because I didn't fall prey to his charms like the others, he had assigned me a spy as a secretary. Thank you, by the way, for disposing of that Rick. I really appreciate it," Ilium said as though Rick had done nothing more than taken out his trash.

"At any rate, I joined the meeting last and had intended to talk them into calling off the manhunt for you and Kendra. I wanted to have them rethink their decision to forgo an exception with Kendra's children. As Rick had said, more outrageous exceptions have been made in the past. Luca somehow had almost all of the Council under his thumb, with the exception of Seraphine, Meekayla, and myself." Meeka shook her head.

"I don't understand why would they work with him, he's new on the Council, what kind of hold does he have over them?" Ilium shrugged.

"I'm not entirely sure about that. They seemed to be under some kind of control." Kendra gasped lightly.

"Rick, you have the ability to manipulate ice, right?" Rick nodded, "Is that something all vampires can do?" Rick chuckled.

"No, but this is hardly the time for a lesson in Vampirology" Kendra ignored his comment.

"Can vampires have other abilities that aren't common among us?" Ilium nodded.

"Yes, that's where special humans inherit their unique abilities from." Kendra paused, the wheels in her head turning.

"Has there ever been a vampire with the ability to hypnotize other vampires?"

Everyone fell silent; the hum of the engine was all that could be heard, and Kendra briefly realized that she didn't even notice the jet take off. Ilium shook himself

"I've never heard of such a thing. Do you have proof of such an ability?" Meeka laughed nervously.

"How could you have proof of *that*?" Rick turned to Kendra.

"What makes you believe he possesses this power?" Kendra chewed on a nail before answering.

"Remember when I told you he had visited me in the conference room after you had left, Rick?" Rick nodded. "Well, every so often, while he was talking to me, I felt a push. It was like me trying to hypnotize someone but the other way around. He was talking about sides and having to choose one. He wanted me to choose 'his side' and in return, he would let me keep my kids. Something seemed wrong about him, though, other than his raunchy smell." Kendra's nose wrinkled at the thought. Meeka nodded.

"See, Ilium, I told you your sense of smell was weak. I noticed it, too, Kendra." Ilium shook his head and ignored Meeka "To have that kind of power … Rick, what do you think?" Rick sat back in his seat.

"I think it's entirely possible, a bit unheard of, but … possible." The cabin was quiet for a time, then Rick sat back up, "Where is Seraphine anyway? You said she was also unaffected, so what happened to the old bitch?" Ilium's eyebrow twitched at Rick's rude vernacular.

"*Councilman* Seraphine isn't here with us now because she was knocked unconscious at the meeting." Rick tensed.

"How?" Ilium shook his head.

"Not sure exactly how the whelp got a hold of it but he used Serum X. She fell like a rock, which means they've tampered with the dosing." Rick's brows furrowed.

"They?" Ilium sighed heavily.

"He wasn't alone, Rick, I got Meeka and I out as quickly as possible when I noticed. There were hunters there, in the heart of Council headquarters. Worst of all, Luca was working with them. I would have never suspected they would go this far." Kendra looked between the two men, "Why would it be hard to believe they would do this? If they are serious vampire hunters, then why wouldn't they want take out the heart of vampire society?"

"Ilium, my friend, she has a point, why wasn't the Council prepared for an event like this? The hunter problem came after I had given my seat up the final time, so it wasn't because of me that there is no plan." Ilium shook his head.

"They were never seen as a threat, Rick. A bunch of humans hopped up on vampire blood would never be strong enough to be on our radar. Or so we thought." Kendra tilted her head.

"I'm sorry, 'hopped up on vampire blood.' What does that even mean?" Ilium gave Rick a hard look to which Rick shrugged his shoulders and Ilium sighed.

"What all do you know about the transmission of vampirism?" Kendra blinked.

"Uh, well I know that humans are naturally immune which is the reason for the bloodletting. I know that the vampire disease carries a powerful mutagen and that's what causes the transition from human to vampire. Aside from that, I'm in the dark." Ilium nodded.

"Well, at least Rick taught you something." Rick grumbled, "I didn't exactly have time; there is a lot she still needs to know." Ilium massaged his temples.

"It can't be helped now. All we can do is fill you in so you'll understand."

"Kendra, I know you work as a nurse, but how knowledgeable are you in microbiology?" Meeka asked, Kendra's brows furrowed.

"Sufficient for my line of work though I am no expert." Meeka nodded.

"Good to know. Now, have you ever seen a vampire hunter?" Kendra snorted, "Three actually and fought them." Meeka blinked.

"Really? What kind? Describe them to me." Kendra briefly described her encounter with Phaze, Zackery, and the crazy one with Rick adding his bits in here and there.

"Ok, so there are three kinds of hunters that we know of. The first you should be aware of is the behemoth, that would be Zachery — big, mean, dumb, and ugly. Behemoths are overly mutated humans — they drank vampire blood and had what we would consider an adverse reaction. They lost a lot of their cognitive brain function in the pursuit of power and can't go anywhere without their handlers. When the virus is constantly introduced into a human's system, it mutates, changing how it changes the host.

"From what we understand, the hunters haven't figured out how to control the mutations. Instead they kill those that don't have beneficial mutations." Meeka continued, Kendra was following it so far but the idea of having to kill someone after turning them into a monster was appalling. "Then, there are the handlers. Their mutations are closer to the virus's true origins. Phaze is one such hunter and a well-known one. He's a wanted criminal among humans as well as vampires and other self-governing species. The downside of the mutation a hunter of his caliber has to face is insanity, and empathy is one of the first things to go.

"Phaze can't empathize with humanity anymore. He hunts vampires for the thrill of it, not even Phaze himself remembers why he started hunting our kind in the first place. The handlers are the worst of the worst. They have every power a vampire has with the exception of a unique ability and on average, have the power level of a dhampir. Phaze, however, is stronger. Some pure dhampirs struggle against him, you taking him on as an untrained blooded fledgling and coming out unscathed is kind of impressive."

"Well, what can I say, she comes from strong blood." Rick beamed, making Ilium chuckle.

"What do you mean, 'strong blood?'" Kendra asked. "It's not like we're related" Rick chuckled.

"In vampire society, we kind of are. Not in the way of being like brother and sister, or father and daughter, mind you. We share a common bond. Even after you've grown out of the actual bond between us, we'll still share a connection. Also, every vampire virus strain is a little different from another. Its DNA doesn't change much from sire to fledgling but there are bigger differences between vampires that don't share the same lineage.

"So in short, no, our genetic code isn't the same, but the genetic code of our viruses is. That's what makes us sire and fledgling. And you can prove genetic relation in vampires just like with humans if you know what you're looking for. On that note, you should know, our genetic line is a powerful one. I'm not entirely sure it's true, but it has been rumored that the virus we share comes from god-like standards." Kendra chuckled some.

"Why, Rick, I didn't think you believed in gods." Rick smiled.

"I don't. However I know a lot of those old stories of gods are due to vampires wanting to be worshiped as gods. It's why, throughout history, bloody sacrifice is a high demand from them around the world."

Ilium cleared his throat.

"Can we get back on subject please? as you had said, there is still more she needs to know and our flight is almost at its end." Kendra blushed.

"Sorry for the change. I remember what we were talking about. Meeka, you told me about two types of hunters, but you said there are three, what's the third?" Meeka frowned a little

"Operatives. We don't have any reported sightings of them but we are sure they exist. The other two are usually a little too out of it to plot and plan, so we believe they are the ones behind the scenes. We believe the operatives don't drink vampire blood in order to keep their cognitive function and hide in society.

"Not drinking vampire blood makes them weak. so their best strategy is hiding in plain sight. They maintain a normal human life, you know, work, socializing, family, that sort of thing." Meeka frowned harder. "At least, that's the theory. Based on what we know of behemoths and their handlers, we know there has to be brains behind them. A puppet master pulling the strings in this morbid puppet show, so to speak." Kendra nodded.

"I can see that. Someone had to have come and picked up Phaze after I … after Zachery died. He was missing from the scene, which means he may still be alive."

"So, out of those categories," Kendra continued, "What would the crazy hunter fall under? The one I met in Rome?" Meeka cocked her head.

"He sounds like a handler, but by your description, he may have been rogue." Kendra blinked.

"Rogue? They can go rogue?" Meeka nodded.

"Handlers can. Behemoths are killed if they can't be controlled, handlers lose their sanity slowly so they aren't always dealt with immediately. He may have slipped away before they knew what was going on. If you hadn't killed him he would have still ended up dead."

Ilium leaned forward. "We don't know much else beyond that about hunters. They aren't a talkative bunch. At one point, we did have special human spies within their ranks to gather intel, but in the late 1800's a truce was made between vampires and witches. With the witches gone from the ranks of hunters, the threat was considered nullified. Nothing more was done and our spies came home. Part of the truce was that the witches would police their own and any witch caught within the ranks of hunters or killing vampires are banished." Kendra shook her head.

"Wait, witches? Now you're trying to tell me that magic is real? I can get behind the science of the vampire virus, but magic? That just seems crazy." She was beside herself, hell even the succubus had a reasonable explanation but this was hard to comprehend. Ilium sighed.

"That subject is more complicated than the last. I'm sure someone will explain it to you later, in detail," Ilium gave Rick a pointed side look then continued, "But right now we have more pressing matters. We don't know what is about to happen in Georgia, Luca has proven to be a little more than unhinged, and we still don't know exactly what his relationship to the hunters is." Rick folded his arms.

"Well, I can tell you a little about what's about to happen. Mr. Miller had had a vision while staying at my house in Rome, it's a bit on the foggy side but I'm sure Luca still intends to have Kendra's children killed. As to why, I might have an explanation on that too, but I doubt anyone will like it." Rick explained the vision to Meeka and Ilium. Both were shocked to learn that he intended to send in Death's Hand and from the sound of it he intended to send in all of the members. According to Meeka, there are only five active Death's Hand members, and the Council's use of the group was lessening.

"Why would he want to send in all five for three small children? It's not like they could put up much of a fight — it doesn't make sense," Meeka said, confusion and worry making her voice higher pitched. "Like I said, I might know what the little turd is planning." Ilium gasped.

"It's a diversion — he's trying to get Death's Hand out of the way and the ruling on Kendra's children provided him with a means." Kendra almost snarled, "That bastard planned this. He knew I wasn't going to give up my children. It was part of his plan all along." Rick leaned back.

"He's a tricky one, but he'd have to have been born a few centuries earlier to fool this old monster." He said with a grin.

Ilium chuckled, "You never cease to amaze me, Rick. How exactly did you find out about this?" Rick shrugged.

"I don't exactly have all the information, but I got what I do know from Susan." Ilium's eyebrows rose.

"You mean the late Ms. Dunski — she spoke to you willingly?" Rick grinned wolfishly.

"Not exactly willingly, no. But once I convinced her to talk …" Rick shrugged again, "She really did have a wonderful singing voice." Rick sighed, still grinning, a little too proud of himself. Kendra was almost sure he wanted to lick his teeth to see if her blood still lingered and the thought made her shiver.

She pushed back the thoughts of the kind of monster she had become, she tried to focus on what needed to be done and a thought occurred to her. Kendra felt the shifting of the plane and the pilot came over the intercom to announce their landing.

"So, now that we know a little about what we are up against, what's the plan?" Rick sat up straight.

"I am glad you asked that. As a matter of fact I do have one. It's a bit complicated but I think it will end up solving everything."

Home

The plan was insane. However, Ilium believes it's just insane enough to work. Kendra sighed, *That's Rick for you*. Kendra took care of her part, she didn't like being alone, but she couldn't be seen with Rick right now. Word from James was that Luca hadn't been seen in the Council Hall since the meeting Meeka and Ilium escaped from. Also, with him gone, James has been working with a few others to get control back. He confirmed that the Council is under some kind of control and that there might be a cure.

The reunion with her children was short lived, but it was a relief to have them home. It wasn't safe for them to be there long, but for Rick's plan to work they needed to be in the home at least some of the time. They spent most of their days either at school with a close watch or at their aunt's house. But when it became apparent that the plan was being put into motion, they were sent to a secure location. Kendra felt bad about all the "convincing" that had to be done with her in-laws but couldn't find any other way around it.

Anton was now in Georgia as part of his reassignment, he had checked in with the local branch of AVIA, at least according to the records Rick was able to get. Shit was about to hit the fan, and all they could do was wait. With the trap set, Kendra walked about her house aimlessly, trying to make it seem like she was going about her daily routine. When it was safe

Rick would come by, but there was little talking. His visits were mainly to train her as best as he could. It was rigorous and random, but he was trying to prepare her for anything. On the occasion, he even ambushed her to make sure she was on her toes at all times. At first he had the upper hand, after which Kendra countered him at every angle.

Kendra felt like the exercises were enhancing her senses; she was constantly aware of her surroundings. So when the day came that Rick didn't show up, she was prepared. It was midnight. She was leaning on her kitchen counter, nonchalantly sipping on her favorite herbal tea, when a knife blade slid under her chin, and a cool hand clamped down on her shoulder. Warm breath hit her neck as a raspy voice spoke into her ear,.

"You move and I'll cut your head off." Kendra set her cup down and the hand guided her to stand straighter. "Where are the brats?"

Kendra bit back her anger, "I don't know what you're talking about — there are no brats here." The knife tightened on her neck, biting into her skin, and it was sharp.

"Don't play dumb, bitch. Where are your kids?" Kendra forced herself to play her part, but the rougher he was with her the madder she became.

"They're in their rooms. Can't you smell them." He snarled in her ear: "No they ain't, I checked, don't lie to me, I'll have your head." Kendra chuckled.

"No you won't, because I already have your balls."

Before the man could get out his "huh?" Kendra put a vice grip on his most sensitive of places, the knife fell and Kendra turned to face him. He was only a few inches taller than her, with a five o'clock shadow and a prominent scar over his left temple. His eyes told her he was a vampire of sorts, but Rick had explained that dhampir eyes were duller. Ilium, he had explained, was a pure dhampir, so judging by this man's eyes, he looked to be a dhampir, plain and simple. His face had taken on a paler that might have something to do with the placement of Kendra's right hand. He succumbed to Kendra's greater strength.

"Hands up. If I see you reach for me, I'll squeeze tighter. You try anything funny and I'll castrate you." He nodded and did as she told him, sweat beaded on his forehead. "Where are the others?" he shook his head.

"There are no others." He yelped as Kendra tightened her grip.

"Don't lie to me. I'll rip 'em off. I know there are others, now give me their locations." His mouth opened and he was about to say something, but the only thing Kendra heard was the whooshing of a bullet as it flew past her ear and the man's skull exploded all over her kitchen.

Kendra cursed as his body fell limply onto her floor, she went to the other side of the room away from the silenced sniper and dug around for one of the hidden earpieces that Rick had left behind. Once in her ear, she moved to her broom closet, switched it on and started telling the operative on the other end what was going on. After a moment, Rick tuned in to the same frequency. After a few words were spoken, the plan was laid into action. Kendra reached into the broom closet and pulled the almost antique stiletto knife out that Rick had loaned her for the occasion.

She had been practicing with it, its sheath still on for safety and Kendra had only seen it out of its sheath once. It was an elegant blade with an all-wood handle and sharpened to a deadly point. She swished it through the air to get the feel of it without a sheath, it was still awkward for her, but she felt she could use it well enough for what needed to be done. Her sensitive ears picked up another swooshing sound somewhat farther away and then the resounding thud of a body hitting the ground from about where the sniper was posted.

That was her queue. She headed out the back-door knife in hand. There was no way these assholes were going to get the better of her. She knew where two more were, but there was at least one still not accounted for. She blended into the shadows of the house and waited for the next signal. The knife was light in her hand, she held it tight but not to the point of her knuckles turning white, firm but not restricting. Kendra thought back on the training Rick had put her through, she wasn't fully ready for face to face combat but there was little that could be done tonight.

The hunt was on. Kendra had her mission: she needed to seek out the missing Death's Hand, the leader. Once he's dealt with, then it's on to phase two. Rick had told her to not face off with him directly, just locate him while the others were distracted; the knife was for self-defense. She needed to seem like she had disappeared. What was it that Rick had told her? *I'm mainly trying to teach you how to be stealthy. You need to become one with the darkness, become the night, Kendra.* With steady shallow breaths, Kendra waited in the shadows, then the grunt and thump of yet another body was her signal.

Keeping to the shadows, she moved to her neighbor's yard and reached out with her senses. Still only one left with the leader still missing. She moved further until finally she noticed him just as the second to last fell. He didn't seem to be wise to the fact that his men were taken down, he was just standing in the road half a mile away. Rick caught up with Kendra and together, they made their way over to him. He didn't budge and the hairs on Kendra's neck began to stand on end; something didn't feel right. Once they got closer, Kendra knew why. There were others — at least eight more hidden in the shadows.

"Alright, Jeremiah. Call off your dogs. Let's end this peacefully," Rick called out, the man began to laugh.

"I'm afraid not, Mr. Blake. You had your chance for a peaceful resolution when in front of the Council. I don't do peaceful." A shadow zoomed past Jeramiah and headed straight for Kendra. She sliced the knife through the air aiming for a nonlethal but damaging blow. The shadowed man evaded it easily and sent the stiletto flying through the air. He was more skilled than the one she had faced earlier and, despite his size, he was fast — really fast.

"Kendra!" Rick yelled, but it was too late. The shadow man had Kendra pinned to the ground with his blade pressed to her throat.

"Don't move, if you know what's good for your fledgling, Mr. Blake. All of my assassins' blades are laced with a deadly variant of Serum X. A handy thing to have in our line of work." Jeremiah grinned wide, and from Kendra's point of view, she could see his features better. His dark skin was what made him blend in so well to the darkness. He had a gold earring in one ear, piercing black eyes, and his pitch-black hair was done in short dreadlocks dangling just above his ear lobes.

Rick snarled, "Look, the Council is in tatters, Luca is taking over, he's ..." Jeremiah laughed harder.

"Oh, I'm well aware of the situation, and it's glorious. Luca is going to lead us into a new era." He chuckled manically. "It's about time we took our rightful place as the leaders of the free world." Rick cursed under his breath. Luca had gotten to him to, and now reasoning was out the window. Kendra was afraid of this. Thankfully they have a plan B, but she wasn't exactly looking forward to it.

Kendra moved only slightly to get into a more comfortable position under her assailant. Shadow man tightened his grip on the handle of his knife, causing the blade to bite into Kendra's flesh. She screamed, the pain that slashed through her was enough to make her see stars and she fought to stay conscious, she knew was going into shock induced by the Serum X. Kendra vaguely heard Rick calling her name; through blurred eyes, she could see Rick on his knees, and she knew he felt it, too.

The pain was unbearable, but she had to work through it; her kids were at stake.

"I know where you've hidden them. My men are already making their way to them. I don't care who it is you've got protecting them. They'll die as well." Kendra pushed out her senses as best she could, calling him on his bluff, and sure enough four of the eight that were hanging back were gone. The anger flared deep in Kendra's being, the man on top of her was using his full body weight to pin her, and it reminded her of what Rick had said about the coffin.

"It's almost too bad I don't get to see the massacre. I have to sit here and babysit the two of you. Wouldn't want you getting in the way, now would we." *Zeke, Sasha, Aveline, my babies. Forgive me. I never wanted this. All I ever wanted was to be a mommy, but now I think I'm becoming a monster.* Kendra's tears fell as she reached deep inside herself to awaken the power she had felt growing there. She wasn't sure what would happen and the thought of unleashing the unknown was scary. At that moment, however, there was no other way; if she didn't fully embrace what she has become, her children would be the ones to pay for it.

"No!" she yelled. "Don't you touch them!" Her power surged to life and sent the shadow man flying. Kendra stood, staring at her hand as sparks of electric current flashed between her fingers. Jeremiah stared at her stunned; Rick's jaw hung open. The leader of the notorious group of vampire assassins hastily called out a retreat to his groups. Kendra wasn't about to let the monster out of her sight, using her new ability she boosted her speed and grabbed him by the throat.

"I'm curious — Jeremiah, was it? What does electricity do to a vampire?" She said looking into his soulless black eyes. He shook his head unable to speak. "How about we find out. If you live through it, you'll have learned a valuable lesson. Don't fuck with my kids." Kendra let her anger be translated into pure power and pushed electrical current through

Jeremiah's body. He convulsed violently, smoke rose from his skin and seemed to seep from every pore. His eyes rolled back into his skull and Kendra could all but feel his life force ebb away.

When his body fell, limp and lifeless to the ground, a tear followed closely behind. The last tear she will ever shed for her lost humanity, only now has she excepted her role. To protect her children from the things that go bump in the night, she became a monster, because only monsters have the power to fight and kill other monsters. She did exactly what Rick told her to do; Kendra became one with the night, doomed to walk the path of darkness for eternity.

"Kendra? Are you alright?" He didn't know what she was going through. There was no way he could. In her mind, she had done the one thing that she had feared doing from the beginning, and the one she blamed was still alive. Luca, she vowed from then on that no matter what it takes, she will take Luca down before he ruins anyone else's life. "Kendra?" Rick was on his feet again, but he wasn't moving; even he was afraid to get too close. *So be it — I'll be the monster, but only for the sake of my children.*

"Let's go, Rick." She said, looking back at him, expressionless. "My kids need me." She didn't wait. There was no pause, she didn't check to see if he was behind her. She just ran as fast as she could without using electricity to push her further. Within moments, they were outside of the old bunker her kids were safely tucked away in. The memory of having to lock them away in this place was hard. She could still hear Sasha crying as little Zeke wined and asked her why.

"Don't be afraid. I need you to be my strong little man. It's your job to keep your sisters safe. I'll be back once I have taken care of the danger." She had ruffled his hair and fought to keep the tears from falling down her cheek. She then left him and his sisters in the capable hands of the baby sisters from AVIA. Kendra was glad that Mr. Pudgy wasn't there, though the twins were a welcome sight. Apparently, they are special humans that share the same ability of telepathic illusion and together they are the most powerful known to exist.

It was their status that let them choose the profession they are in, protecting those weaker than them. Now, Kendra stood outside the barred door and scanned the area. The bunker remained untouched, Kendra could still hear the heartbeats of five individuals inside it, and she could barely make out four others outside.

"It's over, your leader is dead, and unless you want to join him, I suggest you leave." A shadow moved in Kendra's peripherals and landed in front of her. She kept her sights on him at all times.

"You lie! I want proof. There's no way you two took out Jeremiah!" Kendra glared at him; he wasn't much taller than Jeramiah had been. He was light-skinned with dark black hair cropped short on the sides.

"I don't take trophies, so I'm sorry. All you have is my word." The man crossed his arms.

"The words of a woman means nothing." Kendra raised an eyebrow.

"Been burned by too many lady assassins?" Kendra mocked, to which the man laughed and said, "There are no women in our organization." Kendra blinked.

"Well, that's unusual in this day and age. You guys need to get with the times." The man shook his head.

"Women are weak, even vampire women are too weak for what we do." Kendra huffed, "You haven't met many women have you?" Kendra could feel the electricity coursing through her veins. Her hair stood on end and she could hear Rick move back, chuckling to himself.

"Now, you've pissed her off, dude. You better run." Kendra fully flexed her power causing a bolt of lightning to shoot from her hand and hit a nearby tree.

"Didn't your mother ever warn you?" Kendra moved closer to him, the man now fully understood what he was up against, and stood there like a deer caught in the headlights. "Don't piss off the redhead!" She aimed and fired a bolt of electricity right in the middle of his chest. Kendra was finding that anger really got the current to move through her, but somewhere inside, she knew she'd have to learn how to control it better. She reflected on this as she watched the man convulse under her power.

She didn't take any enjoyment from it. This was a matter of survival, her children's survival. This man, and the ones he worked with, were a detriment to that. She needed to make an example of him, as his body fell to the ground, she now understood what Rick was trying to do in the Council Hall that day. Despite their sophistication, vampires haven't left behind their roots, a test of power is what is needed to govern the masses.

If she can show them that she can't be bested than hopefully they'll let her live in peace with her children and put this whole mess aside.

Kendra could feel the others still watching her, probably a bit shell shocked, if nothing else, from having watched their comrade die the way he did. Kendra figured it was now or never. She had to put the fear of an old god into their hearts. "Do I have any more takers?" She asked to the darkness, knowing they could hear her well enough. When no one answered or even moved, she said, "No? Well, ok, then hear this. Anyone who dares to do harm to me or my kids again will wish for death when I'm done with them."

At first, they didn't move. Their lingering was beginning to piss her off further. Then, like a single entity, they moved as one and were gone, hopefully to spread Kendra's message. Kendra breathed through her nose to calm herself before opening the door of the bunker. The inside was brightly lit, and Kendra had to blink to adjust her eyes. Once her vision was cleared, she saw her two oldest running for her, and Aveline was sitting in a highchair happily eating crackers. There was a small table with some cards scattered about where the two quiet, but friendly twins were sitting.

It looked like they were playing a game of cards and despite it being a bunker tucked away in a small mountainside, it looked like a daycare. Either the twins redecorated or this was the work of their power. Regardless, it looks nice, though some of the bunker still poked out here and there; they had given it an almost homey feel. Kendra was at a loss for words. She wasn't sure how she was going to thank them for all their work. Before she could get a grasp on her thoughts, the twins spoke up.

"Don't worry, Mrs. Hughes. It's all in a day's work for us." They said, creepily in unison.

Her kids were smiling up at her and Sasha asked Kendra as she picked her up, "Did you make the monsters go away, Mommy?" Kendra held back tears as she spoke.

"Yes, Baby. I made the monsters go away."

Tactics

The truth of the matter was that the monsters weren't gone; the biggest and baddest of them were still to come. Kendra had all but taken down several members of Death's Hand though she couldn't help but feel like it was too easy. Something big was about to happen, and Anton's vision had yet to be fulfilled. She and Rick tucked the kids into their beds that night and went downstairs to discuss the nights' events. Kendra made coffee and sat down with Rick in her living room. It reminded her of the first night she had spent as a vampire, still trying to figure things out, and she was still just as lost now as she was then.

Rick took a sip of his coffee before he began: "Kendra, I don't think you fully comprehend what has happened." Rick said with a more serious tone than Kendra was used to, this wasn't the carefree Rick she had come to know. "I know I haven't been able to teach you everything you need to know. Life tends to get kind of hectic when you jump species. While all this madness was going on you've learned a few things about vampires. What I'm talking about is weaknesses— vampires have an aversion to tight spaces.

"You also know of Serum X, but I haven't had the chance to explain what that is. Serum X is a drug made from a species of wolfsbane that is supposed to be extinct. Ilium has informed me that there is a variant that has been overlooked, and the hunters may have this variant in their possession. Depending on the concentration, it can be a powerful knock out drug or a deadly poison to vampires. What you don't know, but I'm sure you have suspected, is that vampires are more susceptible to electrocution than humans." Kendra blinked.

"What? Really? Why?" Rick chuckled.

"The mutagen changes a lot in us. We haven't figured out the reason why, but it also makes us more conductive than humans. Even though our internal organs are hardier than what they use to be, they are still not shock resistant. With that being said, a taser is enough to severely incapacitate most vampires — tweak the settings just right and they would be deadly. The power you possess is remarkable. There is only one other vampire that we know of that had this kind of power." Rick paused, seeming to mull over the extraordinary circumstances but the suspense was killing Kendra.

"This other vampire that had the same ability as me, who was it?" Rick shrugged.

"Zeus, who else?" Kendra's jaw dropped.

"*The* Zeus? Like Roman *god* Zeus? That Zeus?" Rick laughed.

"Yes that one, but Zeus was Greek; the Romans knew him as Jupiter." Kendra shook her head.

"So what? I'm still trying to wrap my head around Zeus being a real person and not only that but a vampire. I don't give a rat's ass what the Romans called him." Rick sighed.

"Yes well, unfortunately your power will have its downsides along with the perks."

"Oh? Like what?" Rick snorted.

"Well, you'll definitely end up with a neat little collection of enemies. Not to mention, once the Council has reestablished themselves, there is no telling what they may decide." Kendra hadn't thought about that, but then again, she had already written off the Council as a whole as a potential ally.

"Do you think they would really come after me, after all of this? That doesn't seem like a productive use of their time." Rick shrugged and said nothing more, with the subject dropped, Kendra asked, "So, are there any other weaknesses I should know about? You know, since the real ones are not exactly mainstream knowledge."

"Hmm? Oh, well, I guess that brings us to witches. They aren't considered much of a threat anymore, but if you ever come across a witch that has a vendetta, beware the *Finalem Damnationem Mortis*." Kendra blinked.

"Uh, Gesundheit." Rick chuckled.

"It's Latin, it basically means Curse of the Final Death. It was invented for the purpose of killing vampires and is rather effective. The problem is even the most powerful of witches can only cast it a few times before passing out. The spell is banned as of the treaty, but unfortunately the knowledge of it still persists.

"Also, it's highly unlikely that you'd ever come in contact with one, but since we're on the subject of weaknesses, there is no point hiding it. One of the weaknesses we have as a collective whole is that of werecougar venom. We've managed to keep it a secret from the hunters for many generations. However, I'm afraid that might have changed." Rick sipped his coffee and pondered that for a moment. Kendra snorted, "I'm sorry, did you say werecougar venom? Mammals aren't normally venomous and I'm getting the impression you're pulling my leg."

"Shrews are venomous and they're mammals. Also, some primates are known to be venomous." Rick explained, "I'm not pulling your leg, though it is believed to be a coincidence that they are venomous to vampires. The so-called venom is used as an aphrodisiac among themselves and humans. It's still to this day highly sought after in the werecat community. Werecougars are rare these days, though they are the most docile of the werecats. Vampires had nonetheless hunted them to near extinction.

"At any rate, those are the only known weaknesses we have. Like I had told you before, some have developed interesting allergies after their change, so individual results may vary." Rick shrugged with a chuckle. "Now, if you don't have any more inquiries, we need to talk." Kendra nodded.

"Yes, right. What did Ilium have to say when you spoke to him?" Rick leaned forward.

"Something big is about to happen, I could feel it even before Ilium confirmed it. The guys we took out, with the exception of their leader, were all small fry." Rick had his serious face on again and Kendra was beginning to hate what that face meant. "The ones we scared off, plus the few that weren't there, were called back. Meaning the leader wasn't even in charge anymore — Jeremiah had said all he needed to, Luca is calling all the shots." Rick paused and Kendra could almost see the thoughts racing through his mind. "We don't entirely know what he's up to, the rantings of a devout cult follower are hardly anything to go on. Luca most likely told him what he wanted to hear."

"So, what now?" Kendra asked, "How do we find out what his next move is?" Rick laced his fingers and pressed his forehead into his knuckles. The room was silent for a while, Kendra wanted to throw out some ideas, but she also didn't want to interrupt his thoughts. Instead, she sat there patiently, waiting for his response.

"How is he doing it?" Rick whispered so low that Kendra almost missed what he said.

"Doing what, Rick?" Rick sighed heavily before leaning back onto the cushion of Kendra's couch.

"I know he's the one. It's no coincidence, he's behind that, too. I just can't figure out how." Kendra squirmed.

"What are you talking about?" He shook his head.

"The ghoul attacks don't make sense to me, and, on top of that, they've been way too much of a convenient diversion. Luca is behind them somehow but I don't know how he's doing it." Kendra hadn't forgotten about their ghoul problems, but she hadn't thought too much on it in a while. She already had a lot on her plate and it wasn't exactly that important to her at the time.

"What about that Serum X stuff.? How does it affect dhampirs?" Rick shrugged.

"I'd assume about the same way it affects us, only stronger and possibly deadly. I don't know enough about the stuff to give a good answer." Rick sat up. "It can be modified and has been, but the question is could it do that?" Rick rubbed his left temple, then blew out a long breath of air. With a slight smile, he said, "I may not know enough about Serum X, but I do know someone who does."

***

After a few phone calls, the arrival of an AVIA babysitter, and a quiet drive in Rick's rental car, they were standing outside of a large building in the midday sun. The sign on the building pronounced the place as a Drug

Testing and Genetics Research Lab, which was surprising to Kendra. She almost expected to be standing outside of a worn-down factory and lead into a basement laboratory. When Rick had said he needed to go see an old friend that works in a lab, her imagination got the better of her.

They walked up the sidewalk to the front entrance of the building and went in through the front door. Another surprise to Kendra, being that they didn't go through a back door or a side door like she had thought. Rick showed a badge to the security guard and the guard let them through with only a nod and a good day. *Call me crazy, but this seems more suspicious to me than the seemingly ordinary backdoor is really a secret vampire entrance.*

The downstairs looked like an ordinary doctor's office as they walked by door after door before reaching the elevators. Once they reached their third-floor destination, that changed, with most of the labs having all glass barriers and some only had a window that could be shuttered if privacy was needed. They walked down the hallway, some people were at work in the labs, some of the labs were dark and unused, but all of them appeared to be locked.

Rick stopped at the second to last lab room at the end of the hallway. He knocked on the glass and got the attention of the three occupants inside. Two looked at Rick in confusion, while the third stared at him in almost shock. The woman straightened and spoke to her colleges briefly before heading toward the glass door. She was of average height with brown hair that she had lied up in a loose bun. The square-framed glasses that sat on the bridge of her nose complemented the shape of her face and matched the shade of her light brown eyes.

The door swung open with barely a whisper; her lab coat seemed to dance around her as the suction of the room tried to pull her back inside. The door closed and she turned with a warm smile that lit up her face.

"Richard, it's good to see you again, what brings you here?" she said with crossed arms and a glance at Kendra. Rick smiled.

"It's good to see you, too, Linda. Sorry to barge in here like this, but I need to ask a favor of you. Linda nodded.

"I figured that much, you don't come around here without one." She leaned in closer and whispered, "It's not like the last favor you asked of me, is it?"

Rick shook his head with his hands up in a defensive gesture, "No,

no, not like that at all. This has to do with your work with the Council ..."
Linda shook her head.

"Oh, no, I'm not getting involved with them. Count me out." Rick gently grabbed her shoulders.

"No, I'm not asking you to be involved. I want to talk to you about ..." Rick leaned in and whispered, "Serum X." Kendra had never seen someone's eyes get so big, she could almost see the inside of the woman's eye sockets.

"Are you insane? Richard, what would make you think I'd want to get involved in this again?" Rick let go of her.

"Do you mind if we speak somewhere more private?" Linda looked at him like she couldn't figure out what was standing in front of her. She then looked over at Kendra with an incredulous look on her face.

"What about her?" Rick turned toward Kendra.

"She's fine, Linda, she's my fledgling, and part of the reason we are here." Intrigue crossed her face as Linda looked between Rick and Kendra.

"Fine, follow me."

She led them to the door at the end of the hallway, behind the door was another hallway perpendicular to the previous one making them into a T shape. Linda turned to the left and entered a room to her right with Rick and Kendra in tow. Once in the room, Linda waved her hand in a small arch and the door closed behind Kendra with a slight click, like someone had gently closed it behind them. Linda was a telekinetic, though it wasn't surprising. Kendra wondered how it was this woman wasn't under close surveillance by the Council.

She took off her glasses and set them on the desk behind her. she then hung her lab coat up on a hook and sat down behind the desk.

"Ok, Richard, I'm listening." She laced her fingers together with her palms flat on the desk. Her light brown eye's intently staring at Rick. He sat down in a chair in front of her and not wanting to be the only one standing Kendra took the last chair in the room.

"We have a problem that requires your expertise on the subject of Serum X." Rick began, "I figured that out when you mentioned it to me, now what do you need to know?" She seemed irritated and Kendra wasn't exactly sure why. Rick sighed. "Yes, well, my question is, is it possible to modify Serum X to turn pure dhampirs into ghouls?" Linda blinked.

"Why do you need to know that? What are you planning, Richard?"

"I'm not planning anything. Actually my inquiry is strictly a hypothetical one." Linda snorted, "You wouldn't come in here on a hypothetical basis, Richard. You don't even come to see me on your day off. If this was simply a hypothetical question, you could have just called. You know, like you should have three years ago." There it was. Now it made sense to Kendra; Rick had spurned this woman, and was now asking for her help. *Oh, this is going to go well, where's the popcorn when you need it?*

Rick leaned back and sighed.

"I thought we had put that past us." Linda pursed her lips together.

"You're right. We did. So don't come in here acting like you just want to chat and tell me what the hell is going on." Rick chuckled.

"Some things never change, do they?" Rick sat back up. "Ok, here's the problem, the Council has been infiltrated by the hunters. There is a vampire by the name of Luca Bladimir who appears to be working with them and he has handed over the only remaining vial of Serum X.

"It's the vial you were working with four years ago. There has been an alarming amount of ghoul activity lately and we believe the hunters may have modified it to turn pure dhampirs into ghouls faster as a distraction tactic. I need to know if this is possible. If not, then what else could cause this, and is there a cure in either case?" Linda stared at Rick for a long time before she sat back into her chair.

"I was afraid of this." She breathed.

"You knew this would happen?" Linda shook her head.

"Not this exactly, no. Do you remember the reason I told you why I left the Council Research Lab?" Rick nodded.

"Of course, you said what they wanted you to research wasn't challenging or stimulating enough." Linda nodded.

"I'm sorry Rick, but I lied. I had to. At the time, no one was supposed to know about Serum X. It was top secret. I assume you've looked into the files and when you saw my name, you came here."

Rick chuckled, "Oh, ye of little faith. Linda, love, I didn't have to pull any files to know you were the lead researcher on the team. I knew you were lying to me and I knew the reason why. I'm very familiar with your work, you of all people should know that there is very little the Council does that I don't know about." Then, Rick's features grew dark even as

Linda's face paled. "Which is why I was given a distraction." Rick looked over at Kendra. "They made me blood you to get me out of the way."

Kendra gasped, "The bond. It's a weakness we didn't consider. That's why you had fallen to your knees when I got hurt, you can feel my pain, and they plan to use that against you. Use *me* against you." Rick looked at her, a deep-seeded pain seemed to lurk there, swirling beneath the surface.

"You're right, Kendra. Turns out you're my weakness." Kendra blinked as Rick continued, "One I can't let them use against me." A strange emotion was swirling inside her she couldn't quite identify. She struggled to get a grasp on it just as someone cleared their throat.

"I hate to interrupt this moment, but I may have a solution to this problem." Linda stood, keeping her eyes trained on the left wall. She walked over to stand in front of a diploma hanging next to her bookcase. Linda lifted the diploma off its nail to reveal a small safe with a weird keypad that had no numbers. The woman pressed both of her index fingers onto the pad and it lit up, then the safe swung open.

Inside was lit with LED lights and a small cloud fell from the inside to the floor when she opened the glass door set behind the locked one. There were several vials, in an array of colors, nestled into white plastic holders, and Linda pulled out a vial that stood out in contrast. It was longer than the rest and paler in color to the other vials, the translucent yellow was reminiscent of a urine sample to Kendra.

"This is what I was working on — it's a neutralizer for Serum X. It was designed to render the active properties of the Wolfsbane poison inactive. While I was working on it in the Council Research Labs, I had a difficult time balancing out the beneficial effects with the negative ones." Rick nodded.

"I see. What were the negative ones?" Linda shrugged.

"Total disintegration of vital internal organs in most patients." She said, almost too casually, earning her a couple of horrified stares from Rick and Kendra. Linda looked between the two of them, "What? They grew back. Most of the time. That's beside the point. I've fixed it now."

"To what? Partial disintegration of nonvital organs? That still sounds really painful." Kendra almost wanted to shout at the woman, humans don't test potentially dangerous drugs on other humans and the idea that some vampires had been tested on in such a way was repulsive.

"No, actually I've been able to remove the negative side effects. Now, a pure dhampir becomes a ghoul after a few years of not feeding on blood. The resulting deprivation of hemoglobin results in decreased brain function, turning the individual into a ghoul and is, unfortunately, irreversible. However, if these ghouls are a result of Serum X, there might be a chance to save them."

Linda placed the vial in an insulated sleeve, "I will do some testing and hopefully come back with a finished product." Rick looked at her quizzically.

"Finished product?" Linda nodded.

"I'm going to test and reevaluate the potency needed, increase the volume, and put what I can into a few darts so you can administer the treatment without getting to close to the ghouls." Rick rubbed his chin

"And how long will that take?" Rick asked, Linda thought about it for a moment then answered, "24 hours, more or less."

War

A day hadn't passed before Linda called Rick with weird instructions to meet her on the roof of the lab. Kendra had taken up her usual post at work just trying to get back some semblance of normalcy. Kendra went on break around 1:00 pm, she grabbed her phone and found it had over fifty missed calls and even more unread messages. With trepidation filling her, she called Rick back, "It's about damn time, where are you?"

She felt a sense of *Deja vu* listening to Rick.

"I'm at work, Rick. Why? What's wrong?" There was a pause, then, "Why are you at work?" Kendra frowned. "Because that's what normal people do." Rick chuckled into the receiver.

"But you're not normal, Kendra. Not anymore." Kendra opened her mouth to protest that statement but found that he wasn't wrong. Of course, she wasn't going to tell him that, she wouldn't be able to live it down, so instead she ignored it.

"What do you want, Rick?"

"Oh, Linda called, she wants to see us." Kendra sighed, *Was that so hard?*

"Ok, when?" Rick coughed.

"About two hours ago." Kendra yelled, "*What?*" into the phone receiver and gained herself a few stares from around the cafeteria. She gave them an apologetic smile before continuing her conversation. "Tomorrow's my day off, can we reschedule for then?" Rick sighed.

"Kendra, this isn't a doctor's appointment, not to sound cheesy here, but the fate of the world may be in jeopardy. Look, I'll come pick you up and we'll go together."

"Rick, I'm at work, I can't just take off." Rick tsked, "You're a vampire, yes you can." Kendra could feel the frustration building.

"Fine, how long until you're here?" Rick snickered, "I'm at the main entrance, now get out here."

***

Kendra and Rick were waiting on the roof when the door opened. Linda walked out with a large duffle bag. She set the bag down and looked over at them with a bright smile.

"It's about time you two got here. What took you so long?" Rick shrugged.

"Kendra had work and I didn't see the point in coming here without her." Linda looked over at Kendra.

"Oh, I see, what is it you do?" Kendra looked down at the scrubs she was still wearing, her badge hung from the lanyard from her neck.

"I'm a nurse, I work at ..." Linda scuffled.

"Oh, I'm sorry, dear. I hadn't noticed your uniform." Linda leaned down and opened the duffle bag, "Who's ready for a game of paintball." Linda said. She stood, holding two rifles, one in each hand, and wearing a pair of googles. Rick perked up.

"Cool, but I thought you were working on your neutralizing darts?" Linda laughed.

"This *is* me working on my neutralizing darts. This is just a cheaper alternative to building a rifle around a dart. Paintball guns allow for me to adjust the air pressure exerted on the dart, so fewer materials are needed to stabilize the dart's integrity. In short, it's modifiable for a smoother delivery system. The downside is you have to be within 200 hundred yards for full effectiveness. Now, who's ready for some target practice?" Kendra shook her head.

"I don't understand. What's with the target practice? Our reflexes should be enough to compensate for any inaccuracies." Linda sighed,

"You're bright, but you miss the point. The target practice isn't for you. It's so I can properly calibrate the sights for your personal use. I only have a few of these darts, so accuracy is key. Now let's get started."

***

More training — Kendra had asked for Rick to train her, but now he was pushing for more rigorous routines. She suspected it had to do with his recent epiphany, the fact that Luca was using Kendra to weaken Rick was infuriating to both of them. Kendra trained hard, pushing herself to her limits mostly with her physical prowess rather than her newfound ability. After only a few sessions, Rick had admitted that her ability was too strong to test safely, at least not without a paramedic and a team of electricians on hand.

James had reported in recently to inform Rick that Luca was on the move, the imposter himself was coming to Georgia and they knew a war was on the horizon. It started with ghoul attacks, Anton was deployed to various sights with other agents. He called Rick at every sight, mostly it was massive carnage and, so far, no one was reported missing. This was different than what happened in Italy, though the evidence suggests many of the ghouls responsible were the ones involved with the Italian incidents, which begged the question of how Luca managed to transport them.

The night the ghouls showed up on Kendra's street, she and Rick were prepared. There was a pattern in the ghoul attacks, all suggested their heading, giving Kendra enough time to ensure her kids were tucked safely away at their aunt's house. Rick put a guard on the house in the event Luca had other plans. Dressed in all dark clothes, Rick stood guard on the south end of Samaritan Dr. and Kendra guarded the north end, modified paintball rifles at the ready.

The horde showed up on the north end, closest to Kendra's house as well as the position she took, but they weren't alone. Kendra radioed Rick and walked out into the street. They were still a good 300 yards away and out of her rifle's success range, so she took count. From what she could see, and she could see a lot, there were over 80 ghouls, 11 figures lurking in the shadows, and 3 figures taking up the rear. Some quick calculations in her head told her they were short 30 darts and some of these unfortunate souls were going to have to be taken care of the old-fashioned way. Kendra reported this to Rick. He cursed into his earpiece and a slight echo could be heard down the road. He was close.

Rick didn't want to be noticed immediately, so he was going slower than he would like to, but he caught up quickly. Once Rick was by her side, they took off, planning on taking most of them by surprise. The first shot came from Rick, the second from Kendra. Both made contact and the targets went down. The other ghouls made for the body to cannibalize them, but Rick and Kendra were prepared for that.

They stopped where the bodies fell, loading and shooting one dart at a time and making quick work of the quickly surrounding horde. Kendra lost count of how many darts flew from the muzzle her rifle, so she wasn't prepared for the shock of being out of ammo. She hastily called out, "I'm out!" to Rick, he shot another ghoul and replied, "Me, too." They tossed the now useless rifle to the ground. "We saved fifty of them. Now we need to protect them. They'll be out for a while. Are you ready for this?" Kendra nodded while the remaining horde of 30 ghouls ran at them.

Kendra didn't want to use her power so close to the dhampirs they had saved from being ghouls, so she relied on her strength and Rick's teaching as she sliced through their ranks. Their clothes quickly became covered in awful smelling blood, and it dawned on her why Luca smelled the way he did. Her gut wrenched even as she severed head from body of one of the poor unfortunates they couldn't save. *He was feeding from them!* Luca was a sick bastard that needed to be stopped. That wasn't news to Kendra, but the level of low this man. No, this monster made her sick.

She couldn't begin to imagine how the Serum X in their system may have affected him, she could be wrong, but her nose told her otherwise. Rick took the last kill, his eyes ablaze with the fury that he had to kill so many, the figures in the shadows leaped to the road, challenging Rick and Kendra. She knew they were what was left of Death's Hand, the only ones of their group that died that night was the man who lost his head and the two Kendra had done in herself. The others were being held within AVIA headquarters.

There were five senior Death's Hand, including the leader, and eight that were in training. The man that died in Kendra's house was a rookie, as well as the three others who were taken down nonviolently as to be taken into custody. After those two Kendra had killed were counted for, that left three experienced and three rookies — six Death's Hand all together. However, only five stood in front of them now, putting them both on edge. Two of them stepped forward drawing their weapons. Kendra and Rick waited at the ready, playing defense rather than offense.

Ilium had warned them that their blades may be laced with Serum X now that Luca was in charge. Linda had supplied Kendra and Rick with one dosing of the antidote in an EpiPen like form, but all they had was one each. The assassins charged into battle. Rick clashed with his before the other attempted to slam into Kendra. The blade that narrowly missed Kendra's face glinted in the moonlight; the woman was lithe as she pushed off of Kendra's stomach and landed on her feet even as Kendra stumbled back.

Not giving pause, the woman came back, her blade arching through the air, determined to slice a hole in Kendra's flesh. She blocked the attack and, this time, pushed the woman back, seemingly startling her. Kendra straightened, daring the woman to come at her. Kendra focused on her training and tapped into her vampire power. The other woman came at her again, but this time she psyched Kendra out, jumping over her, the woman landed behind Kendra and made for the plunge with her blade.

Kendra, moving on instinct, slammed her head into the other woman's face. She twisted and grabbed the assassin's wrist that held her dagger, Kendra snapped her wrist with a quick jerk. The woman's scream echoed through the air, even as she pulled yet another dagger from her belt. The glint came as a warning just before Kendra's knee connected with the woman's chin. Kendra picked up the knife that fell from her broken wrist and asked, "Is this a deadly concentration?" The assassin's answer was a glob of blood spat in Kendra's direction.

Kendra had to keep telling herself that what she was doing was to protect her kids. It made it easier for her as the blade slid in through the woman's ribs and into her heart. The woman fell to the ground, slowly dying; the blade pulled free of her flesh allowing the blood to flow freely. The toxin rushed through her bloodstream making a quick end of her. Even as she gurgled her last breath, the thump of the other assassin's body signaled the end of the one Rick fought. Kendra didn't have enough time to process what she had done before the next assassin grabbed her from behind.

Kendra moved just as a long blade sliced through her jacket, she twisted out of his grip, causing the blade to get pulled from his grasp. As it clanged to the pavement, the man pulled out a smaller dagger and lunged at Kendra, not giving her any reprieve. He must have been watching Kendra's fight with his colleague because he was more prepared than she was. Kendra got a glimpse of Rick, who was facing off with the last two assassins at one time.

The blade came to close to Kendra's neck and made her jump back further than she wanted. He had the advantage of momentum and was still coming at her full force, Kendra barely had time to react. The blade skittered across her arm, slicing open the sleeve of her shirt and narrowly missing her flesh. Kendra's heart raced; she wasn't on this man's level; he had had more time than her to hone his skills. She had to make a move and fast if she was going to survive this.

Kendra watched carefully to the way he moved as she dodged him. At first, his steps were precise, but slowly his measured movements were less corradiated. As his confidence grew, his maneuvers became sloppier, he was working toward making a quick end of Kendra and she sought to use that against him. She made her escapes seem narrow the closer he got, trying to conserve her stamina even as he used his to pursue her.

Finally, the assassin made a mistake. He stepped too far to her left to block off her escape, and Kendra pivoted to the right to take advantage of his open ribcage. She slammed her elbow into his side, knocking the air out of his lung, then brought her arm up and over his head. She slammed her elbow into his head right above his temple. The blow disoriented him enough for Kendra to kick him in the back and send him spiraling to the ground.

The man landed with a thump and began coughing, fresh blood coated the air as it came sputtering out of his mouth. Kendra turned him over to find the dagger embedded in his neck, puncturing his jugular. Against her better judgment, Kendra pulled the blade free, with the blood now flowing; his wound healed but the damage was done. Serum X took his life as well, and as Kendra watched the light die in her attacker's eyes, she heard Rick's fight come to an end.

Kendra turned from the dying man, pushing back the darkness that was growing inside her heart, and faced what was to come next. Rick pulled a blade free from one of his victims with a wet popping sound that made Kendra's stomach clench. He tossed the blade to one side and stood beside Kendra. *Then there were three.* One of the silhouettes walked toward them; the sound of clapping could be heard as it moved closer; the moonlight revealed its identity.

"Luca, you traitor." Rick growled to which Luca tsked him

"You misunderstand, Richard. I can't be a traitor if I was never allied in the first place." Rick grunted, "I don't give a damn about the Council. You're a traitor to your species." Luca sighed.

"Yes, well, that part couldn't be helped. If I was going to infiltrate your inner sanctum, some sacrifices had to be made." Luca shrugged and stared at Rick who only blinked in confusion. "Oh, oh my." Luca chuckled.

"So the big bad Rick hadn't figured it out yet? I thought that was what you were talking about." His chuckle turned into more of a laugh, "So it is possible to pull the wool over your eye's, oh how marvelous. Let me explain: I'm a vampire hunter, always have been. The state I have found myself in was a necessity. We needed a way in, and I provided." Rick lunged.

"You bastard!" Luca twitched his hand and a dart thumped into Rick's chest, "Rick!" Kendra screamed. She ran to him ready to use her antidote.

"Kendra, don't", Rick said, as he slumped to the ground.

"But ..." Kendra began, Rick shook his head with a weird look in his eyes and Kendra understood. Kendra looked over at Luca. "What do you want from us?" Luca rubbed his chin with a wide smile, "Well, with the great Richard Blake reduced to nothing, not much, really. I want you to join me. I want to give control of the leading governments back to humans, and the complete annihilation of the vampire race." Luca shrugged, "You see? Nothing major." Kendra nodded.

"Yes, I can see why you'd want these things." Rick groaned and thumped to the ground, Kendra winced and ignored it, she had to keep him talking. "I don't, however, understand what it is you want from me?" Luca tilted his head, "I figured that would be obvious." Kendra sighed.

"Humor me."

Luca chuckled, "Well, how about we start with this." He said arching his hand over the scene behind her, "Your power is unprecedented among fledglings, making you a powerful ally. Your youth, in terms of vampire age, means you could be more sympathetic toward humans. You can understand a hunter better than most. And let's not leave out the ultimate weapon that your unique ability presents."

"You know about that?" Luca chuckled.

"Of course. Did you think the new leader of Death's Hand wouldn't know who killed his men and how?" Kendra shrugged.

"Fair enough. However, I do see one fatal flaw in your plan." Luca grinned wide.

"There are no flaws, my plan is pristine." Kendra shook her head.

"Let's say I join you; let's say we're successful in giving the leading government control back to humans, what then? You want the complete annihilation of the vampire race, but you are forgetting one thing." Kendra was moving slowly closer, trying to fill in the gap that separated them, as Luca stared his smile slowly disappearing. "After you have killed every last vampire, even if you turned on me and killed me, too." Kendra was face to face with him, staring him down, his smile was almost gone. "There will still be one vampire left, Luca." Luca's smile turned into a grimace.

"It's obvious. I'll just kill myself ..." he paused and pondered what he had just said.

"Only you won't, we both know you won't, and with you still alive the vampire race will never truly be annihilated, now will it?"

Luca shook his head. "You're playing with my mind, I don't know how, but you're trying to trick me." Kendra blinked.

"If by tricking you, you mean telling you the truth, then yeah I guess I am." Luca grabbed his head with both hands and fell to his knees.

"No, no, no, no, no, no, the crafty witch lies. There is a way. My plan, it was pristine, perfect, like a crystal lake, I could see all the way to the bottom." And there was the madness, forced to the surface, even the two hunters who stood near-by knew it.

One raised the gun that had shot Rick and aimed at Kendra's chest, but just before the hunter could fire, he was slammed to the ground. Luca stayed on the ground muttering to himself, unaware or uncaring of what happened around him. The other hunter turned to shoot just above his fallen comrade, but no one was there, and the hunter frantically waved his gun around, looking for the attacker. It wasn't until the other hunter was taken down that Rick revealed himself; Kendra was too focused on Luca to pay much attention, but she knew it was him.

Luca stood slowly, looking around himself like he had just woke from a dream. He saw the two hunters on the ground and looked toward Rick and Kendra.

"Oh, you two must think you're so clever, you thought you could trick me? You wanted me to shoot Rick cause he's the only freak with an immunity to this shit." Rick shrugged.

"Who needs immunity when you have great friends?" he chuckled. "Give it up, Luca. You're outnumbered and outpaced. You can either let us take you into custody to face trial or you can continue fighting us, and possibly, maybe, you know, die. It's your choice."

Luca looked between them. A smile started to spread across his face.

"Die? Me? Never. However, I'm not ready to throw in the towel just yet." The grin he had grew so wide that Kendra was afraid it would split his head in two. Then Luca breathed in deeply and shouted, "Team 5, Team 6, now!"

Climax

Within moments, they were surrounded again, but this time it was hunters — lots of them. They were all armed to the teeth. Their guns may have had some live rounds, but Kendra was sure that quite a few had some of those nasty darts.

"What's the plan here, Rick?" Kendra asked as their escape routes were being closed off.

"Fight. Don't get shot. Don't die. Any one or combination of those will work." Kendra rolled her eyes.

"Well that's real damn helpful."

Kendra looked around at the hunters. They seemed eager to take Kendra and Rick down quickly. A few of them carried in some nets. When Kendra looked closer, she saw that the nets were hooked up to a wire — they were electrified.

"Rick, do you see ..." He nodded.

"Yes, Kendra, I see them." While, in theory, Kendra could handle being shocked herself, Rick was another matter altogether.

"Why don't you use your ice trick? It would really save us some time." Kendra hissed. Rick shrugged. "I would if I could, but sadly I'm depleted." Kendra looked around at him as he stood behind her.

"And what exactly is that supposed to mean?" Rick smiled at her.

"I'll tell you when you're older, in the meantime, we have a fight on our hands." Just as he had said that, a large brute came crashing between them, effectively separating them from each other. Rick took on the massive man and Kendra turned to face a group of hunters.

There were four of them holding rifles and two dragging an electric net behind them. The four carrying rifles didn't waste any time, darts flew past Kendra as she dodged them. One at a time, she took down the four riflemen, she knocked the first unconscious with a hard kick to the head, the second she gut-punched and wrenched the rifle from his hand. Her knee met his skull and he was out for the count, the third was a little more prepared, he and the fourth teamed up in an attempt to overwhelm Kendra.

She high-kicked the rifle from the third hunter's grip and jumped behind them faster than they could see. Kendra slammed their heads together with a loud crack and they crumbled to the ground like marionettes without strings. She heard the two net carriers sneaking up behind her and waited. Once they threw the net on her she grabbed a hand full of the thing and wrenched it from their grasp, knocking them to the ground.

Kendra kicked one in the face, knocking him out cold as the other tried to grab her ankle. Kendra grabbed her wrist and pulled the hunter to her feet, then, with the swiftness of lightning, Kendra bit deep into the hunter's neck. She didn't think about it, Kendra just acted on instinct, the smell of blood that permeated the area aroused her blood lust. Kendra knew she wouldn't find satiation in hunter blood, but there was power there and the act of biting into the tender flesh chased away the hunger for a time.

The girl was almost drained when Kendra was wrenched away from her meal. She gave out a fierce snarl only to be met with a strong hand gripping her neck. The haze of feeding cleared as she stared down into the eyes of one angry Luca. The blaze of fury radiated the air as Kendra's feet lifted off the ground, she struggled as her air supply was diminished, though it didn't feel like she was suffocating. He squeezed harder, the lack of air was simply uncomfortable, the pain from his grip, however, was made her squirm. She fought for some control, clawing at his arm.

"Not so powerful, now, are you? I've got your fledgling in a hard grip, you can feel her pain can't you, Rick?" Kendra looked past Luca, Rick was in as much pain, if not more, than she was. He struggled on the ground as two large hunters closed in for the kill, Kendra struggled furiously, she didn't want to use a power she couldn't yet control, but now she had no choice. She reached deep inside herself and grasped the seed of power that resided there.

It was hard trying to release a controlled storm, the lightning that blazed through her and into Luca was powerful, ancient, and not willing to be controlled. It was one thing to let instinct take over and allow the power to flow freely, but this was like trying to control the weather in the center of a tornado. Yet, despite her best effort, Kendra's power all but consumed the both of them in a blinding electrical surge. She couldn't hold back the wave of pure energy that erupted from her.

She could barely hear the scream that came from Luca as he was engulfed in the electrical charge that poured from Kendra. All she could focus on was her kids, the sound of little Zeke's voice as he asked her if the monsters were gone, Sasha's giggles as she played with her dolls, and Aveline's baby babble. Then she was spent, the power no longer flowed from her, she looked down at Luca. He lay in a heap, a tangled mess of burnt limbs and singed clothing. The surrounding ground looked like it had been struck by lightning.

The smell of ozone mingled with the smell of burnt copper and Kendra bent down to look at what remained of Luca. She turned him over and found that his clothes were lined with copper wire so fine it could be weaved into the cloth. He tried to use it to redirect her electricity, but he didn't plan for the intensity of the attack. An underestimation on his part that proved fatal; Kendra's keen senses were telling her there was no life left in him — if there was any life to begin with.

Rick walked over to her, a long metal spike jutted out from the back of his left leg, making him limp. "Kendra, would you mind giving me a hand?" Rick grunted. Without a second thought, Kendra reached over and yanked the spike out of his leg. Rick groaned loudly and dropped to his knees.

"Geez, warn a guy, would ya!" he huffed. Kendra whispered an apology, but she didn't seem to feel the emotion that she should be feeling. She was numb and that should have scared her.

Kendra watched the wound close and still she could not feel, almost like she had poured all of her emotions into killing Luca. Had she become the monster that she feared being? Would this be the end of her emotions?

Are all vampires this dead inside? She looked at Rick, even as he huffed with pain, there was life in his eyes. Rick had emotions; they blazed in his features; there was no way he could fake his feelings with how strong he seemed to feel them. Or could he?

"Rick, is there something wrong with me?" Rick sat down on the ground, rubbing the now healed spot on his leg.

"Hmm? I don't know. I don't feel like you're in pain. You seem fine to me. Why? Is something wrong?" Kendra allowed herself to collapse on the ground next to him.

"I don't know — is it normal to not feel anything at all?" Rick looked at her, worry clearly marked his features and yet Kendra could feel nothing. No, not all vampires were dead inside, just her.

"Do you mean you've lost your sense of touch?" Kendra shook her head.

"No. It's like, I should be able to feel ... something, anything. I feel numb, like I can't cry or laugh or feel remorse. Rick, what is wrong with me?" Even to Kendra's ears her voice came out as flat, practiced, like she was just reading lines with no emotion. Rick's worry lines in his face eased a little.

"Oh, I understand now. It's ok, what you are feeling, or should I say not feeling ... it's normal. You're in shock, love, that's all."

Shock. Kendra knew what shock felt like. At the time, she was in denial, but it was shock that kept her from crying at Travis' funeral. This was different; this was more profound; it was a deeper kind of feeling. Could this be shock? Is shock different every time you experience it? Kendra couldn't recall.

"Oh, there you are!" Kendra was pulled from her thoughts, "We took care of some of the stragglers, but a few got away." Meeka and Ilium walked over to where she and Rick sat on the ground. Ilium was rubbing the back of his neck and Meeka was beaming brightly.

"That was some show you two put on. We got here in time to see Kendra go supernova." Meeka giggled. Ilium rolled his eyes and then narrowed them on Luca's body, "Is he dead?" Rick shrugged and leaned back on his hands.

"You tell me, can you sense him?" Ilium sighed.

"No. No, I cannot. Do you really have to beat around the bush like that?" Rick shrugged again with a smile and said nothing more.

"Anyway, Anton has his ability working overtime here to make sure he can make a full report. Hopefully, that puts an end to these grim events."

Kendra watched them interact with one another almost like she was watching from another place — detached. This was also familiar to her, but no matter how much she tried, she couldn't seem to find her way back. They chattered about the mess, a phone call was made, she muttered automatic responses to stimuli, but she wasn't there. It was like living in a dream. She wanted so badly to believe it was a dream, to believe that she was home in bed. Maybe soon she would wake up to see her kids' smiling faces and make breakfast.

Maybe she would wake up to find Travis lying next to her. She would be snuggled up in his arms, the sunlight shining into the bedroom window, and all would be fine. Life would go on and she could put the bad dream behind her. The dream persisted, a bunch of people were surrounding her, the scene was being cleaned, and a doctor flashed a light in her eyes. She wasn't even responding anymore, what's the point? It's all a bad dream after all, why continue living in a dream when she could wake up and live in the real world.

She was in a car and someone was driving, maybe she was with Travis, they were probably taking the kids to the park. That would mean it's the weekend. They would always take the kids to the park on the weekend ever since Zeke was a toddler. There would be laughing and singing along to kid songs on the radio. They went over a bump and suddenly it was night out. There was some light in the sky like it was dusk or maybe dawn, the car was empty and a man that Kendra didn't recognize was driving.

She felt like she should know him; he was attractive with hair the color of sand and hazel eyes. She knew she was safe with him, but he wasn't Travis. Where was Travis? He was talking to her and she could hear him, he was a part of the dream, he wasn't real. Travis and the kids were what is real. She needed them. She couldn't wake up though, Kendra wondered if Travis was worried about her, or if he still slept, too. The dream man seemed to be as worried as she figured Travis would be, but again it didn't really matter; she just wanted Travis.

***

Rick paced in the living room, listening closely to the sounds of the house. *How much longer before she gets here?* Rick bit a nail and stopped pacing. A slight movement caught his attention. When the sound stopped, Rick sighed and continued wearing a trench in the floor with his feet. After several minutes, Rick sat back down on the couch and tried to calm his nerves. He picked up his pad of paper from off the coffee table and looked at the drawing he was working on. It was a rough sketch that he had drawn and began coloring in, but it was a little bland. It needed a background, and he struggled with what to add to it.

A knock at the door made Rick bolt straight up. He was so distracted that he missed their approach. Rick opened the door to find Anton standing on the stoop with a woman he didn't recognize.

"Is this her?" Anton grimaced.

"No, Rick, this is the Queen of Shiba. she took some time off her busy schedule to help a couple of vampires." He pushed past Rick, leading the woman into the house, "Of course it's her, what kind of question is that?"

Rick wanted to snarl. If he ever met the person who came up with sarcasm, he'd kill them. Anton escorted the woman into the room. Her hair was grey with little trace of its youthful color. Her dark eyes sparkled inside her wrinkled face and something danced in her expression as she watched Rick's appraisal of her. She seemed to be the embodiment of the phrase "Young at Heart" and yet Rick still found himself apprehensive as to whether she'll be able to do what she came to do.

"Rick, this is Mama Terresa. She is the oldest living special human and a telepath. Her powers are extraordinary, even at 176 years old. I believe she can help Kendra." Rick blinked; he had no words. 176 years was a long time for a human to be alive, let alone sane.

"You sure she's in the right mind." The woman looked at him and even though her mouth didn't move, he heard her speak in a clear, almost youthful voice.

"My physical voice had left me long ago but I'm still able to communicate with you. I think I'll manage with helping your friend."

Rick shivered, her voice resonated in his mind like a song he couldn't forget. She smiled warmly at him. She knew the impact her ability had on people, "Now, could a frail old woman ask a strapping young vampire to carry her up the stairs. I'm afraid my tired old legs can't carry me like that anymore." Again, the woman's voice came into Rick's mind. Like warm butter melting on to a cob of corn, it seeped into his consciousness softly and calmed him. Rick looked at her

"I can carry you. What will you do to help Kendra?" A sparkle danced in her eyes.

"I will know once I'm in her head— it's not the same with everyone." Rick nodded, then stooped to pick up her light, fragile body. Once she was positioned comfortably in Rick's arms, he took her up the stairs to Kendra's room. Anton opened the door and pulled the armchair that sat in the corner closest to the bed. Kendra lay on her side, eyes wide open but seeing nothing, like in a trance.

Anton grimaced at the state of Kendra and glared daggers at Rick's back. Rick sat Mama Terresa down in the chair close enough so she could touch Kendra if need be. She reached for Kendra and laid a wrinkled hand on Kendra's temple. The room grew silent and the two men stepped back into the hall. They waited in silence for the telepathic Mama Terresa to finish her work.

Nightmare

Kendra was watching the kids play in the backyard. The glass of lemonade sweated in her hand; the day was hot but perfect. The backdoor opened and Travis walked out with a tray of sandwiches.

"Kids, come eat!" he yelled over the squealing. He sat the tray down on the patio table and picked Aveline up from the wood porch. Kendra watched him take care of the kids with a loving passion. She smiled and took a sandwich off the tray. The kids ate and then took off back to the playset Travis finally got around to building for them.

Kendra got up, walked over to Travis and sat in his lap. She gave him a big kiss.

"What's this all of a sudden?" he asked her with a crooked smile. Kendra shrugged.

"Because I love you and wanted to express it." She giggled and he smiled up at her. He scooched her off his lap and grabbed her hand.

"Come on." Kendra giggled again.

"Where are we going?" He smiled.

"Somewhere private." He pulled her but she resisted some.

"What about the kids?"

Travis looked behind her. "They'll be fine for a bit. Come on," he repeated, and they went inside the house. Only it wasn't their house; it was almost Victorian and very familiar. A beige grand piano sat in the corner of the room and instead of electric lights there were candelabra. She looked at Travis in awe. He was dressed in a white three-piece with long tales hanging off the jacket. He wore a black button-up shirt and waistcoat with a blood-red tie that matched the stitching in the rest of the suit. He stretched a gloved hand toward Kendra.

"You look amazing in that dress. May I have this dance, my love?" Kendra blinked and looked down at herself. She was wearing a silver sequined dress that was snug against her body with a mermaid-style skirt. It was backless and her hair was elegantly done up with pins. She wore long white gloves that went above her elbows, it was the most elegant outfit she had ever seen. She could only imagine what kind of picture she painted.

A song began to play on the piano, Kendra couldn't see who played and didn't care as she took Travis's hand. It was the single most romantic thing he had ever done, and she didn't care how he had pulled it off. Travis pulled her along, taking the lead in their waltz, he smiled at her as he twirled her across the dance floor. He looked into her eyes and the warmness that she was so familiar with was there, shining brightly. All that mattered to her then was this moment, the movement of their feet, the swaying of her dress.

"How long do you think you can keep this up?" Travis asked. Kendra giggled.

"I can dance with you all night long." Travis' smile slipped some.

"No, I mean, this charade. You know I'm only a figment of your psyche." Kendra laughed.

"What in the world are you talking about?" Travis smiled.

"None of this is real. When are you going to stop lying to yourself?" Kendra was confused, she was smiling but she couldn't believe what he was saying.

"Travis, you're not making any sense." Travis pulled her close, his smile waning.

"No, Kendra, you acting this way doesn't make any sense. I'm dead and you're a vampire. You need to live in the present. Our kids need you." Kendra stared at him in disbelief.

"What's wrong with the kids, Travis? Let me go. I need to see them." Travis held her tighter.

"I can't. Not until you wake up, I'll not let you until you come to your senses." Kendra was in a panic, but she couldn't move except to dance. All she could do was let Travis lead her across the dance floor in a perpetual waltz.

She looked around, looked anywhere but at Travis. The room changed, one minute it was the Victorian house the next it was an elegant ballroom, then they were in a field of roses. She could smell the wonderful fragrance just as the scene changed again to a graveyard. The music became a haunting tune that sent shivers up Kendra's spine. She couldn't look anymore, the gravestones were giving her the creeps and yet they still danced.

Kendra looked up at Travis to ask him to take them back to the Victorian house or the ballroom, anywhere but there. It wasn't Travis's face that she saw; it was a different man, someone who was familiar to her.

"Where is Travis? What did you do to him?" the man chuckled.

"You don't recognize me, Kendra? I'm hurt." His hazel eyes were amazingly bright and danced with a fire Kendra couldn't imagine. She was drawn to those eyes.

"Should I recognize you?" The man smiled wide; his eye teeth were pointy and looked sharper than they should be.

"Of course, we know each other pretty well." Kendra blinked at him. He had roman features and sandy-colored hair. He was also a good head taller than Travis and she felt like she did know him but couldn't place how.

"Can't you just tell me who you are? It would be easier that way." He shook his head.

"That would ruin the fun." Kendra pursed her lips together.

"How about a hint?" The man chuckled.

"No, Kendra, I'm afraid you are on your own with this one, I can't help you." Kendra pouted, "Well, can you at least let me dance with Travis? He is my husband you know." The man frowned.

"You don't like my company?" Kendra sighed.

"It's not that, I just know who Travis is, I don't even know your name." The man sighed.

"You can't dance with Travis, love, he's dead. You're with me, now, so you'd better figure out who I am and quick. We're running out of time." Kendra tried to pull away but found it impossible.

"What do you mean he's dead? I was just dancing with him?" She felt like she was near tears, "What happens when time is up?" The man asked her. Kendra blinked.

"I don't know, I didn't even know there was a time limit." The man pointed, "Look they're beginning to rise." Kendra looked around her, they were still in the cemetery and the mounds were beginning to move. Fear seeped into her pores, the dead were going to rise, was that what happens when time is up? Kendra shoved her head into the man's chest.

"It's not real, it's not real, it's not real." She chanted, "That's right, Kendra none of this is real. Now, remember me and this whole thing comes to an end." Kendra whimpered, "I don't wanna die." The man pulled her close.

"Remember me, Kendra, and I can make it all go away." Kendra thought hard, trying to ignore what was happening, trying to remember. Her bedroom door being slammed, sharp teeth, a broken phone, images whizzed through her head: pancakes and syrup, hot coffee, and the taste of blood.

One word shot through her like a jolt of lightning: vampire. She looked up at the smiling man that now held her still, standing in a calm field of roses. She slowly backed away but didn't leave.

"Say my name, Kendra. I know you know it." Kendra blinked back tears.

"Rick, it that really you?" He shrugged.

"Well, yes and no." Kendra grimaced.

"You know I hate it when you talk in riddles." Rick laughed.

"It's time you went home."

He walked up to her and put his hand on her shoulder, then without any warning, he pushed her. Kendra fell and kept falling for what seemed like eternity, falling through blackness. Then suddenly she was gasping for air and looking about wildly, she was in her bedroom and an elderly lady was sitting next to her. Kendra instinctively called out for Rick and the door to her room flew open. Rick, Anton, and Ilium all walked into her room, worried looks on their faces. Meeka joined shortly with a cup of coffee and handed it to Kendra; it was made the way she liked it.

"What happened? Tell me all you know Mama Terresa." The old woman looked around at everyone and then a voice in Kendra's head said,

"I am going to tell you all at the same time. This way no misinformation can be spread. The girl wasn't alone in her head. Someone from the outside had planted a psychic seed in her mind. I have taken care of it, but the culprit has hidden themselves from me. Be wary — the danger isn't over yet. There are still those who wish to do you harm."

Then the old woman collapsed into the armchair and began to snore. Rick picked her up and carried her downstairs, Anton took the woman home as Ilium and Meeka stayed to watch over Kendra. She wasn't sure what had happened, but she was glad it was over. Well, not entirely; she felt like she was mourning the loss of Travis all over again. It was somewhat easier now that she was in her right mind, but it didn't stop the pain she felt from barely healed wounds being ripped open again.

Rick came back into the room and the two vampire councilmen left them alone. Rick sat next to her on the bed; not a word was spoken as Kendra curled up next to him and broke down in tears. She couldn't hold it back anymore, she had lost him again, and Rick let her cry. He held her for hours. After some time he told her about what had happened after she slipped into her coma-like state.

The scene was cleaned up and Luca's body was carted away with the rest of the evidence and the unconscious and dead hunters. James was working on returning order to the Council while the Councilmen recovered from Luca's influence. The news report went out about a transformer exploding and causing massive damage to the area the fight took place. Janet was taking care of the kids for a while so Kendra could have some time to recover. She was going to need it after what happened to her.

***

Two weeks went by and Rick never left Kendra's side. Sometimes she would talk about what had happened and sometimes she rarely spoke. Rick worked on various projects in between helping Kendra recover. One morning, Kendra woke to find him building the swing set that Travis never got to finish. At first Kendra wanted to stop him because it was Travis' project for the kids, but then remembered he could not finish it and let Rick do it.

Sometimes she would ball herself up and cry silent, mournful tears, and all Rick would do is hold her. Other times he'd encourage her to get up and do something just to stay busy, to keep her mind off of her thoughts.

Kendra made dinner one afternoon and brought some to Rick to thank him for his support. She found him in her study drawing at her desk. Kendra looked over his shoulder.

"Wow, I didn't know you could draw."

Rick chuckled, "It's not very good, I mostly do to help me relax." Kendra stared at the drawing.

"Its good, but I thought you weren't very religious." Rick's eyebrows furrowed.

"What does religion have to do with it?" Kendra blushed.

"Well, the drawing … a cross is a religious symbol, and you're drawing a cross with roses intertwining it." Rick laughed.

"You don't have to be religious to appreciate a well-designed symbol." Kendra looked at the picture again.

"Why does that rose look dead?" Rick stared at the picture for a moment then closed his sketchbook.

"Did you want something?" Kendra blinked.

"Oh, yes I made dinner. I thought you'd want some." Rick beamed, "I'd love some." Rick left the room and Kendra turned to follow, taking one last curious glance at the sketchbook. *Artists are weird.*

When the kids came home, Rick went back to work, but he came to check up on Kendra every now and then. James worked with the Councilmen to get everything back in order after they were fully recuperated. Ilium told Kendra over the phone that he was working on a full exception under vampire law for her kids. She wouldn't even have to go back to Rome unless she wanted to.

Life went back to normal. Though Kendra didn't need to, she went back to work. She couldn't imagine anywhere else she would rather be during the day. Every so often, Zeke would ask questions about what had happened, but Kendra couldn't bring herself to have his memories erased. She just hoped that he was young enough to fully forget it as he got older. Halloween was just around the corner — maybe the fun stuff she had planned would help him forget.

***

Rick was rummaging around in a trunk when James pulled up in his sedan. Rick popped his head up to see his "victim" stepping out of the car. He closed the trunk and began to skip over to the black sedan.

"Jimmy, oh Jimmy boy!" he chanted. James immediately took pause.

"Whatever it is, my answer is no." Rick reached him and slapped a hand down on his shoulder.

"Don't be like that Jamsie. This is going to be fun," Rick said with the widest grin James had ever seen.

"Whenever you say that, it usually means fun for you and torture for me. No." Rick stood back and shrugged his shoulders.

"Ok, fine."

A line of ice traveled across the ground and froze a nearby tree solid. The instant cold caused the water in the tree to separate from the wood and a loud explosion sent a shiver down James' back. With heavy regret and a healthy appetite to live, James uttered through his teeth: "Fine. What is it you want me to do?"

666

Rick knocked on Kendra's front door. He stood there, barely able to contain himself and was bouncing on his heels with excitement. When she opened the door he yelled, "Trick or Treat!" He held back a bout of laughter at the look on her face.

"Rick? Is that you? What are you wearing? It isn't even Halloween yet."

"Yes, actually for me it is. Come on. It's time to go," he said, reaching for her arm. Kendra moved out of his reach.

"I can't leave now. What about my kids? I don't have a babysitter." Rick was growing impatient, and the mask to his *Phantom of the Opera* costume was beginning to get hot.

"Don't worry about that. I've brought one with me." He looked behind him, Rick waved toward a shadowy part of Kendra's yard and said, "James, come on, old man. Get over here." Rick could hardly stand the hilarious look that took over Kendra's face when she saw James in his costume.

"I can't believe I let you talk me into this." James moaned as he stepped into the flood of light coming from Kendra's porch. He wore a big, bushy, red matte of curly, clown hair and a matching red nose with a squeaker. His shirt was orange with big blue polka-dots. He had his hands stuffed in the pockets of a pair of ballooning blue pants, bottomed by the traditional overly big shoes in blue. A tie was hanging from his neck that, with the help of a few bendy wires, defied gravity in a zigzag-y way. Even though Rick knew James was not smiling, the clown makeup made it seem like he was always smiling. James looked quite ridiculous, even for a clown.

Kendra burst out laughing. "James, are you under there? Did you lose a bet?" Rick grabbed James' shoulder and said, "Here is your babysitter for the evening. He's great with kids, the loveable lug. So, how about we get out of here, hmm?" Kendra got her composure back, she folded her arms and looked at the two of them inquisitively.

"Not until you tell me what is going on."

Rick rolled his eyes and pushed James into the doorway. At the same time, he grabbed Kendra's arm and said, "No time. I'll explain on the way." Kendra resisted but not completely. Rick knew if she didn't want to be budged, he probably couldn't budge her, but her curiosity was getting the best of her.

"Well, wait, Rick. It's 10 o'clock at night, I need to change, I'm in my pajamas." Rick stopped and looked her up and down.

"So?" but the look on her face said she wasn't having it.

"Don't worry, we'll take care of that later. just come on," he urged. Kendra looked back at the house and asked, "What about my purse?" Rick sighed.

"Baby, you won't need it where we're going" he said with a wink. She gave him an irritated look but didn't protest anymore as he dragged her away from her house.

"You two have fun!" James yelled after them "Don't worry, your kids are in good hands!"

Rick stopped in front of a black van with dark tinted windows.

"What are we doing here?" Kendra asked. Rick turned his head and grinned at her.

"We're getting you something else to wear." His cryptic comment left her wondering what the hell he had in store for her. He swung open the back doors of the van and a light came on. There were trunks inside, some looked genuinely antique and others looked like he bought them at a hobby store, brand new but made to look worn. Rick opened one of the newer trunks and started rummaging through it before pulling out a costume. It was the female role to the *Phantom of the Opera*, the name of which eluded Kendra.

"Voila, you will be going as Christine Daae, the kryptonite to my Superman." His smile was infectious, but Kendra managed to keep her cool.

"You still haven't told me where we are going, besides what if I refuse?" Kendra folded her arms in defiance. Rick's smile disappeared.

"Well, you're more than welcome to one of the other costumes I have in here." He went back to rummaging and came back with two new costumes still in their packaging. Kendra looked at them horrorstruck, one was called sexy kitty and was barely more than lingerie, and the other was a naughty nun with her boobs sticking out of her costume. "Why do you have those?" The moment the question was spoken, Kendra immediately regretted it.

"Hmm? Oh, these aren't mine, their James'." Rick replied.

Horror came crashing down on Kendra.

"That leaves more questions than it answers!" she shouted. Mentally slapping herself, she snatched the Christine costume off the chest where Rick had abandoned it. "Where can I change?" She just wanted this night to be over.

"You can change in the van, the windows are tinted, and I promise I won't look." Kendra grumbled and climbed into the van; Rick closed the door behind her. The costume surprisingly fit like a glove, the wig, however, gave her some troubles. She tossed the wig off to one side after trying to get it to work.

She opened the door of the van and stepped out. Rick helped her down and stepped back to get a good look at her.

"You're not wearing the wig." His words were more of a statement than a question.

"Nope, I'm not, it wouldn't cooperate." Kendra dared him to say something about it, but Rick responded with a warm smile.

"I like it. You're much more suited as a redhead. I wouldn't have it any other way."

She smiled back at him but before she could say anything in return, he slipped a brown burlap bag over her head, tied her hands behind her back, and threw her over his shoulder. It all took her by surprise, and she didn't even have time to react. He began to sprint, jumping and zigzagging, almost like he was trying to confuse her. Unfortunately, it worked. By the time they stopped she was very disoriented and almost couldn't stand on her own. The lights were very bright when the sack came off that she was nearly blinded.

"Where are we?" She wobbled and tried to get her bearings. Rick didn't answer but instead ushered her down a few corridors until they came to a large room. Once inside, she could see that it was an amphitheater with a large stage and what looked like a band that was beginning their preparations. He pushed her down the aisle until they got to about middle of the room and into the middle row. After taking their seats Kendra turned to say something but Rick shushed her with his finger.

Annoyed, she began again only to be shushed once more, and a paper shoved into her hands. She blinked at him before reading the pamphlet, it had the theaters name and below it the name of the play that she was, apparently, going to watch. Not only had he dressed them up in *Phantom of the Opera* costumes, but he had also brought her to see the play. Her mortification at what might have transpired if she had chosen one of the other costumes sank in. The band played a few test notes for about half an hour, during which Rick refused to talk or let Kendra talk, for reasons she could not fathom.

Aggravated at the forced silence, Kendra stood to walk out, but Rick pulled her back down to her seat. Before he could silence her again, she turned to slap him. He tried to stop it mid-swing, but she proved faster than him. Her hand hit home just as the band struck up an actual tune and began to play the intro to the play. Rick grabbed her by the wrist and pulled her close, unfazed by her violence.

"It's just beginning, please take a seat." he grinned.

At first, Kendra was bound to refuse, but when she looked around, she found they were the only spectators in the whole theater. She sat down so she could hear him speak.

"Where is everyone? And don't you dare shush me again or I will leave." He gave her a heartbroken look that seemed rather dramatized.

"Why would you leave, the play is just starting?" She glared at him and, finally, he answered her question with a sigh. "You really like to take the fun out of everything don't you? We are the only ones here because I bought out all the tickets so we could have this place all to ourselves. Other people can make a classic like *Phantom of the Opera* a drag."

Kendra stared at him in awe.

"How can you buy out the whole play? That's ridiculous! It must have cost a fortune!" Rick waved his hand at her.

"Yes, yes, later — the play is starting. The first characters are about to be introduced. We will talk later."

***

The play was wonderful and as they were leaving the amphitheater, Kendra realized they were somewhere in the middle of Atlanta, but the surroundings were unfamiliar. She turned toward Rick in time to see the bag come back out. Kendra zipped away from him before he could slip the bag back over her head. *Fool me once*, she thought and continued to dodge him.

"Stop, Rick, just tell me where we're going. There is no need for the mafia treatment."

He stopped in front of her, Kendra made sure she was just out of reach.

"Fine, I was going to take you to the carnival across town, they're doing a Halloween week and I was hoping we could enter in the costume contest."

"See, now was that so hard?" Kendra asked. Rick perked up.

"So you'll go with me?" he smiled wide.

"Not a chance, I'm going home." Kendra made to move but found her shoes were stuck to the concrete. She looked down and saw a line of shimmering ice flowing from her feet to Rick's. When she looked up, Rick was gone and then the bag was back over her head. He tied her arms and back over his shoulder she went. They bounded again through streets and, knowing Rick, across rooftops.

When her feet touched the ground once more and the bag came off, she was presented with the sight of a haunted house carnival ride. Well, the rear of one, anyway. She turned to leave, but Rick lightly grasped her arm, he pulled her closer to him.

"Please stay, I promise to behave." he wagged his eyebrows and she couldn't help but fall prey to his charms.

"Ok, but only for a little while, I do have to get back home to my kids."

Rick's face lit up as he dragged her into the haunted house. They rode most of the rides and played a few of the games before signing up for the costume contest. They walked through the crowds of people, cotton candy in their hands. Kendra looked over at Rick, his smile was infectious, but something was bothering her. They were about to pass a bench when Kendra grabbed Rick's arm.

"Rick, stop for a minute, please." He turned to look back at her.

"Is there something wrong?" Kendra shook her head, "I want to ask you something." Rick put his hands in his pockets.

"Ok, shoot."

His smile really was infectious, and Kendra almost lost her nerve.

"Rick, why did you want me to come here with you?" Rick's smile faded some.

"What do you mean?" Kendra sighed.

"I mean, why me? Why drag me out here with you? Don't get me wrong, I'm having fun, but I keep asking myself why? And I don't have the answer, you do, so I'm asking you, why?" Rick shrugged and looked up at the sky.

"Kendra, what time is it?"

She blinked.

"What?" Rick continued to look up with a strange look that was almost serene.

"Just indulge me for a moment, ok?" Kendra looked at her watch and couldn't believe it.

"It's almost midnight, oh my god. I didn't even realize it was that late. Sorry Rick but I must get back home to my kids." Rick grabbed Kendra's arm before she could run off, he wasn't forceful, but it made Kendra stop.

"Stay, just a little longer —, please?" He pulled her closer and wrapped his arms around her. The sudden embrace startled Kendra. He held her tight and Kendra began to think something was wrong. *Don't let this be a goodbye. I'm not ready to say goodbye.* Rick pulled back enough so he could look into Kendra's eyes. Kendra saw a longing there she had never seen in the bright amber depths before. "In a couple of minutes, it will be my birthday. I'll be 666 years old. I just wanted to spend the first few minutes of it with you." Kendra couldn't quite process her feeling about that statement, it still felt like he was trying to say goodbye, but now she wasn't sure.

"Kendra, I have a confession to make, and I don't know if it is the right time to do so. I relegalized something when I held you the night your mind was not your own and I have to tell you now. I think I'm falling in love with you." The longing in his eyes seemed intensified by the confession as he waited for her response. But what response could she give him? Did she even know how she felt about this? If she couldn't sort out her own feelings, how was she supposed to express them to him?

"Rick, I ..." she couldn't get the words out of her mouth because, at that moment, Rick's was on hers. The kiss was deep and filled with passion, his tongue probed her lips for entry, and she accepted it. He held her close to him, their bodies almost becoming one, and Kendra realized that this was what she missed the most. The closeness, the intimacy of another person, someone close to her, she wanted to feel loved again.

The embrace, the kiss — it ignited in her the feelings she missed the most, and awakened memories she thought she had pushed aside. Travis. His name was like a whisper through her mind, Kendra slowly broke off the embrace and backed away. "Rick, I ... I can't. I can't return your feelings — now. There is still a lot for me to unpack. I've only been a widow for six months, I still haven't fully processed that yet. I haven't let Travis go in my heart and I don't want to hurt you, Rick." Rick put his hands in his pockets, his shoulders sagged but he still smiled. The sadness in his eyes gave away his real emotions and Kendra almost choked on her next words.

"I just need time Tt sort out how I feel, Rick. I just need time." Rick shrugged his shoulders.

"All we have is time, right?" Kendra nodded "Just don't keep me waiting forever, ok?" then Rick turned and left. At 12:10am, they parted ways and Kendra went home to relieve a very bored clown.

***

James showed up at the condo that Rick was renting in Georgia. He had just left Kendra's house. She refused to talk about what had happened, so he came here to talk to Rick. He was sitting on his couch cleaning one of his prized handguns, a colt army revolver, a gun that hasn't been seen regularly on the market since the late 1870's. This particular gun probably hasn't been shot in almost 40 years, the fact that Rick was cleaning it wasn't a good sign.

James knocked on the post of the entryway, the door was unlocked, and Rick more than likely knew James was already there.

"Rick, are you ok?" Rick started methodically putting the few pieces of the handgun back together, "I'm fine. We were given a new assignment." James nodded even though Rick couldn't see the movement.

"I'm aware."

"Good, we will leave in the morning — about 9 am. Sound good?" James put his hands behind his back trying to relax himself.

"Sounds good. Do you want to talk about what happened tonight?" Rick sighed.

"If you're still peeved about the clown costume, don't be. it was for the kids." James grunted.

"I'm not on about that, Rick. I mean with you and Kendra." Rick loaded the gun slowly, not looking up at James. He stayed quiet and didn't say anything for a long time. "Rick, what happened between you two tonight?" The cylinder clicked into place and in a swift motion Rick pointed the loaded gun at a wall staring down the barrel to check the sights.

"I confessed my feelings to her," he said simply, still staring down the sights at the bare wall.

"I take it that didn't go so well?" James sank a little, realizing that Rick was dealing with some deeper feelings than he was willing to admit. Rick brought the gun down and set it on the coffee table before standing. He looked over at James, a sad smile on his face.

"She wants time to think. She's not sure how she feels." Rick sighed. "Well, whether I want to or not, I have no choice but to give her space. This mission we are going on is going to take a while. I told HQ I'd tell you the parameters of the case due to the sensitive details." James' eyebrows furrowed.

"What are you talking about, Rick?" The other man clamped his hand down on James' shoulder, "My friend, gear yourself up. I need you to be at full capacity for this. We're going after Vivian's killer — our target is Phaze."

EPILOGUE

Evidence Processing AVIA Morgue
October 31, 2016

A man walked into the mortuary and opened the cold locker where Luca's body was kept. The sound of the zipper echoed in the room as he opened the body bag. Luca lay there, paler in death than he ever was in life; the markings on his skin showing the path the electrical current took. The man pulled out an EpiPen like devise and slammed it into Luca's body. After a few moments, Luca gasped and began breathing heavily. Luca opened his eyes and saw the man who brought him back from death, "It's you. You came to save me."

Without warning, Luca lunged up and bit into the man's neck. He didn't scream; he knew what needed to be done. Luca was starved and drank greedily, he only let go once the man was fully drained. Luca slipped off the hard metal drawer and picked up the body. Methodically, he stripped the man of his clothes and put them on himself. Then he zipped the body up in the bag Luca himself was once stored in.

Once cleanup was done, Luca turned to leave. Just before closing the door to the mortuary, he spoke into the empty room.

"Thank you, my friend. I shall not forget you. Your service will not be in vain. Rest in peace Travis Hughes."

ABOUT THE AUTHOR

Trinity Showalter was born in Atlanta, Georgia in a hospital that no longer exists. It was in the 3rd grade that her teachers noticed her talent for writing and encouraged her to pursue it. There were many things that stopped her progression but still she wouldn't let go of her dream. Trinity wrote many tales and poems with some winning awards in school. One poem was rumored to have been published in a magazine but without proof, who knows.

It wasn't until the birth of her first child that the inspiration for Become the Night came to fruition. Sadly, this, like many other works, got put on the back burner so that life could have its way. When Trinity moved to Alaska (Yes Alaska, and no, we don't ride polar bears) it was her soon to be husband that encouraged her to write again.

She gave birth to two more children long after she had decided to have her main character be a mom of three. While the children are not based off of her own kids, her husband is the inspiration of the character Rick. To some degree, it is overly dramatized, but, yes, for the most part he is like that. Trinity's dream has always been to write epic tales and have the world read her work. This is her first book and hopefully it won't be the last.

See you in the shadows.

Printed in the United States
By Bookmasters